Praise for *Eat Cake*

"From the very first pages of *Eat Cake,* readers cannot help but develop an affinity for Ruth, the frazzled wife, mother and daughter whose life we enter during its most trying time. . . . [Ray] does an impeccable job of capturing the ordinary details of one family's life during a complicated couple of months. Besides having written a believable and engaging story, Ray carefully develops each of her characters into a multi-dimensional person whose personality adds immeasurably to the overall plot . . . a delightful refuge."

—*The Tennessean*

"All her books . . . deal with the day-to-day issues people cope with, such as aging, family relationships, living with elderly parents and teens at the same time. They are light, humorous and tender tales, a refreshing change from the angst-ridden, self-absorbed books that seem to fill bookstores." —*Chicago Sun-Times*

"I connected with Ray's characters in a way that not only engaged my mind, it changed my behavior. After reaching, with some sorrow, the final page of the novel, I went out, bought cake pans, and baked the first cake of my life."

—*The Leaf-Chronicle* (Clarksville, TN)

"Enjoyable . . . warm . . . Ray has a proven talent for everyday dramas of family life, and her latest is as toothsome as its predecessors."

—*Publishers Weekly*

continued . . .

D0168304

Praise for *Julie and Romeo*
One of the *Today* Show's "Six Best Summer Reads"

"Smart."   —*Entertainment Weekly*

"Original."   —*The New York Times Book Review*

"A comic gem of a love story . . . completely entertaining."
                                            —*The Denver Post*

"Ray has the perfect light touch. . . . The romance is challenged by hilarious and heartbreaking family intervention and sabotage. . . . Sweet but never saccharine, filled with the hard-won wisdom of people who have lived life and found well-deserved happiness, *Julie and Romeo* deserves to be a summer hit."
                                —*The New Orleans Times-Picayune*

"Captivating . . . charming . . . great laughs."
                                —*The Christian Science Monitor*

"A little jewel of a book."   —*The Philadelphia Inquirer*

"The Bard would smile."   —*Houston Chronicle*

Praise for *Step-Ball-Change*

"Sweet." —*New York Daily News*

"Smart, charming, and funny." —*Chicago Tribune*

"[A] surefooted charmer . . . readers are bound to demand an encore." —*Boston Herald*

"[A] gem. . . . Ray's novel explores what love and marriage mean across the years, how to recognize the 'real thing,' and whether adults can transcend artificial restrictions to seek true happiness. Funny, believable, and full of surprises, this novel, like time with a good friend, is over far too soon." —*Library Journal*

"Snappy . . . an endearing narrator, realistic and self-deprecating . . . [Ray] has a gift for lively dialogue that makes the characters snap into place." —*Publishers Weekly*

"A novel as comfortable and inviting as coffee at your best friend's kitchen table . . . appealing and entertaining." —*Booklist*

Also by

Jeanne Ray

JULIE AND ROMEO

STEP~BALL~CHANGE

eat cake

JEANNE RAY

NEW AMERICAN LIBRARY

New American Library
Published by New American Library, a division of
Penguin Group (USA) Inc., 375 Hudson Street, New York, New York 10014, U.S.A.
Penguin Books Ltd, 80 Strand, London WC2R 0RL, England
Penguin Books Australia Ltd, 250 Camberwell Road, Camberwell, Victoria 3124, Australia
Penguin Books Canada Ltd, 10 Alcorn Avenue, Toronto, Ontario, Canada M4V 3B2
Penguin Books (N.Z.) Ltd, Cnr Rosedale and Airborne Roads,
Albany, Auckland 1310, New Zealand

Penguin Books Ltd, Registered Offices: 80 Strand, London WC2R 0RL, England

Published by New American Library, a division of Penguin Group (USA) Inc.
This is an authorized reprint of a hardcover edition published by Shaye Areheart Books, a
member of the Crown Publishing Group, a division of Random House, Inc.
For more information address Crown Publishing Group, 1745 Broadway, New York, NY 10019.

First New American Library Printing, May 2004
10 9 8 7 6 5 4 3 2 1

Copyright © Rosedog, LLC, 2003
Readers Guide copyright © Penguin Group (USA) Inc., 2004
A complete list of permissions is on page 254
All rights reserved

 REGISTERED TRADEMARK—MARCA REGISTRADA

New American Library Trade Paperback ISBN: 0-451-21197-9
The Library of Congress has catalogued the hardcover edition of this book as follows:

Ray, Jeanne.
Eat cake : a novel / by Jeanne Ray.
I. Title.
PS3568.A915 E2 2002
813'.6—dc21   2002008838

Designed by Lynne Amft

Printed in the United States of America

Without limiting the rights under copyright reserved above, no part of this publication may
be reproduced, stored in or introduced into a retrieval system, or transmitted, in any form, or
by any means (electronic, mechanical, photocopying, recording, or otherwise), without the
prior written permission of both the copyright owner and the above publisher of this book.

PUBLISHER'S NOTE
This is a work of fiction. Names, characters, places, and incidents either are the product of
the author's imagination or are used fictitiously, and any resemblance to actual persons, living or dead, business establishments, events, or locales is entirely coincidental.

BOOKS ARE AVAILABLE AT QUANTITY DISCOUNTS WHEN USED TO PROMOTE PRODUCTS OR
SERVICES. FOR INFORMATION PLEASE WRITE TO PREMIUM MARKETING DIVISION, PENGUIN
GROUP (USA) INC., 375 HUDSON STREET, NEW YORK, NEW YORK 10014.

The scanning, uploading and distribution of this book via the Internet or via any other
means without the permission of the publisher is illegal and punishable by law. Please pur-
chase only authorized electronic editions, and do not participate in or encourage electronic
piracy of copyrighted materials. Your support of the author's rights is appreciated.

For Heather and Ann Patchett

Exemplary daughters,
Extraordinary bakers

Should I, after tea and cakes and ices,
Have the strength to force the moment to its crisis?"

FROM THE LOVE SONG OF J. ALFRED PRUFROCK,
T. S. ELIOT

Chapter One

YEARS AGO, I WENT TO A SEMINAR ON STRESS reduction at the Y. Most of what the instructor told us struck me as either obvious (make lists of what you have to do and check off what you've accomplished) or embarrassing (a series of breathing exercises that made me think of Lamaze class), but there was one thing he said that made the whole class worthwhile, a trick I still use when I find myself getting overwhelmed: He told us we should visualize a place where we felt completely safe and peaceful. He said it didn't make any difference if it was someplace we knew well or someplace we'd only dreamed about, but that we should think about it in great detail, notice everything around us, memorize all the sights and the sounds. Then he instructed us to go to this place in our minds. I glanced quickly around the room. Everyone had closed their eyes and gone to their childhood bedroom or a beach in Jamaica or wherever life was simpler. I had no idea where I was supposed to go. I felt embarrassed sitting in my folding chair, as if the people around me would know that I was still in the conference hall while they were all walking down a white sand beach with the sun glinting off their hair. I ran over a quick mental list: the house on Lake Placid we rented one summer; my own back porch; Paris, where I've never been but would like to someday go.

None of them seemed right, they all seemed to be asking too little or too much. But when I finally closed my eyes and tried, what I wanted came to me with complete clarity. The place that I went, the place that I still go, was the warm, hollowed-out center of a Bundt cake. It is usually gingerbread, though sometimes that changes. Sometimes it's gingerbread crowned in a ring of poached pears. The walls that surround me are high and soft, but as they go up they curve back, open up to the light, so I feel protected by the cake but never trapped by it. There are a few loose crumbs around my feet, clinging to my hair, and the smell! The ginger and butter, the lingering subtlety of vanilla . . . I press my cheek against the cake, which is soft as eiderdown and still warm. This isn't a fantasy about food exactly, at least not insofar as I want to eat my way through a cake that's taller than I am. It's about being inside of cake, being part of something that I find to be profoundly comforting. The instructor told us to take another deep breath, and all around me I heard the smooth shush of air going in, waiting, coming out. I thought I might never open my eyes.

Cakes have gotten a bad rap. People equate virtue with turning down dessert. There is always one person at the table who holds up her hand when I serve the cake. No, really, I couldn't, she says, and then gives her flat stomach a conspiratorial little pat. Everyone who is pressing a fork into that first tender layer looks at the person who declined the plate, and they all think, That person is better than I am. That person has discipline. But that isn't a person with discipline, that is a person who has completely lost touch with joy. A slice of cake never made anybody fat. You don't eat the whole cake. You don't eat a cake every day of your life. You take the cake when it is offered because the cake is delicious. You have a slice of cake and what it reminds you of is someplace that's safe, uncomplicated, without stress. A cake is a party, a birthday, a wedding. A cake is what's served on the happiest days of your life.

This is a story of how my life was saved by cake, so, of course, if sides are to be taken, I will always take the side of cake.

It's a laugh to think that I was feeling stressed when I signed up for that workshop. What was I feeling stressed about eight years ago? My son, Wyatt, was twelve then, still a full year away from the gawky roller-coaster ride of his teenage years. He asked for help on his homework and introduced me to his friends when they came over to go sledding. Camille was a little girl who still crawled into my lap some nights after dinner and let me brush her hair. I called her Kitten. Camille is sixteen now and about as much a kitten as a lioness eating a half-living zebra on a scorching African veldt. Eight years ago, my mother still lived by herself in Michigan and only came to visit twice a year and sometimes not even that. My husband, Sam, was the hardest-working hospital administrator anyone could have imagined, if one was given to imagining such things. I remember it now and hang my head in disbelief. I want to go back to that person I was, take her by the shoulders and shake her. "Look again!" I want to say to myself. "You are standing in the middle of paradise."

I arrived home in the rain, my arms filled with groceries. I tried to bring them all in at once, which wasn't exactly possible, but the rain was beating down with such a biblical fury that I thought it would be smarter to make one incredibly challenging trip than three manageable trips. The paper bags, a foolish choice, were melting between my fingers. My keys were so far down in the bottom of my purse (looped over the left wrist) that they might as well have been in Liberia for all the chance I had of getting to them. Not that I was even sure the door was locked. It might have been unlocked. I couldn't turn the doorknob unless I did it with my teeth. It was very clear that I had shown some poor judgment. I kicked at the door.

Through the window I could see my daughter sitting at the kitchen table reading a magazine. At the second kick she raised her eyes heavily, as if she were in fact not reading at all but had been hypnotized by the magazine. There was a hard wall of rain between us and yet I could still make out the supreme disinterest in her gaze. It was a look I knew intimately. I kicked again. She tilted her head, not entirely sure why I was interrupting her: Clearly, there was the door, I was capable of opening a door; I had keys if the door was, in fact, locked; I could see her weighing all this out in her mind. I felt a critical shift in the balance of the groceries and kicked again, just to speed things along. She sighed, a sound so reverberant with weariness that it made its way across the room and past the door and through the rain to reach me. She lifted her slender frame, a willow, a willow leaf, shuffled to the door, and opened it. When that task had been completed she returned wordlessly to the table and resumed her reading. I pulled myself inside and gasped at the air. One bag, the fifth bag, sensing we had reached the threshold of safety, decided it could no longer bear the burden of its responsibility and split apart, sending tangerines and three packages of frozen spinach and a roll of paper towels and (the kicker) a large plastic bottle of cran-apple juice bouncing over the floor. Not the eggs, not the paper carton of milk, I did not lose sight of the ways in which I was fortunate. I sank to my knees and put the other bags down before they could follow suit. I was profoundly wet. I could not imagine that dolphins ever got this wet.

"I couldn't get to my keys," I said.

"It wasn't locked," Camille said, but she didn't look up.

I got up off the floor and started to pick up what needed to be picked up. There was a great lake forming beneath me.

"Ruth?" My mother came into the kitchen holding a stack of papers in one hand. My mother was always holding papers. They seemed to be a natural extension of her hand. I imagined her sleeping with fistfuls of paper clutched to her chest. "I need you to look at these for me. I've been over them a million times and they just don't make any sense. Does it look like Blue Cross paid the doctor or does it look like I have to pay him? I don't want Dr. Nickerson to think I didn't pay him."

She was wearing a pink warm-up suit that appeared to have been ironed. She was looking at me, but I wasn't sure that she saw me at all. If she had seen me she surely would have commented on the fact that I looked like I had just been dragged from the lake, that I was raising myself up from a fiery ring of tangerines.

"I'll go over them, Mother, but I just got in from the grocery store. I need to put these things away first." I pushed back a wet clump of hair that stuck to the side of my face like seaweed.

"Did you get the dried apricots?"

"Were they on the list?"

She closed her eyes for a minute. "I can't remember. I can't remember anything." She turned to her granddaughter. "Camille, it's a terrible thing to be old. I hope you never get to be my age. Or maybe by the time you get to be my age they will have invented a cure for forgetting things."

Camille made some small humming sound that acknowledged that she had heard her own name spoken but she did not stop reading.

"I'll put apricots on the list for next time," I said.

"And these papers. Will you look at these? If I owe Dr. Nickerson money I think I should pay him."

I scooped up the sodden remains of paper sack and threw them in the garbage. I put myself inside the cake and tried to breathe slowly. I made it a simple lemon cake, no glaze. I was an only child and my parents had been divorced since I was two. My mother had done everything on her own. She had taken good care of me, played rounds of Go Fish, cooked nutritious meals, sewed me clothes that never looked homemade, taught me to play the piano in a passable manner. This was payback time. "The mail has already gone out today. Just let me get the milk in the refrigerator."

"Camille," my mother said. "Come over here and help your mother. We'll get this done in a minute."

Camille closed her eyes and pushed her fingers against the slender bridge of her nose. I could tell she was trying not to scream, and even though I didn't expect her to have much success, I appreciated her minimal efforts at restraint. "When I came into the kitchen to *read,* there was nobody in here. If I were smart I would just stay in my bedroom until it was time to go to college." She slapped her magazine shut, knocked one narrow hip against the table, and was out of the room.

My mother and I watched her, both of us frozen for a moment. It wasn't as if we hadn't seen it before, but it never ceased to be a surprise.

"You never spoke to me like that," my mother said quietly.

"No, I don't expect I did."

"I think I would have had a heart attack," she said. But then she thought about it some more. "Or I would have killed you. One or the other."

"I think that's right." Sometimes I wanted to run after Camille and grab her. *Where is Kitten!* I wanted to know. *What have you done with my daughter?*

"You and Sam need to do something about this. That girl has too many privileges. She talks on the phone all the time, goes out with her friends. She has a car!"

I wondered if my mother thought I hadn't noticed that one.

"How can you allow a child to behave that way and let her have a car?"

"I don't know," I said honestly, because even though I wasn't interested in hearing her point of view at the moment, it was not entirely without validity.

My mother shook her head. "So the groceries can wait for two minutes. Come sit down and look at these forms."

And so I sat down, my raincoat still pooling water in its cuffs, my groceries on the floor. I fished my reading glasses out of the bottom of my purse. "You know, Sam is so much better with these things than I am." I took the papers from her hands.

"Sam's so busy," she said. "He runs a hospital all day. He shouldn't be bothered with medical papers as soon as he walks in the door."

But she would ask him. She always did. I would fill out the forms and then she would ask Sam to correct my work.

"Ruth! You're getting those wet!" She leaned over and blotted the papers with a paper napkin. "Can't you at least dry your hands first?"

On my mother's behalf, I will say that the insurance forms were viciously confusing, and that after sitting there watching me read for a few minutes she did get up and start to put the groceries away, though she held up every other item and asked me where it went.

"I thought so," she'd say, and then put the can of soup with the other cans of soup.

My mother moved in with us a little more than a year ago after her house in East Lansing had been robbed in the middle of the day while she was playing bridge with friends. Whoever did it knocked down the front door. They didn't pick the lock or jimmy open a window, they just kicked the door in, smashed it to bits, and stepped inside. After that she didn't want to go home. She had a new door installed and waited to calm down. She went back to the hostess of the bridge party and stayed with her for a week, thinking the feeling of uneasiness would pass. When it didn't, she packed up what the burglars had deemed unfit to take, including her enormous collection of fabric remnants, and moved to Minneapolis to live with us.

My mother had been a high school music teacher who went back to school to get her certification in history and geography when the state's budget for music programs was cut back. She was practical because she had to be; that was the hand life had dealt her and she didn't complain. A roast chicken showed up as chicken hash the next night and then chicken soup for the weekend. My father, whom she had met at a convention of Michigan high school music teachers during the two weeks he actually was a high school music teacher, played piano at clubs, bars, and wedding receptions, his engagements sending him out later and later, and then farther and farther away, until it seemed like too much trouble to make the trip home. This was the early nineteen fifties, when being a divorced woman with a child was still a cause for sideways glances from other women in the grocery store, but my mother kept her head up and trudged forward. I try to imagine sometimes how hard her life must have been. I know that our life together was hard enough, but children are remarkably adaptable creatures, and if there is little there they settle for little. But my mother was a young woman, working all day, giving private piano lessons in our house on the weekends and after school. Sometimes my father would blow into town, seeming relaxed and handsome and nearly famous, but he always blew out again, and while he may have left behind a box of macadamia brittle or a child's coat that was already too small, he never left actual cash for the gas bill.

When my mother finally retired, it looked like things were going to be fine for a long time. She still gave private piano lessons and collected a manageable pension from the school system. She had her friends, her bridge group, her music appreciation club. She even went on a package tour of Europe that Sam and I had given her for her birthday. I always saw her as one of those women who would have to be dragged out of her home by six policemen when she was ninety-eight. But then, what in life actually works out the way you think it's going to?

I wish I could find the person, the people, who kicked in her door. I never have gotten over my need to tell them that they took too much. The television, the stereo, largely worthless jewelry, six pieces of family silver which included her mother's butter dish that had come over with the family on the boat from Denmark, they could have all of it, but they shouldn't have kicked in the door. That was the thing that changed my mother for good. Divorce and hard work and single motherhood—she was up for all of those challenges. But to be seventy-three years old and know that someone can just kick in your door, that they don't even have to have enough finesse to force the lock, really destroyed her sense of how the world was ordered. It scared her, my mother, who had always been such a brave person. Even after it was long over it left her unsure of things. Now she was living in what was once my guest room and lacked the certainty to fill out consumer questionnaires without my going over them with her.

"Oh, Ruth," my mother said, looking over my shoulder while I tried to wrestle Blue Cross Blue Shield to the ground. "I don't know what I'd do without you."

"I think that's got it." Not that it mattered. Sam would check it. I pushed back from the table. The kitchen floor had only the lightest sheen of water left on it. My hair was half dry. "I should get to work on dinner."

My mother looked at her watch and I saw a familiar cloud of hesitancy and desire pass over her face.

"Oprah's on," I said. My mother was a fool for Oprah. "Go."

"I can help you."

I shook my head. "Dinner's a piece of cake. I'll be fine."

My mother headed off to the den and I was glad. I would take a moment by myself over practical assistance any day. There was a time when Camille used to pop out of her room at five-thirty, eager to mince onions and stir sauce. Then again, there was a time that a wall divided the east and west of Germany. Life was not a static experience. We shouldn't expect things to remain the same.

I held four chicken breasts in my cupped hands. I stared into the cold, translucent flesh, wondering how I could make them sing. I got tired of cooking dinner. Everybody gets tired of cooking dinner. There's too much responsibility. Did we eat this last week? Is this good for you? Is it balanced, is it green, will he like it, will she eat it, do I have the right ingredients, enough time, will this new recipe fail me? Camille wouldn't eat red meat anymore and had recently informed me as I set a plate of chops on the table that pork, so widely advertised as "the other white meat," was in fact as red as a flank steak. "Pigs are more intelligent than dogs," she said. "Why don't we just eat Benjy for dinner?" Lately she had been talking about giving up chicken and fish, maybe even becoming a vegan, which would reduce me to coming up with fascinating ways to cook broccoli every night without benefit of cheese sauce. My mother clipped chilled-salad recipes from women's magazines and taped them onto the refrigerator to voice her own preferences. Sam was deeply suspect of anything that he hadn't eaten before and had been known to pick dishes apart until he could clearly identify each of their elements. Wyatt, my vacuum, the only truly brilliant eater in the family, was a junior in college and enjoying the deep, hot wells of cafeteria food that could be ladled onto a tray. As for me, I couldn't have cared less. I think I would have been happy with a carton of lemon yogurt every night if it meant I didn't have to cook. Dinner, I think, would be fascinating if I only had to do it once a week. Dinner could be riveting if there was a way to make it cake.

I washed the chicken breasts and stripped out their tendons with pliers. As I was beating them flat between sheets of wax paper I started thinking about making a carrot cake. I had plenty of carrots. I had been planning on making glazed carrots for dinner but there was no reason why I couldn't shred them instead. My family tended to grumble when there was too much cake in the house. As a rule, they liked to see cakes go right out the door, to school bake sales, to sick friends, for someone's birthday. When Camille's friends came over they told her she was lucky. "My mom wouldn't know how to bake a cake if you threw a box of Duncan Hines at her," her friend Becca said as she lobbed off a hunk of chocolate chiffon, but Camille only snarled. Still, if I made the carrot cake without frosting, if I put a minimal amount of sugar in it and baked it on a sheet pan so that I could slice it into squares, I could practically pass it off as cornbread. It hadn't been a great day, and no one ever objected to cornbread. I left the chicken for a minute and got out the flour. There were raisins and walnuts. I held two cold eggs in one hand and felt the knot between my shoulders start to unravel the tiniest bit around the edges.

An hour later Oprah had said her piece and my mother came into the kitchen and sniffed the air. "That's a cake." She pushed the oven light on and peered inside.

"Carrot bread." I pulled the pot holders out of their drawer.

"There is no such thing. Really, I'm going to be the size of a house if you keep baking this much."

"I've always baked this much and you've never been heavy a day in your life."

"That isn't true," my mother said, pouring herself a vodka and orange juice. "I looked like a snowman when I was pregnant with you."

"That was a long time ago. Nobody remembers it."

"I remember it," she said darkly.

I picked up the phone in the kitchen and called Camille's room. She had her own line with call waiting. No matter how remote Camille could be in person, she always answered the phone, which is why I strictly forbid her to have caller ID.

"Dinner," I said.

"Is Daddy home?" She wanted to know so that she wouldn't get stuck waiting in the kitchen. That was my other rule after no caller ID: We all ate dinner together.

I was about to answer truthfully when I heard the back door open. "Yes," I said, and she hung up.

The rain had not abated. Sam came in with sleek tributaries pouring off his suit jacket. He looked nearly drowned. He leaned toward me and I thought he was going to whisper something in my ear, but instead he pulled me to him and held me tightly in the great, wet walls of his arms. I hadn't been dry so long myself but I felt oddly dazzled by the spontaneity of his gesture. The water off his coat soaked through my blouse, and once he had kissed me and pulled away, I looked like someone had dumped a bucket of water on my chest.

"I'm sorry," Sam said. "I've ruined you."

"I dry very quickly."

"Hollis!" Sam said to my mother. "You have a drink. Be a pal and fix me one of those." It was my father who had started the tradition of calling my mother Hollis, her last name, rather than Marie, her first name. She said it was the only thing from their relationship that had stuck, other than me.

"It isn't orange juice," she said with some embarrassment.

"I didn't think it was orange juice. Did you think I thought you were drinking orange juice every night?"

"I did," my mother said. She looked a little confused and I wanted to tell Sam not to tease her.

He shook his head. "I know what you're drinking and I want to join you."

"On a Tuesday?" she said.

"This Tuesday." My soaking-wet, handsome husband seemed to be a bundle of life this evening. "Ruth, are you having a drink?"

"I wasn't planning on it."

"But you would," he said. "Things happen you don't plan on." Sam's blue eyes looked all the brighter for the rainwater still clinging to his lashes.

"Are you all right?"

"Never better," he said, but his voice didn't convince me. "Hollis, we want two of whatever you're having."

So my mother returned to the cabinet where the vodka was kept and assumed the role of bartender. She went back to the dishwasher to retrieve the shot glass. My mother believed that mixing a drink without a shot glass was tantamount to putting the bottle to your lips and tipping your head back.

Camille shuffled into the kitchen and for a second I thought I saw Sam's great good mood crumple a little at the edges. He seemed so moved to see her there that if it weren't for all the rain he was wearing, I would have thought he was tearing up. I held out a dish towel but he ignored it. He went to Camille and folded her in his arms.

"Daddy!" she cried, and wrenched away from him with some effort. "Are you *insane*? Look what you've *done* to me." Camille was wearing a T-shirt and some sweatpants and as far as I could see he hadn't done any real harm.

"Your father is in a hugging mood."

"He hasn't hugged me," my mother said to herself as her steady hand took the vodka right to the rim of the jigger.

Sam made an easy turn in his puddle of water but my mother took a giant step away.

"I'm *soaked*." Camille put a hand on either side of her head. It was as if she had been sent to live in a house of friendly chimpanzees and she was constantly astonished by the indignity of it all. Then she turned around and was gone again.

"Well, now you've done it," my mother said, handing Sam his drink. "You frightened her off. You know it's going to take at least a half an hour to get her to come out of her bedroom now. We could starve before she changes clothes."

"What are we doing here," Sam said, "taming the little fox?"

"I only try to hug her when she has a fever," I said. I was joking, of course. I was sort of joking.

Sam looked at the door through which our daughter had disappeared. "I think we should be more affectionate. That's one of the things we need to work on."

"Work on it yourselves," my mother said. She gave me my drink. She'd thrown in a splash of cranberry juice to make it pretty. I have to say it wasn't bad.

Sam hung up his coat on the back porch, where it could drip without consequence, and I put the chicken on the table. Camille came back in record time wearing a blue cotton sweater and a pair of low-slung jeans. She pointed at her father. "Don't."

He raised his hands to show that his intentions were honest.

"Doesn't this look good?" my mother said to the plate of chicken, which is what she said every night regardless of the meal.

"Chickens are shot full of antibiotics," Camille said. "And it's not just that. Girls are starting their periods at, like, seven now because the chickens have so many hormones in them."

"Everything is a health hazard if you want to look at it that way." Sam speared a piece of meat and put it on Camille's plate, where she looked at it as if it were a squirrel hit in a mad dash across the road. "Walking across the street is dangerous. Driving a car, very dangerous. Think about what's in the water, or in the air for that matter. For all we know we're sitting on top of the biggest source of radon in Minnesota. Did you ever think about that?"

"You're so morbid," Camille said morbidly.

Sam shook his head. "Not at all. I'm just sticking up for the chicken. My point is, you never really know what's good for you or what's bad for you. Have you done the right thing or the wrong thing? You never know what's going to get you until it's too late."

I put down my fork. My mother and daughter put down their forks as well. We all stared at Sam. "What in the world happened to you today?"

Sam sliced, chewed, reflected. "Nothing much."

"May I be excused?" Camille said to no one in particular.

"You haven't eaten," my mother said.

"I ate something," Camille said, though she must have meant she ate something for lunch because clearly she hadn't eaten her dinner.

"Stay put," Sam said.

"At least have a piece of cake," I said.

"Cake!" Camille cried. "You know I can't have cake. Why do you keep making cakes? This isn't a bakery."

"This isn't a bakery," Sam repeated quietly, as if it was news to him.

"She can't have cake if she hasn't eaten her dinner," my mother said.

But I was already on my feet, already heading over to the pan on the kitchen counter. The debate was still raging but I had a knife in my hand. It was carrot cake, after all, which is practically a serving of vegetables.

"I'm going to be the size of a house," Camille said.

"You are currently the size of a coat hanger. A house is a long way away." Sam reached forward and pulled her plate toward the middle of the table and I smoothly set the cake down in its place.

Usually he would complain about the cake too, but tonight he backed me up. Camille was grumbling, but up came the fork and she took a delicate bite.

"Cake when she hasn't had any dinner at all," my mother said. It was wrong. It was the moral equivalent to pouring vodka without a shot glass.

Camille's eyes fluttered and then closed. The cake was warm and her fork went down again. "Oh," she said quietly.

There was a time I cared: a meat, a vegetable, a starch, some cake. Life had an order, but now the point only seemed to be eating. Here was my daughter, eating, devouring, she was almost through with the cake.

"Did you make this with honey?" Camille said. There was something in her voice I nearly recognized. It sounded like interest, kindness.

"I did."

"Because sometimes—" She couldn't finish her sentence without stopping for another bite. "You use brown sugar?"

"It's another recipe."

"I like the honey."

"The problems they're having with bees these days," Sam began, but I held up my hand and it silenced him. There was too much pleasure in the moment to hear about the plight of the bees.

My mother took a long, last sip of her drink and then went to the counter to get the cake, the knife, and three more plates. "First the two of you are having a drink on a Tuesday, now we're all eating cake before we finish our dinner." She cut four pieces and gave the first one to Camille, whose plate was empty.

"It's madness. Anarchy. It must make you wonder what's coming next," Sam said.

My mother handed me my plate. I don't eat that much cake, but I never turn down a slice.

The four of us ate, pretending it was a salad course. Camille was right to pick up on the honey. It was the undertone, the melody of the cake. It was not cloying or overly sweet but it lingered on the tongue after the bite had been swallowed. I didn't miss the frosting at all, though it would have been cream cheese. I could beat cream cheese longer than most people would have thought possible. I could beat it until it could pass for meringue.

When we were finished with our cake we were all as happy as babies.

"Well," my mother said, laying down her fork.

"Perfect," Sam said, and ran his fingers over his plate for the crumbs.

Camille reached forward to her dinner plate and cut off a small piece of chicken.

So what if it hadn't been such a good day? There we were, having a good moment. A good moment is all that anyone should ask for.

"Sam," my mother said. "I'm sorry to bother you with this, but could you look over some insurance forms for me after dinner? Ruth did her best but I want to make sure that they're right. It never hurts to get a second opinion." It was her little medical joke and she made it often.

It wasn't such a serious question. My mother asked Sam to double-check her papers at least twice a week, but Sam mulled it over for a long time.

"I'm not sure I'm the best person to ask," he said finally.

"Of course you're the best person to ask."

Camille seemed to smell some impending family conflict and stood up from the table, but she wasn't quick enough. Sam told her to stay for a minute.

"I was going to wait until later. I was going to tell Ruth first."

"Tell Ruth what?" my mother said.

"Just tell Ruth," Camille said. "Don't tell us now."

"But we're all together, and you're going to find out sooner or later." Sam took Camille's wrist gently to stop her; she was edging toward the door.

"We aren't all together. Wyatt's not home," she said. "You should wait."

"Wyatt won't be home until summer vacation. That's still two months away."

"'Don't be in such a rush.' Don't you tell me that six million times a day?"

I realized I was holding my breath and I forced myself to exhale. I have to say, I was with Camille on this one; whatever it was, I wanted to push it off for a little while, but I knew that wasn't going to happen. Something had been set in motion and now there was going to be no stopping it. We all looked at Sam.

"I lost my job," he said.

"Fired?" my mother said.

Sam scratched the back of his neck. "Fired sounds very personal. This wasn't personal. You see, it was everyone, really, almost everyone." He looked at my mother, who was listening to him with extreme concentration. He tried a different approach. "Yes, I suppose you could say I was fired."

Sam's Lutheran hospital had been bought by a huge for-profit chain two weeks before. We had sat up at night talking about what could happen. In our worst-case scenarios we imagined a pay cut or even a transfer. Camille would have to switch schools in the middle of her junior year. She may never speak to us again. Those were the things we had been worried about. We had been thinking in terms of inconveniences. Turns out, our fears hadn't even been in the ballpark.

"We're going to have to sell the house, aren't we?" Camille said. "I'm going to have to go to public school."

"I don't think we have to worry about that right now."

Camille's eyes welled up with tears. She had a tendency to take things personally.

My mother stood up and came over to Camille. "We should let your parents talk."

Then plink, plink, one giant tear rolled down each of my daughter's porcelain cheeks and fell onto the empty cake plate. She and my mother put their arms around each other and left the room.

Sam picked up his glass and went to fix himself another drink. "That went badly."

It did go badly. I wanted to ask him, What was with the levity, the jovial attitude? Wouldn't the news have been easier to take if he had limped in the back door holding a handkerchief to his forehead? Maybe not. Maybe he was trying to give us all one last good time. Certainly this wasn't one of those moments we had any training for. My father had lost his job, my father lost his job every week. But as a musician, losing his job was just part of the cycle, like leaves falling from the trees but more regular. I thought of Willy Loman. I tried to remember what Willy's wife had said, if she had been supportive. I had no memory of her at all. "You seem to be taking it really well," I said. My voice was kind.

Sam leaned over and took my hand. He kissed my fingers. "To tell you the truth, I have no idea how I'm taking it. I think I'm in shock. This big group of corporates that have been there all week going over the books started calling people into the office, and one by one they're going in, Steve and Jordan and Diane—"

"They fired Diane?" She was always so nice to me at the Christmas parties. She had three kids.

"They went in like lemmings going for a swim. It was everybody. And I sat at my desk watching all of them and I'm thinking, This is criminal, this is awful, but, Ruth, it never once occurred to me that I was on the list. Even when they called me, I went in there thinking they wanted me to help the others with some sort of transition. I just went right on in, and everybody was watching, and everybody had figured it out except for me. What kind of ego is that? I never saw it coming."

"Well, there wasn't any warning." Not any warning for him or for me. Sam was home now and he didn't have a job.

"But you're not going to worry," he said. He could read my mind sometimes. When you live with someone for twenty-five years it isn't exactly a magic trick. "There are plenty of jobs for me. This only happened"—he looked at his watch—"three hours ago. Less than that. Two hours and forty-five minutes I've been unemployed. I don't think we should start panicking yet."

"I had no intention of panicking."

He kissed my hand again. "Let me fix you another drink. I thought it was good with the cake. We'll drink and eat cake and in the morning we'll come up with some sort of plan. I think it would be good if we didn't try to figure it out right this minute."

There was a dull, rattling fear in the lower part of my abdomen, but the calm in Sam's voice covered it like a soft layer of snow. Sure, we would figure this out. We had figured out plenty of things before this.

Chapter Two

THE MORNING WAS A DIFFERENT STORY. PANIC HAD set in during the night like rigor mortis. Sam was staring straight up at the ceiling, his eyes unnaturally large, his fists holding on to the edge of the sheet like it was the only thing keeping him from being flung against the ceiling.

"Bad night?" I said quietly.

"We are in big, big trouble," he whispered.

I propped up on one elbow. "Sam, that isn't true. We're going to take some time to figure this out, remember? That's what we decided."

"I have to find a job."

"You'll find a job."

He rolled over to face me, curling his pillow under his cheek. "What if I don't know how to do anything else? I'm old. They manufacture these kids now. They're geniuses. They live off of those big fancy coffees and a couple of protein shakes and they don't go home or want time off. All they know how to do is work. They were actually engineered to not have a life. How does someone like me compete with someone like them?"

"Were you up all night?"

"We're going to have to move, Ruth. We're going to have to sell the house. We can't afford to keep a house like this."

"You have a severance package, right?"

"It hasn't been completely negotiated yet. Anyway, we aren't living in the nineties anymore. Or the eighties. In the eighties they fired a man and gave him half of the company in stock options. Today you're just out there. Two months of health insurance and you're on your own."

"You know it's not going to be like that," I said, trying to comfort both of us. "There's going to be money and there's going to be time." I put my hand on top of his white knuckles. They were practically frozen. I tried to wiggle my index finger into his fist to loosen up his grip and get a little blood in there. "This is a hard thing, I know that, but it's happened to a lot of people before. We're going to get through it." We're going to get through it? Is that what people really said to one another when something bad happened? I hadn't worked outside the home since Wyatt was born. When I quit my job as a high school history teacher, it was because I was eight months pregnant and ready to start a new phase in my life, it wasn't because the principal was walking me to the door and handing me the contents of my desk in a cardboard box. When I left my job they threw me a party with cupcakes and all the kids made a big banner saying, A FAREWELL BASH FOR MS. NASH! The end of work was a celebration. After all those years of loyal service Sam hadn't been given so much as a cupcake. Frankly, I thought he was too good for them.

"It's possible," I said, "that this might turn out to be a good thing."

"I don't see how that would be possible." He wasn't blinking. I hadn't noticed that before.

"Well, the truth is you haven't exactly been in love with your job for a long time, and you probably never would have left on your own, even though you thought about it plenty. So what if this is the thing that forces you out of the nest?" This was pure improvisation on my part but it was starting to sound good to me. It was sounding right. "There's a perfectly good chance that this is a day you're going to remember for the rest of your life. This is the day when you got your second chance, when everything changed."

"We have a mortgage, a son in college, a daughter in private school who is about to go to college, sizable credit-card bills, and a pitiful savings account. I think I'm going to remember this day for a long time."

I mulled this over, trying to find the hole in his reasoning but not coming up with one. I scooted over to Sam's side of the bed and put my arms around him. "You just need to relax. Take some time, think about yourself for a change. When you're ready there's going to be a great job for you."

Sam slipped one arm beneath me and sighed. "You're very charitable for a woman whose husband is unemployed."

"Temporarily unemployed," I said. "You don't exactly have a long history of slacking off."

Sam kissed me and for a second I had the distinct impression that the mood in the bedroom was about to shift from desperation to romance, but then the phone rang. Sam sat straight up, the sheet still knotted in his fists. The panic was back. "What if it's them?" he said.

"Them?"

"What if it's the hospital? What if they changed their minds?"

"Sam, it's not the hospital." Whoever it was was calling too early. It wasn't even six o'clock in the morning. I leaned over to get the phone.

"Wait," he said. "Don't answer it. I don't know what I'm going to say."

"You won't have to say anything. I don't want to wake up Mother and Camille."

The call was collect and so it was my father, who had never been awake at quarter till six in his life unless he hadn't been to bed the night before. The operator never said it was Guy calling for Ruth. He always had to make the names up, Mahler calling for Alma, or Rosencrantz calling for Guildenstern. This morning it was Sacco calling for Vanzetti, which made me think he was probably in some sort of trouble. I said I would accept the charges. Sometimes he called twice in a week and then we wouldn't hear from him again for ten months. It was hard to track him down. His home was a series of hotel rooms and mail pick-ups. At seventy-five he was still playing piano in bars and on cruise ships. A couple of times I had encouraged him to think about the future and he'd had a good laugh and we'd dropped it. My father wasn't anyone I knew particularly well and so his future wasn't any of my business. I was hoping this call had nothing to do with money. It wouldn't be the best morning to call this house for money. The operator connected us and my father said my name. In the background I could hear all sorts of squawking and overhead announcements, but I couldn't tell what they were announcing, exactly.

"Dad, it's so early. Are you in a bus station?" I asked.

"Not a bus station. Do you want to take another guess?"

I listened harder. Normally I wouldn't have enjoyed this game but I wasn't so eager to get back to the business at hand.

Sam tugged at the sleeve of my nightgown. "Your father?" he mouthed.

I nodded. I listened again.

"Hurry up and guess," my father said, his voice full of booming good nature. He must have been up all night, in which case he could not possibly be sober.

"A casino."

"She thinks I'm in a casino," he said to someone, and I heard a woman's voice laugh and repeat the funny sentence to another woman, who also laughed, from farther away.

"Okay," I said. "I give."

"Darling girl, your old dad's coming for a little visit."

Now I sat up in bed. I twisted the cord around my wrist and pulled it snug. "Well, that wouldn't be the best plan because as you may remember my old mom lives here now."

"She's still there? I thought she would have found her own digs by now."

"These are her digs."

"Can you tell him you'll call him back?" Sam said. "We're in the middle of a crisis here."

"Dad?"

Sam reached up and put his hand over the receiver. "But don't tell him what happened."

"I wasn't going to tell him."

Sam let the phone go and fell back on the mattress like a coconut falling out of a tree. He made a soft thud.

My father cleared his throat. "I'm sorry about your mother, I know that makes things a little complicated for everybody, but we'll work around it."

"It doesn't make things complicated. It makes things impossible. I don't mean to be coldhearted here, but you remember that Mother hates you, right? This is her home now. I can't just—"

"Ruthie, listen again."

This time I imagined my father holding the phone up to the ceiling and suddenly I could hear quite clearly what the intercom voice was saying. "Dr. Lewis, please report to the ICU." It was the way he would break some sort of bad news, to make a riddle out of it, to come around to the information by the most circuitous route possible.

"Dad, what's happened?"

"I had a little accident."

"And you're hurt?"

"I'm fairly hurt," he said, his voice as chipper as ever. "It isn't an impossible situation but I am going to need to come and stay with you even if it means we have to grind up a few Valium in your mother's Metamucil."

"How are you hurt?"

"I broke my wrists."

"You broke your wrist?" That didn't seem so impossible. A person could still get around in the world with a broken wrist.

"Wrists. Plural. Both of them. I've got a lovely nurse named Gina who's holding the phone for me right now."

"You can't hold the phone?"

"I can't hold a fork."

"Let me talk to Gina." I pressed the phone against my chest and whispered to Sam, "This isn't good."

"She wants to talk to you, darling," I heard my father say, and then Gina said hello.

"Are you Guy's daughter?" Gina had a big, solid smoker's voice. I imagined her heavyset, bleached, with frosted lipstick. My father's type.

I owned up to being the daughter and asked her what the problem was.

"The problem is your dad has three sets of pins in each of his wrists. They did the surgery when they brought him in last night."

"Surgery?"

"Those pins don't get in there by themselves."

"This is serious."

"This is pretty serious. Bones don't heal so quickly when you get to be a certain age."

"You think I'm too old for you?" I heard my father say in the background.

Gina didn't answer his question. "The doctors think with time and a good bit of physical therapy he should make a solid recovery."

There were a million questions to ask but none of them came to mind. I just saw my father propped up in a hospital bed, his arms plastered straight out in front of him, and for reasons I could not explain I felt guilty. Maybe he hadn't been much of a father but I certainly hadn't been much of a daughter. Suddenly there were tears in my eyes and Sam was whispering to me, "What happened? What happened?"

"What happened?" I said to Gina.

"It seems to be a pretty complicated story. We've had a couple of versions since last night. The bottom line is he fell and smashed his wrists."

"But nothing else."

"His wrists, his right elbow. I think he's got one shoulder that's sprained. It was enough."

"Oh, Dad," I whispered. "Let me talk to him again."

"He's taking a good bit of Percocet for the pain right now. He may not sound entirely like himself."

But he had sounded exactly like himself, which made me

wonder if he had been taking Percocet for a while. "Dad? Can you hear me?"

"I didn't fall on my ear, darling."

"I didn't know if Gina had the phone up."

"She's doing a great job."

I almost couldn't ask it. The question got halfway up my throat and then lodged there like a chip of crab shell. "Do you know if you're going to be able to play the piano again?"

And then my father roared. His laugh was huge and round and I could hear the nurses laughing with him even though they wouldn't have known why they were laughing. He sputtered and coughed, trying to bring himself down again. "Ruthie, you're a genius! That was the first thing I said. I'm smashed to bits and they're taking me off to surgery, all these doctors are poking and prodding, and right before they put me under I say, 'Doc, will I ever play the piano again?' And the man looks at me with contempt. Contempt! He says, 'I wish you guys could come up with a new line.' Like I'm taking up his time by even asking."

"That's terrible."

"So I say, 'You have to understand, this is how I make my living. I play the piano.' And he tells me to lie still. Some other kid, I swear to you not a day over sixteen, comes in calling himself the anesthesiologist. He comes at me with a mask and saying I should start counting backwards from one hundred. By this point I'm irate, and I say, 'Bring a piano into this operating room at once and I'll show you who's kidding around!' My old wrists are splattered all over the gurney, of course, but I would have rallied them for one last round of 'Moonlight in Vermont.'"

I could hear the nurses gasping in the background, they were laughing so hard. My father had an audience, a full house. He was high on Percocet and surrounded by nurses and had his daughter's undivided attention. "So the doctor says, 'What's the opening chord for "Rhapsody in Blue"?' and I say, 'C sharp minor, you jackass.' And then he blinks at me. It's three in the morning and I swear to you, Ruthie, until this instant the guy had been completely asleep. He tells the junior anesthesiologist to hold off for a second. He asks me who I play and what kind of piano I like. It turns out this guy has a Beckstein in his living room. Some rich surgeon who can probably just barely pick his way through 'Chopsticks.' A Beckstein! Such a waste. But now his heart is in the game, and he says he's going to make a real pianist of me yet. He says I'll be playing Rachmaninoff when he's through with me. He thinks I can't play the Rach."

I was wondering if he actually could play Rachmaninoff when all of a sudden my father was quiet, and the quiet alarmed me.

"Dad?"

Then I heard Gina's voice again. She said that my father could tell me the rest of the story when he got here, that he needed to get some sleep.

"Ruthie?" Gina said.

"Ruth," I said.

"Ruth, we'll check in with you after the doctor comes by and let you know when your father is going to be discharged. Then you can come pick him up."

I closed my eyes and tapped the earpiece of the phone against my forehead a couple of times while Sam watched with real interest. "Could we speak privately?" I asked the nurse.

"Sure."

"I mean, not in front of my father. Could you go to another phone?"

"Your father is out like a light. I can't believe he stayed awake this long. He isn't going to hear anything we say."

Was it possible to fall asleep so quickly? Again I saw him, small in the bed, his arms swallowed whole by his casts. I tried to picture myself inside the cake, and when that didn't work, I tried to picture my father inside the cake, casts and all. That seemed better. "How important is it that he come to stay with us?" I said. "I don't want you to think I'm a monster, but my father and I aren't close, and my mother lives with us, and my father and mother *really* aren't close, and it's going to create—"

But Gina stopped me. "It's not my business to pass judgments one way or the other, so let me just speak medically here. Your father is old enough that going into a nursing facility is probably going to be hard on him. A lot of people his age go in seeming pretty young and they just don't come out. His chances for a full recovery are going to be better if he's with family. His chances of not winding up with some problem he didn't go in with are going to be better. Now, if you can't do that, you can't do it. Only you know the answer to that question. If you have to put him in a facility, you're going to have to think about the cost. I don't know what your father's financial situation is, if he has good insurance, but if he doesn't, then that creates a whole other set of problems. I can pretty much guarantee you that money is the key to good care in a situation like this one."

"Right," I said. "I understand."

"You've got some time to think about it," Gina told me. "At least a couple of hours."

"I don't even know where you're calling from."

"Mercy Hospital," she said.

"No, I don't know what state you're calling from. Where is he?"

"Des Moines," she said, and then added for greater clarification, "Iowa."

"He broke *both* his wrists?" Sam said.

"That's the story."

"How did he fall?"

"I didn't get any of the details." Des Moines wasn't too far away. He could have just as easily been in Tucson. I wondered briefly if he had been meaning to visit.

Sam shook his head. "I guess he's coming here, then."

"How can he?" I pulled the pillow over my head and pushed it into place. *Pull the mask down firmly and cover your nose and mouth,* a voice instructed in my head. *Breathe normally.*

"It's not so much a matter of how can he," Sam said, gently removing the down pillow from my head. "It's a matter of how can he not?" His nose was only a few inches from my nose. He looked resigned but not particularly upset. I was now the one who was upset. "I may not know your dad well, but I can promise you two things: He doesn't have supplemental health insurance and he doesn't have anyplace else to go."

I wanted to protest, Who doesn't have supplemental health insurance? But the clear, unadorned truth of what my husband was saying didn't leave me much room to argue. "How will I tell my mother?"

"I have no idea about that one, but if you promise to wait until after I've left the house to do it, I'll go pick him up."

Under normal circumstances, say, yesterday afternoon, Sam would not have readily volunteered to drive to Des Moines, but this morning was a different story. He was depressed, adrift, and he saw my father's problem as one that was bigger than his own. He seemed almost perky as he took his shower and moved around the room getting dressed.

"Don't you think you should wait until the doctor calls?" I said. I didn't want him to go until I had told my mother. I wanted to be able to present the visit as a possibility rather than an inevitability that was barreling up I-35 toward our house.

"The doctor will call and tell us to come and get him. End of story. He's Medicare. They aren't going to want to keep him in that bed a minute longer than they have to."

"But you don't know that. He could need more surgery."

Sam looked at his watch. "I've been an unemployed hospital administrator for just over fourteen hours. I doubt the drill has changed too much since I got out of the business."

"Wouldn't you at least rather fly?"

Sam shrugged. "I have the time. Besides, the driving might actually be easier on him."

I stood up and put my arms around my husband. "You're an awfully good guy to be doing this."

"An awfully good guy would stay here and break the news to your mother while you drove to Des Moines. I'm not so good."

"It's just that—" I stopped in hopes of finding a better way of saying this. "I know you have a lot of other things on your mind."

Sam kissed my forehead, something he had done on our first date when he couldn't work up the nerve to kiss me good-night. Ever since then I have found it to be a gesture of supreme tenderness. "This will give me a chance to think some things through, like where I want to work. Then I'll come home and start looking for a job. I bet it's all going to turn out great."

I had to hand it to my father: He was still sedated in Des Moines and he had already managed to settle Sam's nerves in Minneapolis. "I know it will."

I encouraged Sam to put a couple of things in an overnight bag, even though he assured me he wasn't going to be gone overnight. "When you get back from picking up my dad, you should take a couple of days and go sailing."

"It's too cold to go sailing now."

"So don't go on the lakes. Go down to Florida. Maybe your brother would meet you, or you could take somebody from work."

"I know some guys who aren't very busy." Sam smiled. "But I think we should be saving our money right now. I'm talking about having to sell the house and you're telling me to go on vacation."

"It might be good. You know, relax, think things over." Sam had grown up on the lake in Chicago and had sailed all through his youth. Being out on the water relaxed him like nothing else. There was hardly ever time to do it now, but every time he stepped off a boat he looked ten years younger.

"We'll see," he said, and picked up his bag.

I pulled on my bathrobe and together we went down to the kitchen. My mother was up, but as far as I knew she was always up. She was up when we went to bed at night and she was up when we came down in the morning.

"Are you going into the office?" she said to Sam. After all, he clearly had the look of a man who was going somewhere with great purpose.

"I don't have a job," he reminded her.

My mother was flustered and she knit her fingers around the edges of her coffee cup. "I know that. I just thought that maybe, I don't know, that you were going back for papers or something."

Sam assured her it was nothing like that.

"Of course, you're not wearing a suit. If you were going to work, you'd be wearing a suit."

Sam laughed. "Hollis, you missed your calling. You would have been a brilliant detective." He headed for the door.

"You aren't leaving already?" There was a trace of panic making a sharp edge around my words. "You haven't even had a cup of coffee."

"I'll pick one up," he said. "This way I'm still ahead of the traffic."

Sam left the house every morning and I have to say his departures were hardly an event, but this morning I wanted to throw myself around his ankles.

"You girls have fun," he said, and waved to us. Just like that, he was gone.

"Ruth," my mother said in a low voice. "I think that something is terribly wrong."

I looked back at my mother. I could make her a list of what was wrong. "What?"

She leaned toward me even though we were alone together. "He had a bag," she whispered.

"A bag?"

"He had a *suit*case."

I looked back out the window and watched Sam's car pulling away in the bright clear light of early morning. Wouldn't that be something if this was all a ruse, if Sam was taking his small duffle bag and making a run for it? "I know," I said. When there is no good place to start, you just have to pick something at random. This was going to be it. "I packed it for him."

"Is he leaving?" my mother said. There was such fear in her voice, and all at once my heart went out to her completely. How must she have felt when my father left her? Both of her parents were dead, she had a small child, a schoolteacher's salary. What was I thinking, telling my father he could come here to stay? But then there were those casts. I straightened up in my chair and tried to pull it together.

"Sam is driving to Des Moines."

My mother started to react to that, a drive she would have felt was too long to make alone, whatever anxieties she might have had that this meant we were all moving to Des Moines, but I held up my hand to stop it before it started. "He is driving to Des Moines to pick up Dad."

She cocked her head to one side like a dog that was trying to make sense of some unfamiliar sound. "Dad as in your father Dad?"

"Dad had an accident," I said. I waited to see a flicker of pain or anxiety cross my mother's face but nothing came. She could have cared less if my father had been run over by a bus in Des Moines and Sam was going out to make funeral arrangements. I reached over and took my mother's hand. "I don't completely understand what happened, but he fell and broke both of his wrists. He isn't going to be able to take care of himself for a while and I told him he could come here. I'm sorry about this, I really am. I know this is going to be hard on you, but when the hospital called this morning, I didn't know what else to do."

My mother looked at me for a minute and then she took her hand away. "Well then," she said. "I guess I'll have to find a place to live."

"Mother."

"It doesn't give me a great deal of time, but when I put my mind to something, I can usually get it accomplished. It's not as if I've never been on my own before."

"Mother, you're not moving out."

"What choice do I have? You invite my ex-husband in to live with us. Do you really think I can just stay here?"

"Mother, please. I didn't invite him to live with us. He's very sick. He needs my help. I know he's your ex-husband, but he's also my father, and I have some responsibilities to him."

My mother looked at me in a way that made me shiver with cold. "He never had any responsibilities to you."

I closed my eyes and nodded. This was a very difficult conversation to have, and without a cup of coffee, it seemed almost impossible. "I know you're right. I will try to make this as quick and as comfortable for everyone as I possibly can. I'm really, really sorry."

"I never would have done this to you," my mother said quietly. On one hand she couldn't. I didn't have an ex-husband. On the other hand I knew what she was saying. She was always true to me. She put me first.

At the moment when I saw our conversation moving toward the more practical details of sleeping arrangements, there was a terrible scream that came from the back of the house. My heart froze. My instinctive reflex was to take it personally; *what had I done to cause screaming?*

"Seven thirty-five!" Camille came into the kitchen wild-eyed, her dazzling yellow hair twisted into a plastic clip, her pajama bottoms trailing over her feet. Her face was so pretty like this, without makeup. She looked like she was twelve. "You didn't wake me up!" She was howling.

I looked up at the kitchen clock. "Honey, I—"

"I have to *shampoo* this morning. I have a test." She pressed her fists over her eyes while the huge injustice of her life pounded her down. "Forget it. Forget it. I don't know why I even bother trying. I'm going back to bed. I'm not going to school."

"Honey, I'm sorry I forgot to wake you up. There's been a lot going on here this morning." Honey, I have bought you three alarm clocks and shown you how to use them. Honey, I am a human being, not an alarm clock. "You have to go to school." I tried to make my voice peaceful, neutral.

"If you thought my going to school was so important, then you might have remembered to knock on my door this morning."

"Camille," I said.

"You can't make me go to school like this."

My mother picked up her nearly empty cup of coffee and slammed it down on the table hard enough to break the cup free of the handle. It spun around twice and then fell over on its side, making a pool of milky coffee on the table. She lifted the small ceramic U still curled in her fingers and pointed it toward my daughter. "You are sixteen years old. This is not a hotel. Get yourself dressed this instant and get out of here."

Camille suddenly wore the same bewildered look my mother had had three minutes before, and while she opened her mouth, she said nothing. She blinked, turned, and went back to her room without so much as slamming the door.

I looked at my mother in disbelief. I didn't even know she was capable of sounding so angry. "Thank you," I said.

"It's all in the surprise factor," my mother told me. "If I did it all the time she wouldn't listen to me, either."

Chapter Three

MY FATHER WOULD SLEEP IN WYATT'S ROOM. MY mother didn't like this. Wyatt's room was Wyatt's room regardless of whether or not he was away at college. She followed me from the northwest corner to the southwest corner of the bed while I stripped off the sheets. She did not offer to help.

"This says to Wyatt that he is no longer a member of this family, that his room doesn't mean anything to you." She picked up the framed picture of his high school basketball team and wiped her sleeve across it, implying dust.

"Mother, Wyatt could care less. Call him. Ask him."

"Put your father somewhere else."

I stopped, my arms full of the blue-striped top sheet and pillowcases. I strongly suspected they were clean. "Okay, we're not going to put him in Camille's room. He's not going to sleep with me and Sam. Something tells me that your room isn't a likely candidate—"

"I'm not talking about putting him in another bedroom. The couch in the den is all he needs. He's probably been sleeping on park benches for years anyway. If you put him in a nice bed like this, he won't know what to do with himself." But then something much worse occurred to my mother. She put down the photograph. "Or he might *stay*. Don't you see it? This is probably all a ruse. He'll come here, make himself comfortable in Wyatt's bed, and the next thing you know we won't be able to get him out of here with an exterminator."

"What do you think? He broke his own wrists out of some desperate desire to come and visit us? You can't put a man with two broken wrists on a couch. Logistically it doesn't work. There wouldn't be room for him." I snapped off the fitted sheet.

"Did I say the couch? Put him in the garage. We'll make up some sort of bed for him out there. We can rent a roll-away. You can leave your car in the driveway. That's sacrifice enough."

I put down the bundle of laundry in Wyatt's desk chair and opened a dresser drawer. "You're not even being serious now." I scooped out an armload of sweaters.

"What are you doing?"

"Well, I figure he'll need some drawer space."

My mother turned pale. She put a hand on the headboard to steady herself. "He is going to stay, isn't he?"

"For a while, just until he's better."

"You're lying to me. You've been lying to me all along. You think that once he's in, there will be nothing I can do about it. He's moving in here."

I put the sweaters down on the bed and went to my mother. Her eyes were filling up with tears behind her glasses. "I know this brings up a lot of bad memories, but you have got to trust me."

"Trust you?" My mother stepped away from me. "How could I ever trust you?"

When she turned and left I did not go after her. There was nothing else I knew to say. A few minutes later I heard her banging out an especially angry Beethoven piano sonata in the living room, the notes swarming the air like a cloud of wrathful bees. Either this visit was going to be the most painful, horrible thing that had ever happened or it would just be bad. I picked up Wyatt's baseball glove and slipped it on. I balled up my other hand and beat my fist into the glove until I felt something that surpassed a sting. Wyatt was a lefty.

The truth of the matter is I didn't bear my father any particular ill will. I had for a short time when I was young. I thought he was a terrible man. But as I got older it occurred to me that just because someone isn't cut out to be a husband or a father doesn't make him terrible, only terribly disappointing. Sometimes my father came to Minneapolis. He played piano at the Marquette Hotel downtown and I would go and hear him. It happened once after my mother moved in with us, and I lied and told her I was going to a book club. They weren't life-changing events, those evenings, but they were nice. My father was a funny guy who liked a lot of attention. He played the piano with the same kind of unself-conscious elegance with which Fred Astaire danced. He could make the piano tell jokes. He never looked at his hands. I sat at the bar and nursed a very weak white wine spritzer and every now and then my father would lean into the microphone and say, "Ladies and gentlemen, do you see that beautiful woman over there? Would you believe me if I told you she's my daughter?" The first couple of times it had mortified me, then after a while I came to see that the only thing to do was nod and give a little wave. My father's fingers wandered off into the high notes, remembered what they were supposed to be doing, and then made their lazy way back down toward the melody again. When my mother played the piano, which she did beautifully, she always had an expression on her face like she was trying to unscrew an especially tight lid off a jar. I never once saw her play a note that wasn't written on the sheet music. I never looked at my parents and wondered why they broke up. I looked at my parents and wondered how they had managed to get through one entire meal together without killing each other.

To be honest, I didn't know all that much about my father, or I knew as much about him as anyone who bought a gin and tonic and sat at the bar. He was born in San Diego, he started playing the piano when he was four, he started playing in clubs when he was fourteen, sometimes hitchhiking up to Los Angeles and then later up to San Francisco. He liked to tell these stories into the mike. It occurred to me now I didn't even know if they were true. He painted himself as a skinny boy in dusty jeans, his dark hair combed back with Vaseline, his one suit for playing folded neatly in the bottom of a paper sack while he waited by the side of the road for a ride. My father, it seemed, had two talents in his life, one for music and one for mobility. He traveled as effortlessly as he played. The slightest possibility of a job was reason enough to get him back in his car in the years he had a car, back on the bus when he didn't, or on a plane in his few phases of being flush. I really doubted that he cared when a job was over. It just meant that there was a chance at another job in a new town. I tried to imagine him here, his wrists decked out in casts. I wondered if he would be able to turn a doorknob.

Wyatt's room was clean but the air seemed a little off. With some real effort I managed to pry open a window. It was March in Minnesota and there was still some late spring snow on the ground, but the cold air was wonderful. When I started to look around I was able to locate the source of the stuffiness: Wyatt's room was full of sneakers. I found eleven odd shoes in the bottom drawer of his dresser. I found dozens of pairs under the bed and piled up in the closets. They were old, peeling rubber, missing laces. Their insoles hung halfway out like the tongues of overheated dogs. They represented every trend in athletic footwear in the past ten years, puffy white high-tops that looked like big marshmallows, techno running shoes with clear windows in the soles, preppy boating shoes with smooth bottoms. I wanted to throw them all away, but then I wasn't sure. Was he keeping them for a reason? Was he sentimental about one thing? Was it all right to get rid of old shoes without my son's permission? Was it all right to store my ailing father in a room full of shoes? I went to the kitchen and got a big black Hefty bag. I would put the shoes in the basement for now. That was a compromise. After my father left I would put them back, and then at some point I would talk to Wyatt and ask him about his collection.

"Are you throwing those away?" my mother said, popping up out of nowhere. My mind was a million miles off, in some piano bar. I dropped a small blue Ked, a child's Ked, and covered my heart with my hand.

"Were you in the closet?" I asked her. Why hadn't I noticed the Beethoven had stopped?

"Those are Wyatt's shoes!"

"I'm just clearing them out for now. He's kept every pair of shoes he's had since he was six."

My mother looked at me like I was burning his birth certificate. "I didn't expect this of you," she said. And then she was gone again.

How had I come to this point? I couldn't comfort my husband or discipline my daughter or help either of my parents. I couldn't even decide if it was okay to throw out a pair of shoes. I sat down on the bed and felt a terrible lump coming up in my throat. Then just when I thought I was going to really break down for a good cry, I remembered a large bag of pistachio nuts in the back of the pantry. I don't know what made me think of them. I had hidden them beneath several packages of dried pasta. Sam liked pistachio nuts. I bought them for a cake recipe I had seen in *Gourmet*. I stood up like a sleepwalker, my hands empty of sheets or shoes. I would take care of all of this once the cake was in the oven. The recipe was from several months ago, I didn't remember which issue. I would find it. I would bake a cake.

My father liked exotic things. On the rare occasions we went out to dinner together over the years, he always wanted us to go to some little Ethiopian restaurant down a back alley or he would say he had to have Mongolian food. He would like this cake. It was Iranian. There was a full tablespoon of cardamom sifted in with the flour, and I could imagine that it would make the cake taste nearly peppered, which would serve to balance out all the salt. I stood in the kitchen, reading the magazine while the sharp husks of the nuts bit into the pads of my fingers. I rolled the nut meat between my palms until the bright spring green of pistachios shone in my hands, a fist full of emeralds. I would grind the nuts into powder without letting them turn to paste. I would butter the parchment paper and line the bottom of the pan. It was the steps, the clear and simple rules of baking, that soothed me. My father would love this cake, and my mother would find this cake interesting, and Sam wouldn't be crazy about it but he'd be hungry and have a slice anyway. Maybe I could convince Camille it wasn't cake at all. Maybe I could bring them all together, or at least that's what I dreamed about while I measured out the oil.

Once my nine-by-twelve was safely in the oven at 400 degrees, the phone rang. I wondered if the caller had somehow sensed that he or she needed to wait.

"How would you feel about living in Des Moines?" Sam said.

People in Minnesota don't go to bed at night dreaming that one day they'll live in Iowa, but I figured I wasn't in any position to be close-minded. "I'm open to all discussion," I said diplomatically.

"It turns out I know the guy who's the head of this hospital. He used to work with me, it must have been ten years ago."

"You're at the hospital already?"

"The roads were wide open," Sam said. "I made great time. This guy, Dick McKenzie, he seems to think my situation may not be so desperate. In fact, he thinks it's the right time to make a move."

"Sam?"

"Hmm?"

"How's my father?" On the other end of the line I could hear the P.A. system calling out for one doctor or another. It was like I was talking to Sam at work.

"Oh, Ruth, I'm sorry. You must think I've lost my mind. Maybe I have lost my mind. Your dad's in good spirits. I'd say if you forgot to look at his arms, he'd be his same old self."

It wasn't much information, but then Sam had spent even less time around my father than I had over the years. "Is he in a lot of pain?"

"Let's say he's in a lot of pain management. He couldn't feel too bad. He's trying to pick up all the nurses."

"When do they think they'll let him go?"

"We're waiting on a discharge now. The doctor already told me he'd get sprung this afternoon. We'll be home tonight. Did you break the news to Hollis?"

"It was not our finest hour."

"Your dad is a wild card," Sam said with a sigh. "I think this is going to be hard on her."

From somewhere in the distance I heard a whoop.

"I think it's going to be hard on all of us," Sam added.

"Are you there with him now? Can I talk to him?"

"No, I'm down the hall at a pay phone. Guy was going to have a bath. He said he'd rather I gave them some privacy."

"Sure," I said. "Listen, you're an absolute saint for doing this."

"It had to be done. You won't completely discount Des Moines?"

"Not if you promise we can leave my parents in Minneapolis."

"We can sneak out in the middle of the night. Camille can take care of them. She could whip them into shape."

I wouldn't have minded sneaking off with Sam. After all, how many men would not only accept the fact that his divorced in-laws are moving in but actually go to pick one of them up? Considering all he had on him at the moment, he was unfailingly game.

After I got off the phone I had a heightened sense of resolve. I was going to be as game as Sam. I got the sheets washed and the tennis shoes stored away. I moved the little television out of the kitchen and into Wyatt's room. I even went out to the side of the house and cut a fistful of the few brave crocuses that were still standing and put them in a glass beside the bed. When Camille came home from school I spelled it all out for her: her grandfather, her grandmother, and the inherent limitations of the mix. I begged her to try to be helpful.

"Great," she said. "My dad's unemployed and I live in a nursing home now."

I told her to go and straighten up her room.

The last time I had lived in a house with my father I was two years old. Even before I was two, I gathered, he hadn't been much in residence. Good or bad, this was all the experience I was probably going to get in my life with my father, and no matter who was against it, I decided to give it my best shot.

Given how long it takes to get discharged, all the various conversations there were bound to be about medicines and rehab and follow-up visits, I assumed that they would be late, that Mother and Camille would be in bed and that I would be waiting up alone when they came in. I had not expected that Mother and Camille and I would be sitting in the kitchen eating lasagna (made with steamed vegetables and tofu as per Camille's request) when the back door swung open.

"The return of the natives," Sam said in a weary voice. In either hand he held a ridiculously old-fashioned suitcase with sharp corners and smooth tan sides. He set them on the floor and flexed his hands back. He looked like a man who had just run over to Kosovo for a loaf of bread.

My father, who had always seemed so much larger than life throughout my childhood, was in fact not such a large man at all. He was thinner than usual, and his white hair, which he liked to wear too long, fell down in his face. He had on a pair of tuxedo pants, black patent-leather shoes, and a hospital gown that tied up the back. He teetered slightly toward the dishwasher and Sam slipped his hand under one armpit. It was not what I had been expecting. I had been thinking casts, hard and white and plastered up in a tidy manner. The most dramatic thing I had imagined was maybe a sling. The truth was considerably less cinematic: Both arms were surrounded by silver halos, bright rings of Saturn through which thin metal rods pierced into his skin. His hands and wrists, puffy and scratched red, were suspended and eerily still. On the right side the apparatus reached higher. His elbow was pinned as well. Camille made a tiny sound and I gave her knee a gentle squeeze under the table. My father held his arms at an awkward forward angle as if he were coming in for an embrace or warding off another fall.

"Ruthie!" he said, trying to put some boom into his voice. "Let me look at you, girl!"

But we all just kept looking at him, staring in exactly the way that one would try very hard not to stare if he were a stranger you were passing on the street. There was just something so unfinished about it all, as if the doctors had realized he only had Medicare halfway through the surgery and so had chosen to just walk away. I gave my husband a helpless glance, but Sam looked pretty washed out himself. Someone just coming in on the story might have thought that whatever they had been through, they had been through it together.

"Dad," I said. "Are you okay?"

Behind me I heard the fast scrape of my mother's chair pushing away from the table.

"Hollis," my father said. "Not even a hello for your old husband?" He turned his body toward her and his arms leaned out for their embrace.

"Go to hell," my mother said. I had never seen such a look of fury on my mother's face. She was completely unmoved by the obvious display of physical trauma. In fact, for a minute I thought she was going to go in to break his leg.

And so the kitchen became paralyzed, the women on one side, the men on the other, my father reaching out for us, Sam holding him up. I wanted to go to them, to kiss them both, but I was afraid that would be the very thing that would send my mother into the abyss. To my deep amazement, it was Camille who crossed the linoleum, put her arms around my father's neck, and kissed his scratchy cheek. "Hey, Grandpa," she said.

He looked at her and then he looked at Sam. "Don't tell me this is Camille. Don't tell me you're little Camille?"

"I'm little Camille," she said.

"You're a butterfly," he said. There was no bravado in his voice. "Hollis, did you see how beautiful this child is?"

"I see her every day," Hollis replied, every word an ice cube thrown at his head.

Camille leaned forward and whispered something in her grandfather's ear that made him smile hugely. "I would ruffle your hair, dear child, but I am completely unable."

"That's all right," she said lightly. "I'm pretty much over the hair-ruffling thing."

I couldn't even remember the last time I heard Camille make a joke. "She's getting back at me," my mother whispered to me. "It's because I yelled at her this morning."

"That looks like it really hurts," Camille said, peering down at the place where the pin met the skin.

"It would, my love, were it not for pharmacology."

Finally my own feet became unstuck from their place on the floor and I went over and kissed my father. He still smelled like Bay Rum. I wondered if one of the nurses had put it on for him or if he had such a buildup in his system over the years that he would smell like Bay Rum in his grave. For a moment I touched my face against his neck while he held out an arm on either side of me. "Welcome home," I said.

"Ruthie, you're a champion, taking your old man in like this. Sam was telling me on the ride up that you two have problems of your own. I was sorry to hear about that. Sam is a fine man. Hard to imagine what kind of ninny would fire him."

I saw Sam look queasy. Something told me it had been a long drive. "We're all going to be fine," I said.

"Fine!" my father said, his voice so glad you would have thought I had actually said something of substance. "That's right! You're a champion, Ruth. She's a champion, isn't she, Hollis? You did a fine job with this one."

"Camille is a butterfly and Ruth is a champion," my mother said. "You've got it all figured out." The configuration in the kitchen had changed. Now Sam and Camille and I were standing with my father and my poor mother was left over by the plates of half-eaten lasagna.

"I don't suppose there's any chance of your letting bygones be bygones?" my father said.

"Not one chance."

He nodded. "Okay, then what are the chances of getting a glass of Wild Turkey? Des Moines is in another state, you know. That's a long ride."

Camille trotted off to the liquor cabinet with great authority, but my mother saved her the trouble of looking. "No Wild Turkey," she said. "It's not anything we stock."

"Is it all right for you to have a drink?" I asked.

"A drink? A drink is good for me. That's what the doctors all say now. I'm not talking about a scandal, just one drink. How is it you could have such a nice house and no Wild Turkey?"

"I'll go get some!" Sam said, and jingled his car keys in his hand to prove that he was good to go.

"Oh, Sam," I said, "after all the driving you've done? Relax, have something to eat. I can go to the liquor store."

Sam gave me a look of sheer desperation. I knew immediately what he wasn't saying: He had driven across Iowa with my father and now he needed an excuse to be alone, if only for the amount of time it took to drive to the liquor store. "I'll be two minutes."

"Get the big bottle," my father said. "They've got a plastic one. You could drop that sucker on the floor all day long and you're not going to break it. There's some money in my wallet. Here, just reach in my back pocket." My father turned around, offering up said pocket, but Sam declined to reach in.

"Well, it's good to see you haven't wasted your life," my mother said. "You've managed to learn something."

"Put a sock in it, Hollis," my father said lightly. "I come in peace."

I heard the back door click closed and realized Sam had left without any of the social formalities of departure. Without him, the remaining members of our party stared at one another with unbridled awkwardness. I tried to remember the times I had been in the room with both of my parents. There was the year that my father drove halfway across the country for my birthday. He showed up at the door with a doll in a grocery sack, a pink paper hat on his head, a noisemaker hanging out of the corner of his mouth, which he blew into hard when my mother opened the door. That in itself almost scared her to death. She started yelling at him and he started saying, "For God's sake, it's the kid's birthday." Which it wasn't. My birthday had been a month earlier. It wouldn't have been awful, his getting the date wrong, but as it turned out he had a job to play at a club in town. He was planning on being there anyway.

"How about some dinner?" I asked.

"Oh sure, dinner would be good. It smells good." My father stood there, arms out, as if he were waiting for someone to tell him when he might be allowed to unscrew them.

I took a light hold of his upper arm and walked him over to the table where he sat down in Sam's chair. Camille pulled up a chair next to his.

"All those pills they give you, they make your stomach feel a little funny, you know. I think some food would take the edge off things."

"I thought that was the Wild Turkey's job," my mother said.

I glared at her. "Do you have medicine you should be taking now?" I picked up plates and put them in the sink. I had the feeling we were all done with eating.

"Sam's got the pills. A whole suitcase full, you wouldn't believe it. That Sam, he's as good as a doctor. I guess when you hang out with them long enough, you know all the right questions to ask, but everybody was really taken with him in Des Moines. I told him on the way home, I think he should go to medical school. Wouldn't that be something, Ruthie? You could be married to a doctor after all."

"Dad's too old to go to school," Camille said.

I cut off a piece of lasagna and put it on a plate with some bread and a little salad. My father had gotten so frail. I was glad to have the pistachio cake.

"You're never too old to learn something and you're never too old to start over, right, Hollis?"

My mother stared down at him. She hadn't taken up her seat at the table again. "Would you stop turning to me for confirmation on everything? If you want to make proclamations, make them on your own."

"Right," he said, not listening to her at all. "Perfect." I put down the plate of food and some clean silverware in front of him while he rested his wrists against the table. He stared at his dinner for a minute and then he looked up at me and smiled. "Really great."

We all waited.

"See, the thing is, I can't pick the fork up, and if I could pick the fork up, I couldn't get it anywhere near the neighborhood of my mouth." We all looked at his fingers, all of which appeared to be about half a size too big. They were deathly still.

"Oh, God, Dad, I'm sorry. I don't know what I'm thinking about." I picked up the knife and the fork and cut off a bite. Then I blew on it a little, thinking it might be too hot.

"What are you going to do, chew it for him?" My mother wasn't being helpful.

"It takes a while to get the swing of it all," my father said. "Trust me. This just happened and I don't have the swing of it yet myself. I know that I'm hungry but there isn't much I can do about it."

I raised the fork to his mouth and he took the bite and chewed.

"Wow," Camille said.

My father nodded at her in recognition of all her "Wow" implied. "This is the way it is, kiddo. This is why people have families. You never know when you're going to fall and smash your wrists and not be able to get a fork in your own mouth. It wasn't such a long time ago your mother was spooning in the chow for you."

I wanted to say that's what I was thinking of. I knew that's what I should have been thinking of, feeding Wyatt and Camille with tiny spoons and Gerber jars, but I have to say the two experiences had nothing in common. There was an incredible sweetness to putting stewed apricots into those tiny mouths, their fat pink cheeks, their wide-eyed pleasure at being loved and cared for. But this, this just seemed sad. Dad's upper bridge was out, undoubtedly at the bottom of his overnight bag wrapped in plastic. He was short on teeth and I was grateful for the soft lasagna. Feeding my father didn't make me think about how cute my children were when they were young. It made me think about how dependent my parents were going to be as they got older, how dependent Sam and I would be one day on Wyatt and Camille. Frankly, the whole business broke my heart.

"So I haven't gotten the story yet," Camille said, "about what happened to you. What kind of accident was it?"

"Could I have a bite of the bread?"

"Butter?"

He shook his head. I held up the piece of French bread and my father bit into it and chewed thoughtfully. For a poor kid with a hardscrabble past, my father had lovely table manners. I always thought it was all the time he had spent playing in fine hotels. When he had finished chewing I reached up and dabbed the corners of his mouth with his napkin and he thanked me. "I was walking across a floor and I slipped. I guess they must have just waxed it. Down I went. Bang. That's the story."

"In a club?" Camille said. "Were you playing?"

"That's right."

My mother rolled her eyes. "And the Wild Turkey had nothing to do with it?"

My father tilted his head. "Why, Hollis, are you implying I was drunk?"

"If the highball glass fits. . . ."

"And by implying that I was drunk, are you then implying that it's my own fault that I'm in this hardware, that it was my own bad judgment that brought me here to screw up your domestic bliss?"

"You aren't as impaired as I thought you were."

I put down the fork. "Mother," I said in a tone of tentative authority I used with Camille.

My father sighed and shook his head. He still didn't wear glasses. I would guess he was too vain for glasses. Did he wear contacts? My God, would I have to fish his contact lenses out of his eyes?

"You weren't there, you old bag," he said without energy or malice. "You don't know what you're talking about. Lasagna please."

I cut off another forkful and served it up. "Try to be nice," I said to no one in particular.

"There is such a thing as an educated guess," my mother said in her best schoolteacher-patiently-explaining voice. "I know why you fell in the past and I think it's a fairly safe assumption why you fell this time."

"You barely knew me fifty years ago. You couldn't presume to know a thing about me now. Though I have to say you are in every sense remarkably unchanged." My father looked around, glancing over his shoulder to the kitchen door. Maybe he had figured coming here wasn't his best idea. I wondered if he was planning on making a run for it. "You would think that Sam would be back by now."

"Dad never goes anyplace in a straight line," Camille said. "He's probably wandered off to look for a magazine or something."

"Need that drink now?" my mother said in a nasty tone.

My father's head snapped around and he looked at her with such vicious focus and clarity, I felt quite certain his eyesight was still good. "I need to go to the bathroom."

"Oh," I said. "Oh, of course. You know where it is, don't you? Let me show you where it is."

Now my father sighed with what I could only assume was exasperation with me. "I need some help." He enunciated every word so clearly that they hardly fit together as a sentence.

"I bet Dad's going to be back any minute," Camille said quietly.

My father tapped the toe of his shoe on the floor in lieu of being able to tap his finger on the table the way he meant to. "It's one of the many inconveniences of growing old. There is less time to wait."

We all looked at each other for a minute.

It was a moment that most children of aging parents get to and maybe I was getting there a little earlier than some other people, but that was all right, right? Sooner or later there would be this moment, and if it was now, then there was nothing to do but step up to the plate. I did not put myself inside a cake. I didn't want to bring the cake into this. "Well, okay then," I said. "Let's go."

My mother stood up. "No."

"Mother, please, let's not make this—"

"I'm not going to have you touching your father's penis."

"Hollis, for God's sake," my father said.

"I have homework," Camille said, and with that she stood up and left the room without the slightest hint of a good-bye.

"Come on, Dad." I pulled out my father's chair and helped him up. My mother came around and put a firm hand on his upper arm.

"I'm not kidding," she said.

"So your final moral triumph is going to be to see me piss myself on the kitchen floor?"

"Shut up," my mother said, and started to steer my father away from me.

"You're taking him?" I said.

"I'm sure this will come as a great surprise to you, but I have seen your father's penis before, and as much as I had looked forward to spending the rest of my days without ever seeing it again, it looks like I'm not going to be that fortunate."

While I waited for my father to object, a look of such pure gratitude came across his face that I realized how close he had come to the biggest humiliation of his already humiliating day. Together my parents toddled off, arm in arm, toward the bathroom.

Chapter Four

THE NEXT MORNING I UNPACKED MY FATHER'S suitcases while he sat on Wyatt's bed and watched me.

"I've checked into a lot of hotels in my day and I've never once watched somebody else unpack my bags." My father's face was fixed in an expression of pure pleasure. Looking only at his face, a person would never know he had steel rods driven through his arms. "I went to Japan once, and the bellboy opened the bags up for me. Looked to me like he meant to unpack them, but I thought then I'd owe him one hell of a tip, so I shooed him away."

"I remember that trip. You sent me a postcard." I took out five rolls of socks, five pairs of underwear, five T-shirts, everything in a neat row. I laid them in the top drawer. "You don't have to worry about me hitting you up for a big tip."

"No tipping. I'm in the best hotel in the world," my father said. "Hotel Family. Great service."

"Where do you keep all your things?" Five shirts. I put them on hangers. Two short-sleeved, one long-sleeved plaid flannel, one dress shirt, one tuxedo shirt.

"I had another shirt for my tux but they cut it off of me in the hospital. I told them not to. Blood washes out. I know that. But the nurse said it was all torn anyway. Couldn't be fixed. I'm lucky, though, I wasn't wearing my good one. That one there is real Egyptian cotton. I won it from a guy in a poker game. Just my size, how about that?"

And no ruffles. Maybe he was lucky. "Aside from your other tuxedo shirt. Do you have an apartment somewhere? Do you keep your things in storage?"

"What things?" he asked. He wasn't following me at all.

"I don't know. Chairs. You must have a chair someplace. A bed? A toaster, a clock, a plate? People acquire things, you know. It's part of life."

"No," he said. "I don't have things like that."

I took my hands out of his suitcase. The contents suddenly seemed to signify too much. "How is that possible?"

He shrugged, and then he winced a little. He was deeply sore. "I've had those things before. I've had them a couple of times. I'd get some things together and then something would happen and I'd have to get rid of them. Once I got a storage unit. I was out in Utah. I figured it was dry out there and the stuff would be better off. It wasn't like I left it all in Florida. I went to a little town where I got a good rate and I paid up five years in advance. In five years I thought it might be time to settle down. I'd come back and get the stuff, maybe rent an apartment in New York. But it never turned out that way."

I waited for the rest of the story. My father smiled at me. None came. "What happened to the stuff?" I asked.

He shook his head. "I think I waited too long. When I finally got back there the storage place was gone. Then I started worrying that I wasn't remembering the right town. I'd lost the key, hell, years before that. For all I know it wasn't even Utah. It's not that I'm senile, this was ages ago, but I've never been real keen on details."

I asked him what he had lost.

"I had a box of records in there and a record player. That's what I really missed. I had been so careful not to hold on to too many records, to only keep a few that really mattered." Then my father stopped and he smiled at me. "But it turns out life was fine without them."

"But you've had other things since then, right? I mean, you must buy things. And I send you Christmas presents."

"Oh," he said, eager not to hurt my feelings, "and I've loved them. I keep them for a while. I use them. That gray sweater you sent last year, the cardigan? It's in the bigger bag."

"So this is it? These two suitcases?"

"A man doesn't need very much if the hotel is good. They give you everything now, you wouldn't believe it, soap and razors and shampoo. Half the time there's a barber in the lobby. And they always give you those little sewing kits. I used to save them but now I know that there's always going to be another one in the next place I go. I can really sew. At least I could. I bet I could have fixed that tuxedo shirt."

Was it possible that my father was homeless? And was it really being homeless if you played piano every night and did not aspire to owning furniture? He seemed so completely matter-of-fact about the whole thing, and still it seemed impossibly sad to me. "Aren't there ever things . . . I don't know . . . things that you want?"

My father nodded toward the big suitcase. "Look in there, all the way in the bottom. The flat thing. There you've got it."

I pulled out a brown leather folder that turned out to be a frame when you opened it. On one side there was a picture of me. It was a studio picture. I am possibly four years old and I'm sitting on a little stool holding a white rabbit on my lap, looking dreamy and well behaved. I remember the day it was taken. I had misunderstood the arrangement and had cried for an hour after they took the rabbit away. On the other side there was a picture of my mother and father standing close together, both of them very dressed up. My father is holding a big white bundle of a baby in his arms and my mother is smiling hugely for the camera. He is twenty-three years old and my mother is twenty-one. Around the edges there are smaller pictures, a snapshot of my wedding, Wyatt and Camille as babies, two women I did not recognize, one of whom was in a bathing suit and waving.

"I put that on the nightstand wherever I am. It's the first thing out of the case and the last thing to go in, and I've never left it behind anywhere, not even once. That's all you need to make a place seem like home. You just need your family. I've got you all there."

I nodded my head, my eyes glued down to the very thin record of our lives. It seemed to be so little and yet I could see how it could be enough. "I'll put this up," I said weakly, and set the frame on top of the dresser.

"Put it up there, that's fine," my father said. "But I don't need it now. If I want to see my family, all I have to do is walk through the door."

I emptied out his cases. Five pairs of pants, two sweaters, some knit gloves, three pairs of shoes, nail clippers, a black suit, a tuxedo, a paperback mystery novel from the seventies, the smallest odds and ends of life. I planned to go out immediately and buy him some new clothes. It was fine if he wanted to leave them behind eventually, but while he was here my father was going to have some extra things.

"It's great to be home, Ruthie," he said, giving me his best smile.

"It's great to have you," I said. At the time that I said it, I'll tell you, I meant it absolutely.

Having my father move in would have been a lot to adjust to, but he was not the only new resident in the house. Sam was sitting in the kitchen for hours every morning reading the paper long past the time he should have gone to work. Plus, he and my father had discovered some mysterious cable channel that showed nothing but sports programming twenty-four hours a day. They watched the entire 1985 Lakers–Celtics playoffs in one gulp. The ambient noise of the house was now the low fuzz of roaring crowds, whistles and buzzers, the fast squeak of sneakers on a polished court, not to mention the constant commentary of Sam and my father, who were given to yelling helpful directions at the television set even though the game had been recorded the year Camille was born.

"Look at their shorts!" Sam kept saying. "Look how tiny Larry Bird's shorts are!"

"Stop focusing on that," my father told him. "It's a perversion."

"It would have been a perversion if I'd noticed it at the time. Back in the eighties their shorts never occurred to me."

"Don't you think they could have better music with the basketball games? All of that dum-dum-dum-dum, dum-dum-dum-dum, it gets on my nerves. Basketball is an elegant sport. Couldn't you see it with some light piano jazz in the background? A little Beegie Adair?"

"Do you think it would be unreasonable to have a beer with lunch?" Sam asked my father. "If I had a beer would that make me some unemployed guy drinking in the afternoon?"

"Technically, yes, it does, but I don't see that it makes any difference, as long as it's just the two of us who know about it. One beer does not exactly mark the exit ramp onto the road of steep decline."

"What about you? Are you going to have one?"

"I don't mind if you don't mind. You feed beer to an old guy without arms, you're just making more work for yourself."

The two of them had a good long howl over that.

Sam stuck his head in the kitchen. "Just going to grab something."

I was making them sandwiches. I was, at that very moment, putting the pickles on the plates. "Sam, I can hear you in there, you know."

He came over and kissed my cheek. He took a pickle off a plate and nibbled at the end before putting it back. "I've become completely debauched," he said. Then he took me in his arms and we made three short circles in the kitchen. "Why did we never take ballroom dancing? We used to talk about it, remember? Your dad says he loves to watch the couples in the bars who really know how to dance. Maybe we could start dancing after dinner."

"You think we should do a floor show?"

"It could be a new career for both of us. We could go into people's kitchens and dance for them while they digested their food."

I laughed and went back to the sandwiches. "I'm not sure my father is the best influence in the world."

Sam rested his chin on my shoulder. He seemed so lighthearted that I realized for the first time what a toll his job must have been taking on him all these years. Maybe for a little while unemployment wouldn't be such a bad thing. "The old guy's having a rough time of it. I'm just trying to cheer him up."

"I appreciate it. I really do." I handed Sam the two sandwiches, but he put them down and piled all of the food onto one plate. What difference did it make if they ate off the same plate since one of them was handling all the food anyway? With his free hand Sam grabbed two beers and a straw. The extra-long bend-neck straw had proven itself to be a real friend to our family. With a straw, Dad could at least drink without having to ask someone to lift up his glass. He even had lukewarm coffee through a straw. It gave him a sense of independence.

My father had been in our house for five days now and things were not going at all as I had expected. I had not taken into account the enormous amount of work it would be to have a man with useless arms around. It was like having a baby with perfect verbal skills, a baby who could say, I need my nose blown (often), or, I have an itch on the side of my neck. So far he did not appear capable of doing anything for himself, and a human being, no matter how pleasant, who can do nothing for himself must be carried by those around him. I felt like I was running every minute of the day, bringing in a pillow to wedge against his aching back, counting out pills, making the bed, driving him to the doctor, washing his hair. But I never lost sight of the myriad ways it could be worse. It could, for example, have been my mother with two broken wrists. My father was grateful, not overly demanding, and he complained about exactly nothing. The closest he came to reminding us that he must be in excruciating pain was the fact that he disappeared regularly to take naps. He didn't talk about the future. Still, there was something about the way he seemed not too entirely displeased about things that got to me, the way he let out a sustained, "Ahhhhhh," when he spread his wingspan over the sofa, the way he made frequent references to the fact that *this* was the life. Any doubts I may have had I kept to myself, but my mother kept nothing to herself.

"How do we even know they're broken?" My mother caught me later that day while I was folding clothes. She was having to watch Oprah on Camille's little TV now that the big one in the den was permanently occupied. She stayed in a bad mood. "Surely there's some bum doctor out there who would stick pins in your arms for twenty bucks. He could have won them in a card game."

I shuddered at the thought. My mother was the only one who never seemed to notice that the steel sticking through my father's flesh looked like it hurt—a lot. The doctor who examined him at the hospital where Sam used to work said it was one of the worst collections of breaks he'd seen in years. I still found myself wincing as I dabbed the antibiotic ointment on the pin sites three times a day. "Sam picked him up at the hospital, remember?"

"Which leads me to my next point: The amount of time Sam spends with your father is a little worrisome."

"Worrisome?" I said. "Just be grateful. Sam is the one cutting his meat, getting him dressed." I looked at my mother meaning-fully. "*Other* things."

"He's sainted, I'll give you that. But doesn't it seem like Sam is, well, changing?"

I picked up two white socks and balled them together. "Sam is Sam," I said, not entirely unaware of what she was talking about.

She took the socks out of my hands. "These don't match." She unrolled the bundle and threw them back in the pile. "You don't pay attention, Ruth. You've always lived in your head. It's time to come down to the real world. Sam has been a hardworking man his whole life. Now all of a sudden he's lying on the couch eating cheese puffs and watching basketball? I think that's a pretty significant change. He should be out there looking for a job or at the very least polishing up his résumé." She turned the pile of laundry over a couple of times as if she were looking for evidence to support her case. "Look at this. There's not a single dress shirt in here."

"Listen, Sam has been working nonstop for as long as I've known him. He hardly ever gets to go sailing or even read a novel. I can hardly remember him ever taking a nap. So why not let him relax for a little while?"

"You're starting to sound like your father. Your father is a virus, you know that, don't you? Everything that's bad about him spreads."

I looked at my watch. "Your program is on," I said. It was like throwing a pork chop for a dog. That was all it took. My mother dropped her line of reasoning and went scurrying down the hall toward Oprah.

I could see my mother's point, but I thought it was more important to stick up for my husband than it was to agree with her. Sure, Sam wasn't himself, but were any of us? What about my mother, who had suddenly gone from being awkward and indecisive to being someone who was extremely certain of what she wanted? Or Camille, whose enormous personality was no match for my father's? I hadn't seen her lose her temper once since my father's arrival and not, I suspected, because she was any happier. I thought back to my stress-reduction class. The instructor said that one of the most challenging things that could happen to a family was to gain or lose a member. "Think of a mobile," he told us. "You take a piece off, you put a piece on, none of the other pieces are in balance anymore." So Sam wasn't in balance. Wasn't that normal?

Of course, abnormality is easier to take in normal times, which these weren't. Sam was also out of a job. I couldn't help but think that something had happened to him on that drive to Des Moines. He had left the house feeling frantic and resolved to find work and had come home completely at peace with his unemployment. I wanted him to have some peace. I also wanted him to get a job, but I figured there would be plenty of time to discuss that in the future.

But now that my father lived with us, there was very little danger of having to wait around for things to be discussed.

"I've been trying my best to talk Sam into going to medical school," my father began at dinner that night. I was sitting next to my father, spearing chunks of paprika chicken and mushrooms onto his fork.

"Not medical school again," Camille said, pushing her plate away. She was wearing a tiny tie-dyed T-shirt with dizzying spirals of fuchsia and aquamarine. Every time I saw it I thought *peace*.

"Eat your dinner," my mother said.

"Don't panic," Sam told her. "There's no chance of me going to medical school."

Sam was fifty-three. I figured two years for pre-med, four years for medical school, three years for internship and residency. That put him comfortably past sixty. God help us if he wanted to specialize.

"I had never realized what a smart man your husband is," my father said. "I didn't get to see enough of him over the years. If I had had a son, a son who wasn't musically inclined, I would have wanted him to be a doctor. I think it is a very noble profession."

"But wait a minute, you had a daughter." Camille squinted at him, her burgeoning feminist logic telling her that something was fishy. "Why didn't you want Mom to be a doctor?"

I was incredibly touched that either Camille thought I could have been a doctor or that she was sticking up for me. I was also interested in the answer.

"I guess I never thought about that," my father said in a puzzled voice.

"What a surprise," my mother said into her orange juice.

My father opened his mouth to make a smart comeback and I took the opportunity to give him another bite of his dinner. He didn't think his daughter who was now cutting his meat was smart enough to be a doctor, but how do you say that at the dinner table?

"Even if I did want to be a doctor," Sam said, holding up his hands, "and believe me, I don't, I know what direction health care is going in. I wouldn't want any part of it."

I put down the fork. "You mean you don't want to work in hospital administration anymore?" I tried to keep my voice steady. I wasn't sure what else Sam knew how to do.

Sam looked behind him as if the answer were floating somewhere in the back of the kitchen. "I don't think so."

"What about the job in Des Moines?"

Camille let her fork drop with a clang against her plate. "We're moving to Des Moines?"

He shook his head. "Didn't pan out."

Camille sighed with relief. "I would die in Des Moines."

"Did you ask your friend there about other hospitals?" Had I been counting on that in the back of my mind without even realizing it? A fallback plan in Iowa?

"It's so old," my father said, offering Sam an exit from the awkward moment. "He's done all of that. What would the point be in going back and doing it again?"

"Money," my mother said.

My father looked at her with utter exasperation. "After all these years I would have thought you would have learned a new song. Money, money, money. That's what tore us apart, you know. You never had any vision. You thought there was only one means to measure the value of a man."

"I thought our daughter should eat regularly," my mother said. "Call me old-fashioned."

"A complete lack of vision," my father reiterated.

"So why haven't you found another job if you think change is such a vital part of life?" my mother asked.

"Because I still enjoy my job. I'm still good at it. Fortunately, playing the piano is one field where you get credit for being older. People look at you and think you must be accomplished. They see some young kid playing and it makes them uncomfortable having a cocktail, like they might be corrupting him. They see me and think, That old guy has been in a bar all these years and he still looks pretty good. I inspire people to order up."

"So what do you think you might be interested in?" I said to Sam. I passed him a bowl of sautéed spinach. It was his favorite. I wanted him to know I was thinking of him.

My father tapped his foot against the floor, which is how those without hands get attention. "You can't *ask* those kinds of questions now. A man has to find himself. Sam has been supporting this family for twenty-five years. Now he has to take some time, learn to listen to himself again. He has to take some time to think about the direction he wants to go in."

"Dad, it hasn't been twenty-five years. I was a teacher—"

But he wasn't interested. "You understand my point. A little more chicken please."

I cut off another bite and fed it to him.

"So Dad doesn't have to work anymore?" Camille said. She seemed genuinely interested in the conversation now that it was clear we weren't going to Iowa. I could tell she was listening when she stopped twirling her hair through her fingers.

"Of course I'm going to work again, honey. Your grandpa is just saying that it's important to think things through."

"That's right." My father nodded in support.

"So what if you don't go to work again anytime soon? What if it takes you a long time to find yourself or whatever it is you're doing? Where do we get money until then?" Camille's voice was shaking a little and I couldn't tell if she was frightened or angry at the thought of not being supported.

"Why is the money always the man's responsibility?" my father said. "Why is that Sam's burden? Isn't it enough that he's provided for you all these years? When I was your age I had been supporting myself for years. I didn't ask anyone else to take care of me."

"Your grandfather was hatched alone on a beach," my mother explained to Camille. "He kicked his way free, ate his own shell, and then slithered off to conquer the world without a moment's assistance from another reptile."

My parents had a remarkable ability to simply not hear one another most of the time. It was as if they both spoke in a frequency that the other one was incapable of registering. "Don't you think you're old enough to get a job?" my father said to Camille.

"Um," Camille said, looking down at her plate. "I guess. I don't know."

"Do you think she should drop out of high school? Start washing cars?" my mother said. "Stop giving that old man food. Look at you. You're a fine one to be giving lectures on independence and self-reliance. You can't wipe your own mouth."

"At least I had a dream," my father said. "At least I didn't play the piano like I had never stepped foot outside a Methodist church my entire life."

Suddenly they heard each other.

"Here we go. You think you play the piano better than I do. That's where your superiority comes from. You think just because you're banging it out in some smoky gin joint, you're making art, and because I'm playing in a school with children, I'm the drudge, the talentless drone. But I'll tell you something, Guy, you were never half the pianist that I am, and if you had any wrists I'd prove it to you right now!" My mother was standing up, leaning over the table toward my father.

"I'd play with my toes!" my father roared. "If you want a competition I could beat you without my hands."

Camille sat with her mouth open, looking from one side of the table to the other as if she were watching a tennis match.

Bang it out? Gin joint? Toes? Who were these people who claimed to be related to me, and what were they doing living in my house? My nerves were shot. I imagined my kitchen a crime scene, the neighbors coming in and finding all of us torn apart as if a pack of angry wolverines had broken in through the back door. People could not live like this, not for the amount of time it took bones to heal. Someone, something, needed to restore order to our lives.

"Cake," I said.

"Cake?" Sam said.

"What kind of cake?" my father asked.

"Apple spice."

"When did you make a cake?" my mother said. "I didn't see you make a cake."

"Mom," Camille moaned, but I raised my hand to stop her.

I got up and took the cake out from under its cake-shaped cover. I had made it at three o'clock in the morning in a desperate attempt to comfort myself. And it was an enormous comfort, standing alone in the kitchen in my nightgown, sifting fresh ground nutmeg with allspice and cloves by the little light over the sink. I peeled the apples with ridiculous care, taking the skins off in long, even ribbons that spiraled down to the floor without breaking. I didn't think of any of them while I peeled those apples. I didn't work anything out in my mind. I just relaxed into the creaming of butter and sugar, the sweet expansion of every egg. I had hoped the mixer wouldn't wake anyone up. The last thing I had wanted was company.

I cut off big, hulking slices and slid them onto dessert plates. The apples were soft and golden, the cake was a rust color. I hadn't even cleared the table. I just pushed one course aside and made room for another, then I dropped into my chair and started to eat. I did nothing to help my father and Camille got up to feed him his cake. For a few peaceful minutes we said nothing to one another. We simply ate.

"You always could cook, Ruthie," my father said dreamily. "Especially cakes."

"She didn't get it from me," my mother said.

My father shook his head. "Sure she did, Hollis. You were a fine cook. I remember you made the best lemon meringue pie."

"Ruth probably made it."

"This was before Ruth," my father said. Suddenly there was so much kindness in his voice that everyone at the table lifted their heads and looked at him. My mother looked away.

The truth was, my mother was neither a good cook nor a bad one. Her food was economical and nutritious. It reheated well. She did not believe in luxury or embellishment, so she saw little cause for baking.

"Camille, did you know that when your mother was a little girl she baked her own birthday cakes?"

"That's weird," Camille said.

"At first she baked birthday cakes for all her friends in school and then one year, I think she was nine, I was having a party for her and she asked if she could bake her own cake. Nine was very young, I thought. It was a complicated cake. I don't remember what kind it was now. I think she made it up."

"Do you remember what kind of cake it was, Mom?"

I shook my head no, but of course I remembered. The first cake I ever made for myself was a landmark in my personal baking history. It was a lemon glow chiffon that I sliced into twelve half-inch layers, spread with strawberry jam, reassembled, and covered in seven-minute icing. Looking back, such a cake would appear to have been a monstrosity, but to a nine-year-old it was a glamorous, ambitious cake that had the aura of something very French, even though I had no idea what that meant at the time.

"Well, that's what your talent is, baking cakes," my father said, his voice suddenly heavy with disinterest. "You never got very far on the piano, did you?"

"Ruth plays nicely," my mother said.

"No," I said. "I didn't get very far."

I shaved off a few thin slices for seconds. I knew how to cut the cake in a way that no one would object to having a little bit more. As for the piano, my father was wrong. I could play, I just couldn't play in front of other people. I may have inherited some of my parents' talent but I got none of their stage presence. Some of the most soul-carving moments of my childhood centered around group recitals where I had to play "Clair de Lune" to a living room full of bored parents and restless children. The hours before those small, humiliating performances were the only times I seriously considered running away from home. But I played in the locked practice rooms in college every night after I left the library, and the hours would slip by without notice. When Sam and I were married I played the piano whenever I got home from work before he did. I played when the children were little and then played even more when they were in school. Really, my father would be surprised. I was a pretty good pianist for a housewife. It really was when my mother moved in with us that I stopped playing because I couldn't imagine playing in front of her and there never seemed to be a time when I was in the house alone anymore. It wasn't my passion, but it was a comfort. I have to say I missed it. I baked a lot more cakes now that I wasn't playing.

"What about you, Camille?" My father pointed toward her by turning his entire arm in her direction like the metal needle of a compass.

"Pass."

"I've been trying to give her lessons for years but she just won't stand for it," my mother said.

"Maybe the piano isn't your instrument," Sam offered. "It isn't the piano for everyone."

"I think the guitar would be kind of cool." Camille's voice was small and I immediately understood she was saying something that she actually wanted to do. If Camille wanted to play the guitar, I would get her guitar lessons tomorrow.

"You need to start an instrument early," my father said. "You should have taken up the guitar ten years ago."

Camille's head dipped ever so slightly and she nodded. I could not understand it for the life of me. My father adored Camille. It made no sense at all that he was undermining her this way.

"Let me understand this," my mother began slowly. "Sam here, who—forgive me, Sam—has very likely passed the middle point of his life, is free to start down any path he chooses, is encouraged by you to start medical school so that he could be a doctor just in time to draw Social Security, while our Camille, an ancient junior in high school, is too old to take up the guitar. For heaven's sake, Guy, at least be consistent. Madonna was forty-two when she started playing the guitar."

Camille bloomed, smiling so wide we were treated to a rare glimpse of every one of her perfect white teeth. "That's right!" she said. My mother could not have made more of a celebration out of the moment if she'd uncorked a case of champagne. Who would have thought she was a denizen of popular culture?

My father sighed. "So corrected," he said. He bent back his head in such a way that made me think he would have rubbed his neck had he had the hands with which to do so. "I think the medication is making me fuzzy. I'm sorry. Please don't hold me accountable, Camille."

"I don't," she said kindly, and patted his good shoulder.

"I think I've gone too far. I think I should finish my delicious cake and go to bed."

Camille took her cue and forked another, larger bite of cake into his mouth. I got up and gave him his pills, dropped them on his waiting tongue, and then waited while he washed them down with milk pulled up through his straw.

"I'll get you to bed." Sam pushed back from the table.

My mother shook her head. "I'll take him in," she said, as if it were the most natural thing in the world.

My father swallowed hard. "Will you brush my teeth?" He wasn't being funny. "I need to brush them after all this cake."

"I'll even floss them," she said.

"I never floss. I hate to floss."

My mother smiled with some real and secret pleasure. "Tonight," she said, and tapped the table to mark the exact moment in time, "you will begin to floss."

"Don't forget to put on the antibiotic cream," I reminded her.

"I know," she said, shaking me off. "I know."

Good-nights were said and departures were made. I had no early memories of my parents walking in the same direction. Once they were gone, my husband and daughter and I sat at the table and looked at each other like members of an over-informed jury.

"This is what it was like when you were growing up?" Camille said.

I shook my head. "It wasn't like this at all."

"They were nice to each other then?" Camille leaned forward. This was going to be her bedtime story.

"They were divorced when I was so little I don't even remember them being together. My dad would show up every now and then and they would argue, but most of the time, no, it was pretty quiet." I looked over my shoulder, down the hall to the closed door of Wyatt's room. "Maybe if they had fought more then, they could have worked it out of their systems."

"Or they would have killed each other," Sam said. "One way or the other there would have been more resolution."

"Promise me that you two won't ever get divorced," Camille said, her voice low and serious. "I don't think I could stand this."

I looked at Sam. I knew it was an easy question, like when Camille was six and asked us to promise her that there was nothing under the bed that planned to eat her up after she fell asleep, but suddenly it occurred to me, these were hard times, really hard times with lots of changes, and that our marriage was something we needed to be very careful with.

"I promise you," Sam said, looking at me. He took my hand and squeezed it. "I absolutely promise you that."

"Good," Camille said. "Because I feel like I'm getting a look at what it would be like to have divorced parents and I have to tell you, I'm not interested." She gave us both a hug and kiss goodnight and that made all of the day's discomforts worthwhile. After she was gone, Sam and I cleaned up the kitchen together.

"Hollis is taking her time in there," he said, peering down the hall.

"Flossing is hell," I said.

We went to our bedroom and brushed and flossed our own teeth, then we got into bed. Once it was dark, Sam started in on a different kind of bedtime story, one that did little to wind the listener down for sleep.

"I did some checking on your father's insurance situation," he said heavily. "He doesn't qualify for a home health-care nurse."

I felt a deep pang of disappointment. We had been talking about the home health care we couldn't afford. I was hoping there might be a little help out there. "What about physical therapy?"

"The doctor said it would start after he got the pins out, but I don't know. I think he needs to be working his fingers a little bit if he expects to have a job when this whole thing is over."

"Is he going to have a job? Do you really think he's going to go back out on the road and start playing the piano again?" I thought of the empty suitcases waiting in the closet. Would he simply fill them up and start over? "Which thought is worse, my father wandering the earth looking for a good piano bar or my father staying exactly where he is?"

Sam sighed. "I don't know what I think. I can't imagine this is it, that we're going to spend the next however many years watching your parents duke it out at the dinner table every night."

"Till death do us part."

"I know an occupational therapist at the hospital, Florence Allen. I did her a favor once a long time ago. Maybe I could get her to look at him and give us some advice."

"I'd try anything," I said. I liked to think that occupational therapy would make sure my father had an occupation again someday.

"There's something else," Sam said.

"And it's more good news."

"I talked to my friend in Des Moines and had him pull up your father's records. Medicare only covers eighty percent of the hospital stay, do you know that?"

Maybe I knew that. I had spent enough time looking at my mother's insurance papers. I felt distinctly cold in the bed. "Meaning exactly?"

"Exactly eight thousand nine hundred seventy-two dollars and fifty-eight cents. They won't be sending the bill out for a few more weeks. But it's coming."

I got out of bed and took two Tylenol PMs. It was either that or go to the kitchen to make a seven-tiered wedding cake covered in sugared violets. When I got back in I gave two pills to Sam and handed him a Dixie cup of water. He swallowed with gratitude and we lay there side by side in the dark.

"What are you thinking about?" Sam asked me.

I told him the truth. I was thinking about Q-tips. "There's

something about cleaning out his ears that completely undoes me. It's just so . . . so . . . ."

"Intimate."

"Well, yes, that too, but I'm always afraid I'm going to stick it in too far and rupture his eardrum."

"Then he would be a deaf pianist with broken wrists."

"It just goes from bad to worse."

The moonlight fell over the bedspread in the shape of window panes. I put my head on Sam's shoulder and he put his arms around me and for that moment I felt safe, like I was standing inside a cake.

"Ruth?"

"Hmm?"

"You're not going to divorce me because I lost my job and drank a beer in the middle of the day, are you?" Sam asked.

I propped my chin on his chest. "You're not going to divorce me because my incredibly difficult divorced parents are both living with us, are you?"

Sam kissed me. "Let's call it a draw," he said.

"Tell me one thing, though," I said. "I'm only asking you this because my father can't hear us. Is there something you're interested in? I mean, if you could really turn your life around and follow your dreams, if you didn't have to worry about us or the money, what would you want to do?"

"You already know what I want to do."

I tried to stifle a yawn but I failed. "I do?"

"You said it—well, you sort of said it, that first morning after I lost my job."

My eyes were closed. That was before my father was living with us. That was seven lifetimes ago. "I don't remember." I could feel the wave of Tylenol PM breaking down over my head and pulling me out in the dark tide of sleep. Even as I was asking him the question, I was forgetting what I was saying. I did, however, hear his answer, which he whispered into my ear.

"Sailboats," he said in the enormous darkness. "I'd like to build wooden sailboats."

Chapter Five

MY FATHER WAS USED TO GOING TO BED AROUND four o'clock in the morning. Staying up late was actually part of his job description. Piano players who worked in bars could not be members of the early-to-bed, early-to-rise set, not unless you wanted people to start hanging out at piano bars at nine o'clock in the morning. I understood it, and I understood why old habits would be hard to break. Still, the fact that he wanted his breakfast at one in the afternoon took some getting used to. My father commented often on the aggressive sunniness of Wyatt's bedroom, which lacked the blackout shades hung over every hotel window nationwide. My mother commented on the fact that most adults had completed half a day's work before Guy had flickered an eyelid. I was just grateful to have a little extra time to run errands and get the housework done before he was up and underfoot. Once my father was awake, the second half of my day began. Sam and my mother and I split up the tasks. In short, they took care of bathing, brushing, and any other bathroom matters. Once they got him toweled off and into his shorts, they gave a heavy sigh and turned him over to me. I was standing at the edge of my father's bed, the bed I no longer thought of as Wyatt's bed, with a bunched-up sock in my hands, when I saw them. I stopped, frozen, sock aloft.

"Ah," my father said. "I know. They've gotten pretty bad."

"Do they hurt?" I didn't know how he'd been walking around.

He shook his head and flexed back the balls of his feet to see for himself. "Oh no, I don't even notice them. I guess that's the problem. I wasn't so good at keeping up with them when I was able to do something about it. Now, my hands, my hands always looked first rate. I always got a manicure every Thursday afternoon no matter what city I was in. But I'll have to admit I've let the toes slide." I glanced at his fingernails, which were a little long, but the toes were in a league of their own.

"How did I not notice this before?"

He shrugged. "Who pays attention to feet? You've got things to do, you just want to get that sock on. Go ahead," he said, and pointed out his foot like some gruesome version of Cinderella. "Let's just cover them up."

I sank down to the floor and for a moment I thought I was going to cry from some complex combination of exhaustion and grief and anger and guilt and love. Every one of those feelings surprised me. What kind of person would let her father walk around with a shoe half full of razor blades? His toenails were heavy, yellowed, and flaking. They twisted up and left and right and down, each one with its own specific set of problems. Even if I had never seen my father's feet, which I had from time to time since he moved home, I should have been aware of them. I thought of the morning not too long ago that I had stood in this very room with my mother. She had told me that my father meant to come and stay, that once we let him in there would be no getting rid of him. Now I could see she was right. I didn't think he would live here forever, I thought at some point he would get well and move on, but I knew now that I would always be worrying about him. For the rest of his life I would be calling him up in piano bars asking him if he had remembered to cut his toenails.

I patted the top of his pale foot, which seemed too cold, which worried me also. "I'll get you an appointment with the pedicurist. I'll tell her it's an emergency." Most men you couldn't take to the pedicurist, but I figured my father wasn't most men. Still, he balked.

"Just leave them. They don't give me any trouble. Once we get this hardware out, I'll take care of it."

"In another six weeks they're going to be cutting out the front of your shoes."

"They'll be fine."

"Why wouldn't you want to get your toenails clipped?"

"It's just . . . you know I don't like to go out. It can all get so complicated. It's one thing if I'm out with Sam, but for me to go into some beauty shop . . ."

I understood. It was about the bathroom. More and more my father was becoming afraid of not having anyone around to take him to the bathroom. There had been one afternoon when he was taking a nap and everyone went out and when he woke up and needed to go . . . well, I probably wouldn't have felt any differently. "So I'll cut them."

"Really?" His face brightened. "You could do that?"

"You don't need a degree for toes. If I don't do a beautiful job, who's going to see?"

"That's the spirit," my father said, and gave one foot an appreciative stomp. "Nobody's going to see my toes."

"I'll get a pan of water. I think we ought to soak them first."

"Soak them in lye if it would make it any easier on you." My sockless father stood up. He stopped to tap the top of my head lightly with the tip of his finger, what had come to pass as an affectionate gesture from a man who could make very few affectionate gestures. "I'm going to go in the den. I can watch a little hockey while you work."

"Sure," I said. "It's all the same to me."

So I got some towels and a plastic basin and every size of clipper and file and cuticle scissor I could find hiding in the back of various bathroom drawers. I got some cuticle cream and a package of orange sticks from Camille's room. I filled the basin up with warm water in the kitchen sink and threw in a handful of Epsom salts and took the whole production into the den, careful not to slosh the water while I walked. My father was safely ensconced in his chair with the television on. He'd become very comfortable with working the remote with his fingertips.

"Ruthie, you'll never believe this. It's the Maple Leaves playing the Rangers in Toronto, nineteen seventy-nine. I was *at* that game! Can you believe that! Sam!" he shouted. "Where's Sam? What a game that was. I even remember where I was sitting. Hey, maybe I'll be on TV."

Sam walked in looking a little bleary-eyed and I wondered if he had been back in our bedroom taking a nap. He turned and looked at the television while I spread two towels out over the floor. "Are those the 'seventy-six Maple Leaves?"

"'Seventy-nine!" my father said triumphantly.

Sam sank into a chair, his eyes fixed on the screen. "I can't believe this. You just turned it on?"

"I was *there*."

Sam looked at him. "No."

"You don't even like hockey," I reminded my husband.

"I did in nineteen seventy-nine," Sam said. He picked up the remote control and turned up the volume. I rolled up the cuffs of my father's old khaki pants and then picked up his feet and set them into the water.

"Is that too warm for you?" I asked.

"You could put my feet in the fireplace," he said. "Right now I couldn't care less."

My mother came into the room wearing her blue warm-up suit. She knotted a fist against each of her hips in an attempt to become a caricature of a little old woman irritated by loud television. "Some people are trying to read a book." She raised her voice to a small scream, as if she had to strain to jump up over the volume. It was not *that* loud.

"Sorry, Hollis," Sam said, and reached again for the remote.

"Go for a jog," my father said to her. "You're dressed to go running. So go running." I wondered how he even knew what she was wearing. He hadn't taken his eyes off the screen.

I reached back into the water and extracted one heavily clawed foot. My father did nothing to help me with the lifting. I patted it dry with an extra towel and studied his cuticles, which were in serious need of taming.

My mother was appalled. "For God's sake, Ruth, what are you doing?"

"What do you think I'm doing?" I held his big toe between my thumb and forefinger, turning it from side to side in hopes of finding the proper angle of approach. The light was imperfect. It looked like what I would need was a hacksaw.

"You're going to let her cut your toenails now?" my mother said.

"It was her idea," my father said.

"Ruth, you said you were going to take me to the fabric store this afternoon. They're having a sale on remnants."

"Remnants!" my father howled. "Don't tell me you're still collecting remnants! Stupidest damn hobby in the entire history of stupid hobbies."

At that moment the first goal was blocked and my father's foot shot out of my hands like a caught fish that sees its chance to make a break back for the water. Sam stood up and cheered. "I *remember* that block!" my father shouted. "Wasn't that brilliant!"

"I could have told you it was going to wind up like this. Exactly like this." My mother gave me a particularly cold stare, as if I had broken my father's wrists myself as some kind of social experiment in family reconstruction. Then she turned to leave the room.

I grabbed his foot and held it tightly in my hand. I was willing to do this, but I wasn't going to let it eat up the rest of my afternoon. My mother was right. I had promised to take her out. I took a pair of clippers and made my first incision. The sound was not a snip so much as a crunch. My father flinched and then jerked. "Hold still," I said.

"Hey!" he said. "That's too close!"

I felt my palms starting to sweat and I hoped I could hold the clippers steady. "Watch the game. See what the goalie can do."

Sam and my father both glanced at the screen. A toenail flew past the parameters of the towel and I picked it up and dropped it back onto the terry cloth. With no one to scream along, the television seemed as loud as my mother had said it was.

At the next clip my father jerked hard and made a little squeak. "Watch it there!"

I stared at him until he relented.

"It didn't hurt," he said petulantly. "But you're getting too close."

I went back to work. It was the moment I reached my personal low, my dark night of the soul. Not that anyone else noticed it, but I suddenly felt I couldn't go on with all this, that I didn't have the energy for one more toe. Suddenly the thought of getting in the car and heading north to Canada, home of the Maple Leaves, seemed to me to be the only rational thing to do. Not that there was any money, but I could find a job in Canada. There was a long and noble tradition of my fellow countrymen heading to the great frozen north when things got tough at home. Focusing on the inside of a cake didn't really cut it for me anymore. I needed to envision another country, someplace with vast open spaces where no one went looking for family members. That's where I was when the doorbell rang.

I waited half a minute, thinking my mother would answer it, and then threw in another fifteen seconds thinking Sam might respond. When I came to my senses I picked my father's foot off the floor and dropped it back in the tub, making a significant wake. "Soak," I said with little kindness in my voice. I dried my hands of the whole thing.

The woman I found standing on my front porch was six feet tall, not including the crepe soles of her shoes and the two inches of lift she had in her hair. She had broad shoulders and big arms and hands that could have popped walnuts out of their shells all day long, but her legs were delicate and pretty, even if they were cased in serious white stockings. She was a dark-skinned black woman in a very bright white dress, and I have to say the whole effect of her, height and width and white and black, was nothing short of dazzling. She had an enormous tan leather bag slung over one shoulder and it was easy to imagine that inside that leather bag was the answer to every problem, Mary Poppins style.

"I'm Florence Allen," the woman said. She held out her hand to me and I shook it. "I'm a friend of Sam's."

"Oh, Florence, I'm Ruth. I'm Sam's wife." I glanced quickly over my shoulder, still holding her hand. I willed the television to be turned off, the den to be picked up, my father's toenails to be clipped and filed. "I didn't know you were coming today." I thought that Florence Allen was in the neighborhood of my age. She had a nice face but she kept it serious, businesslike.

"Didn't you get the message?"

"Message? No, we aren't so great about messages around here." I had until recently been a meticulous, some might even say zealous, housekeeper, but times had changed. You could not make out the pattern on my sofa, there was so much clean laundry encasing it. I suppose I should have been grateful it was clean laundry. I stepped back to let her into the ruins of my home.

"I spoke to a girl yesterday."

"My daughter."

Florence Allen raised her hand. "I threw it into the message void, didn't I?"

"I'm afraid so."

"I have daughters," she said. She had a very soothing voice.

"Goa-*lie!*" my father shouted.

Sam banged his beer bottle against the edge of the coffee table in agreement.

"You could drive the puck right up that guy's ass and he wouldn't know it!" my father said.

"Dad." I leaned into the den, trying to shield our guest with my back, but she was too tall for that.

"Ruthie! Ruthie, watch this. They're going to show it again. Here it comes, here it comes." But when it came my father threw his head back and closed his eyes. "Christ Almighty. Have you ever seen such idiocy in all your days?"

The blinds were down in the den, and despite the brightness of the day, the place resembled nothing so much as a cave, my father and husband the two overfed bears. "I have, yes. Dad, this is Florence Allen."

When Sam looked up a flash of real panic cut across his face. He put his beer bottle on the floor behind the leg of the coffee table and hopped to his feet. "Florence!" he said, and held out his hand to her. "I'm so glad you came by. This is my father-in-law. This is Guy."

My father smiled his best piano-bar smile and raised one metal-cased arm. "Hello there."

"Sam," she said, smiling. "Mr. Nash." She nodded her head politely toward my father.

"Oh now," my father said, turning his torso toward her, his arms jutting out with welcoming affection. "None of that Mister business. It's strictly Guy here. You say you're Florence?"

"I say I'm Mrs. Allen, actually."

"A tough one!" my father said. "I like that."

Sam shot my father a look, but I could have told him my father was impervious to looks. "I thought I was going to bring him in to see you. You didn't have to drive over here."

"I was on my way to work," she said. "Today's my half day. It's not any trouble."

Mrs. Allen went over and looked into the pan of water my father's feet were resting in.

"I was just working on his nails," I said apologetically. I didn't want her to think I was neglecting him, that I simply left his feet in pans of water all day. Check it, I wanted to say. It's still warm.

"Have your feet been swollen long, Mr. Nash?"

I came over to look into the water, as did Sam. My father's feet were two balls of rising bread dough. Had they just now expanded? Had they somehow sponged up the water? Was I so consumed by the horror of his nails that I neglected the horror of his feet?

"Oh, they get a little puffy. I'm not a young man, you know, things puff up from time to time." He added an unseemly chortle.

"I don't think they've been this swollen before," Sam said.

She slipped her hand into the bath and took the pulse of both of his feet. "It's probably the medication. I can get some compression socks for you to wear but you'll need to be mindful about keeping them elevated."

"I need to be mindful of my feet? Isn't it enough that I'm being mindful of my arms?"

"I suppose you're smart enough to do both things at once," she said.

"Is there something I should be doing?" I asked her, feeling suddenly guilty that I had ever thought of running off to Canada.

"It would be a good idea to massage his feet," she said to me. "It will help with the swelling."

"A foot rub!" my father said, clicking his heels together in approval. "Now, there's an idea."

Florence Allen simply didn't seem to hear what she wasn't interested in. It made her seem very calm. "Let me take a look at those fingers," she said. He laid his fingers carefully over the edges of her fingers and she studied them. My father watched her watch them.

"What do you think?" he said.

"I think you have nice-looking hands," she said, and my father smiled. "Sam tells me you were a pianist."

"I *am* a pianist," my father said. "I am an injured pianist."

"Have you moved your fingers much since your surgery, Mr. Nash?"

"The doctor said I should wait until I was ready. I don't think they're ready quite yet." My father looked at his hands as if they were old friends he was worried about but didn't want to let on, friends for whom he put on a brave face.

"And when do you imagine they will be ready?" She took the index finger of his left hand and began to move it in tiny circles. We all held our breath.

"I'd rather not rush it," he said tentatively. Like the toenail clipping, he was waiting for the pain to come. He was braced for it.

She moved on to the next finger. "I'll tell you, Mr. Nash, if you don't rush it, these fingers of yours are going to turn into cement and they're going to stay that way. The time to go to work is right now. You must have practiced the piano a great deal in your life to be able to make your living playing."

Practice was something my father didn't like to admit to. Practice was what my mother forced on her students. He billed himself as a natural. He didn't practice, he said, he played. He had always just played.

"I've practiced plenty," he said, reversing himself. "If this is the talk where you tell me what work is, I'll save you the effort. If what this is going to take is work, then we won't have any problems."

"Then we won't have any problems." She moved on to the next finger. "Watch this." She motioned for me and Sam to stand beside her. "You need to rotate them for him. Clockwise and then counterclockwise. Do you see that? Just gently for now. We'll get them loosened up again. We'll have you back on the piano in no time."

"I've never even heard Guy play," Sam said. "Can you believe that? You've got to start back just so you can play for me."

My father looked at my husband with real affection. "After everything you've done for me, the very least I could do is play you a song."

"Just keep it simple," Florence said.

"I don't plan to start with 'Chopsticks,'" my father said.

"You start where you start. Just keep your fingers moving. I want you to do this three times a day, more if you can take it."

"I can take it," my father said.

"I'll come back again in a few days and see where you're at. We should be able to start pressing and bending pretty soon."

"Is that it?" my father asked disappointedly. Maybe he thought he was going to get the chance to make some progress on this first visit.

"That was a good start for today." She looked at her watch. "I should get going."

I noticed that my father still had one unclipped set of toenails sitting in the water basin. I decided they could wait.

"Come on and have a cup of coffee before you go," Sam said.

Florence shook her head. "It's not like the old days around the hospital," she said. "I don't know the boss anymore."

Sam smiled. "I can still write you a note."

"You got out of there just in time, I mean it. You're going to be glad you're gone."

"Maybe I would have come to that conclusion if I had some-place to go." He looked around the den, at my father, the television, the plate of half-eaten sandwiches left from lunch. "Not that I'm not perfectly happy to be home."

"You'll have a place to go," Florence said. Her voice was kind and yet it didn't have the slightest trace of pity in it. "As soon as you're ready, the perfect job is going to find you."

"I hope you're right," Sam said.

I felt like my heart was going to break for Sam. I hadn't thought of how it might be hard for him to see an old friend from work.

"I'm always right about these things," Florence said.

"Sam's going to come out of this one back on top!" my father said. "No more working for the man." My father looked over at the television screen. "Look at that. I think there's blood on the ice. Sam, turn up the volume."

"Good-bye, Florence," Sam said, reaching down sadly for the remote. "Thank you."

She waved to him and my father and we left them on the frozen blue rink.

I knew the polite thing to do would be to walk Florence Allen to the door and let her go, but I turned us toward the kitchen instead, hoping that she might relent for the coffee if it was just the two of us. I realized that I had been so consumed with meeting the needs of my family that the only nonrelatives I had talked to in the past week were the check-out girls at the grocery store. Here was an adult, an intelligent adult I did not know, right in my own kitchen.

And Florence Allen seemed to want to go to the kitchen. She wanted to talk to me in private as much as I wanted to talk to her.

"How's he doing?" she said in a quiet voice once we were alone.

"He doesn't complain, really. He's not the easiest man in the world to have around, but given all he's been through, I think he's holding up pretty well."

She shook her head. "When they fired Sam they took away the spirit of that hospital. There's nobody to stick up for the people anymore."

"Sam? I thought you were talking about my father. Sam is a very easy person to live with, all things considered."

"You have a crisis overlap here," she said.

"I'm not even sure I know how Sam is doing." I pulled out a chair and sat down at the table. Florence followed my lead. "I know this is terrible for him, but to tell you the truth, we don't really talk about it. I don't want him to feel like I'm pushing."

Florence sighed and stretched her long hands out on my kitchen table. She studied them for a while, trying to figure out how much she wanted to say. "Sam saved my job once. It was about five years ago. They were cutting back the whole physical therapy department. They said it was going to be cheaper to contract out the work, and Sam went to bat for me. He said I'd be his mission, and he did it. I'm still there."

"I didn't know that," I said. I wondered what I was doing at home five years ago when Sam was at work saving Florence Allen's job. Probably driving Wyatt to hockey practice.

"He's a very good man, your husband. Everybody thought so."

"I always thought so."

"He went through all that to make sure I'd have a job and now he doesn't have one. How does something like that happen? And now on top of that I wonder if I'm going to have to leave anyway. It seems like all the hospitals are the same these days. It's all about the bottom line."

"It sounds like a tough job."

"You're the one with the tough job," she said. She took off her heavy bag and rested it on the kitchen table. "Did your father live with you before his accident?"

I shook my head. "Only my mother."

She raised one eyebrow, a talent I have always admired and do not possess. "And your father did not live with your mother."

"Correct."

"A very tough job." She nodded her head like a detective who was just beginning to put together the gravity of the crime.

I agreed. "Would you have a piece of cake?"

"Cake?" she said.

"Do you eat cake?" Maybe as a medical professional she was opposed to cake.

"I should probably be going, but thank you."

I didn't want to seem desperate, but I was. I wanted to sit down with someone who was not a member of my family and have a regular conversation. "I made it myself."

"A scratch cake?" she said. I thought there was a flicker of interest in her tone.

"Always."

She looked at her watch as if it might give her approval. "I don't see that one slice would hurt."

I took down two plates from the cupboard. In the next room I heard the volume on the television rise again and I was grateful for the privacy it gave us. "We really appreciate you coming over."

"That's my job," she said.

I sliced the cake. It served well, no breakage, few crumbs. "Well, a lot of people wouldn't want that job. I would think you'd have to be a pretty generous sort of person to want to take care of other people. I don't think I could do it." I set two pieces of cake down on the table. "Would you like something to drink with that?"

"Wait a minute," she said. "I just take care of people in a hospital. You do it in your home. You don't get to leave work at the end of the day like I do."

I sat down and handed her a fork. "But it's my father. See, that's the difference. I didn't sign on for this. I was born into it."

Then Florence Allen did the most remarkable thing. She put her hand on my wrist, just set it there like it was the most natural thing in the world to put your hand on the wrist of someone you barely knew. She looked at me squarely when she spoke. "Everybody has parents. Very few people take care of them."

Gently and smoothly, her words pricked the edge of the enormous well of emotion that had been pressing on my chest since the day my father arrived. I tried to hold myself together but I didn't seem to have the energy to manage it anymore. Great tears welled up in my eyes and I had to pull my hand away from hers to get a paper napkin from the holder. "I'm sorry," I said. "I have no idea why I'm doing this."

"Honey, if I was you I would have been crying a long time ago." She clearly was someone who was very used to being around the fully displayed emotions of strangers and it didn't faze her in the least. She went ahead and ate her cake.

When Florence Allen took a bite of her dessert the expression on her face changed completely. She looked puzzled at first, as if she wasn't at all sure it was cake that she was eating. She cut herself another bite and then held up her fork and looked at it for a minute before slipping it into her mouth. She chewed slowly, as if she were a scientist engaged in an important experiment. She lifted up her plate and held it up to the light, studied it from different angles. Then she dipped down her nose and inhaled the cake. "This is sweet potato."

I dabbed at my eyes again and told her that it was.

"Sweet potatoes and raisins and . . . rum? That's a spiked glaze?"

I nodded.

She took another bite and this time she ate it like a person who knew what she was getting into. She closed her eyes. She savored. "This is," she said. "This is . . ."

"Easy," I said. "I can give you the recipe."

She opened up her eyes. She had lovely dark eyes. "This is brilliant. This is a brilliant piece of cake."

In my family people tended to work against the cake. They wished it wasn't there even as they were enjoying it. But Florence Allen's reaction was one I rarely saw in an adult: She gave in to the cake. She allowed herself to love the cake. It wasn't that she surrendered her regrets (*Oh well, I'll just have to go to the gym tomorrow,* or, *I won't have any dinner this week*). She *had* no regrets. She lived in the moment. She took complete pleasure in the act of eating cake. "I'm glad you like it," I said, but that didn't come close to what I meant.

"Oh, I don't just like it. I think this is—" But she didn't say it. Instead she stopped and had another bite.

I could have watched her eat the whole thing, slice by slice, but no one likes to be stared at. Instead I ate my own cake. It was good, really. Every raisin bitten gave a sweet exhalation of rum. It was one of those cakes that most people say should be made for Thanksgiving, that it was by its nature a holiday cake, but why be confined? I was always one to bake whatever struck me on any given day.

Florence Allen pressed her fork down several times until she had taken up every last crumb. Her plate was clean enough to be returned to the cupboard directly. "I've made sweet potato pies," she said. "I've baked them and put them in casseroles, but in a cake? That never crossed my mind."

"It isn't logical. They're so dense. I think of it as the banana bread principle. Would you like another piece?"

She folded her long fingers over her stomach and shook her head. "I don't want to ruin it by making myself sick."

"Take it home, then." I stood up and took out a package of the extra-heavy, extra-large Chinette paper plates I had become so fond of over the years. It is a universal truth: No matter how trust-worthy they are, people don't return cake plates.

Florence Allen looked at me as if I had pulled off my engage-ment ring and offered it to her. "You can't give me your cake. Your family will want that. What would they think of me if I took their cake?"

"They'll think you're doing them an enormous favor," I said. "They want it out of here. The truth is I have plenty of time to bake something else to have with dinner."

"Is it somebody's birthday?"

"Somewhere I figure it's somebody's birthday. It's always somebody's birthday." I pulled a sheet of Glad wrap over the cake and pressed it into her hands. I was glad to see it go. "I appreciate your help with my father. I appreciate you liking the cake."

"I shouldn't take your cake," she said. "But I want it. My daughters, my husband, they won't believe it." She held it up on the flat of her palms and looked at it.

I smiled. I thought about telling her how happy I would be to bake her a cake every day for the rest of her life if she was willing to come back and help me with my father or even just express an interest in what I was doing, but then I thought there was no need to tell her. It could scare her off. A guaranteed future of cakes was more than most people could really understand.

We said our good-byes and Florence Allen left with the cake. My mother came into the kitchen just in time to watch her walk down the driveway toward her car. She craned her neck forward to get a better look.

"Is that a nurse?" she said.

"Kind of."

"A nurse for your father?"

"She's an old friend of Sam's from the hospital. She just came by to give Dad some advice about working his fingers." I picked up the plates from the table.

"So she's not going to come and take care of him?"

"No, I think that's still up to us."

"Up to you," my mother said. "I'm touching the old man more than I think is appropriate." My mother kept watching Florence Allen until finally she had to move to the other side of the window so she could see the picture from another angle. "Ruth, look, I think she's taking the sweet potato cake."

"I gave it to her."

"You gave her the cake and she took it?"

"She seemed glad to have it."

My mother nodded her head in approval. "Well, I like her already."

That night I lay in bed and thought about cake. I was thinking about what I would bake for Florence Allen when she came back again, something she might eat with equal enthusiasm. I wanted a cake that would in no way be a logical followup to the sweet potato cake. I wanted a cake that would come completely out of left field, something that would astonish her. But I wouldn't just be making it for her. I wanted something for myself, a cake that was complicated and beautiful, a cake that would take up time I didn't have with enough tricky steps to keep my mind completely off of the matters at hand. I thought about a chocolate layer cake with burnt orange icing and the orange in the icing made me consider a Grand

Marnier cake instead. Finally, in a complete non sequitur, I settled on a charlotte. I would make a scarlet empress. I closed my eyes and imagined myself making a jelly roll, the soft sheet of sponge cake laid across my counter. I spread the cake with a seedless raspberry preserve and then I rolled it up with even ends. I was nearly asleep. My parents were floating away from me. I took a knife and started slicing off the roll, but I didn't let it end. No matter how many rounds I cut, there was more there for me, an endless supply of delicate spirals of cake. It was the baker's equivalent to counting sheep, lulling myself to sleep through spongy discs of jam. There were enough slices of jelly roll for me to shingle the roof, to cover the house, to lay a walkway out to the street. In my dreams I made the house a cake, and inside that cake our lives were warm and sweet and infinitely protected.

Chapter Six

WHEN WYATT WAS FIFTEEN I FOUND TWO *PLAYBOY* magazines circa 1989 in his sock drawer. I had not been snooping. I always returned his clean socks to the drawer. I had been doing it with his full knowledge since he was old enough to wear socks. But on this particular day I was depositing an unusually large collection of small bundles to the dresser and could clearly see Miss June staring back at me with an expression that could only be described as brazen. She was barely covered by a couple of mateless tube socks that always stayed behind.

What I thought at the time was that I wished Wyatt could have been a little cannier about hiding his belongings, but as it turned out, I seemed to have a talent for finding things. Lately, a different kind of magazine had been turning up around the house. I found them slipped under sofa cushions and hidden in bathroom cupboards, copies of *Wooden Boat, Classic Sailing,* and *International Yachting.* Sam had always liked the occasional boating magazine, so I doubt I would have noticed them if they had just been lying around in the open. But somehow the fact that they were wedged into the middle of a stack of towels made them seem suspicious, almost dangerous. I made no attempt to look for them and yet I seemed to find them everywhere. Finally I took a copy, closed the bedroom door, and flipped through one. It was filled with glossy pictures of elegant boats: boats cutting through white spray, boats reflected in a glassy lake, boats tied humble and obedient to their docks. Sam came in the room without knocking. After all, it was his room too.

I tried to keep my perspective. They were only boats. "Are these yours?" I asked him.

He took the magazine I was holding and rolled it in his hands. "Where did you find this?"

"In an empty shoe box in the garage."

"Why were you looking in empty shoe boxes?"

"I was going to mail Wyatt some brownies. That's why I save the shoe boxes." I tried to imagine myself in the garage just looking around to see if I could find someone else's secrets. Did anyone have time for things like that?

Sam tapped the magazine against his leg. He seemed very uncomfortable. "I like to look at boats, that's all."

"So look at boats," I said. "But why would you want to hide them? It's not like I've never seen you look at a boating magazine before."

Sam sighed and sat down on the edge of our bed. "I don't have much of a sense of privacy right now. Somehow everything feels different. I'm not used to being home all the time. It's not like I'm trying to hide something, it's just . . . I'm trying to figure something out is all. I just need to think it through."

We hadn't talked about boats again since that first night he mentioned them to me. I was so sleepy that night I had half wondered later if I had dreamed the whole thing up. "Think boats through?"

He looked up as if I finally understood him. His eyes brightened. "Yes."

"Okay."

"Did I ever tell you about my first boat, the first boat I sailed in?"

"I don't know."

Sam got up and put the magazine in his bedside table drawer. "It was with my uncle Nick. He kept his boat on Lake Michigan."

"Uncle Nick, sure."

"I loved being out on the water with him. I would say those afternoons with Nick were some of the happiest times in my childhood. He explained everything to me, all about sheets and lines and how to tack. He was a great teacher. Sometimes I wonder if it was the water that I loved or if it was just the sound of Nick's voice." Sam stopped and shook his head. "I've been in a lot of boats since then, some great boats, but since I lost my job, since everything's been falling apart, I don't know, every time I feel myself getting panicked I think about that boat. I just close my eyes and I'm sitting in the Oday with Nick and as far as I can see in every direction there's water, and then I feel better again. It's like I can breathe."

The boat was his cake. But I had never told him about my cake visualization. Now I wished I had told him years ago when I first started. I thought it was too late to try to go over it now. Of course he had his boating magazines. Didn't I sit down at the kitchen table and pore over every page of the *Baker's Catalog* the minute it came in the mail? Everyone has a private life, the things they love and think that no one else could really understand. I felt so close to Sam at that moment and yet there was no good way for me to explain it. "I understand." It was all I could say.

Sam smiled and kissed my forehead. "Thank you," he said finally. "I'm glad we could talk about this."

I should have just left it there, in that nice moment between us, but I didn't. "Do you want to take up sailing?"

Sam looked utterly defeated by the question. "Oh, Ruth, I don't know."

I wanted Sam to be happy. I wanted it more than anything. But at the same time I had been going over our finances and things were not looking good, not in the short term or the long term. There was tuition, a mortgage, my father's outstanding hospital bill. There were five people costing money in this house, six if you counted monthly checks to Wyatt. As a group, we were not bringing very much in. I didn't feel like I could say anything to Sam. He knew what we had and what we owed, and I didn't see how reminding him was going to be helpful. Still, a boat? "Aren't boats very . . . expensive?"

"Not all boats," he said.

"I guess I just don't understand if you're thinking about this as a hobby or a job." I didn't understand if he was thinking about it as something to do here or something to take him away. Minnesota was the land of ten thousand lakes, but for the most part they weren't the sort of lakes that were conducive to international yachting. If I had found stacks of canoeing magazines hidden around the house, I might have thought he was on to something.

Sam fell back on the bed and stared up at the ceiling. "It really is like your father says. Sometimes you have time to sort it all through. Is it enough to just find a job that will take the place of my other job? I'll tell you, Ruth, I think about it now and I'm not so sure I was happy in the other job. I think I was just on autopilot the whole time. I don't want to go back to that life. I want to try to figure out what I'm supposed to do, what I might be good at. I really want to be good at something, to feel passionate about it. Do you understand that? Your father says that's the best chance a person has to make a real living in this world."

"Tell me the truth here. Just tell me what you want to do. Whatever it is, I'm going to be behind you." I was hoping that he didn't plan on following my father's example. I had a mental image of Sam on a boat far, far out in the ocean. He looked tan and calm and happy as he sliced through a field of limitless blue water. The very thought of it scared me to death.

"I told you, I'm not sure."

But I knew Sam, the way he was pressing his thumbs together, the way his shoulders bent in. This was more than just boats. "There's something else."

Sam sighed and rolled over on his stomach. He was facing away from me, which I thought was a very bad sign. "I'm getting two months' pay as severance," he said.

I had the feeling that the ground was suddenly loose under my feet, loose and slowly slipping down into some invisible drain beneath the bed. Two months was nothing. It was a sneeze. We had used up almost two weeks already, nearly twenty-five percent, without even realizing what we were doing. "Can you negotiate?"

"It's the same for everyone," he said. "There might be a lawsuit but that's not exactly the kind of thing you can take to the bank. The whole thought of a lawsuit makes me feel pretty uneasy anyway."

I lay down on the bed next to my husband. I put the palm of my hand on the flat of his back. I was terrified. I loved him. "So what do you think we should do?"

Sam was quiet for a long time. He seemed to be taking very shallow breaths. "Can I talk to you?" he said. "If I say something, can you just agree to think about it for a while without telling me what a bad idea it is? I know it's a bad idea, but I just don't want you to tell me so the minute I say it."

"Okay," I said, trying to keep the tentative dread out of my voice.

"Well, the way I look at it, we have two choices." He kept his head turned away from me so that I would think it was really the wall he was confiding in. "Either we take that money and just live on it for two months like it was a regular paycheck and I try to find another job I don't really like so I can bring in other regular pay-checks, or . . ."

But then he stopped. Nothing came after the "or." I waited until the moment had taken on the tinge of something unbearable. "Or?" I said finally, hoping to remind him where he had left off.

"Or I take that money and buy a boat. I fix the boat up and sell it for a lot more money and we make a profit."

I tried not to breathe, as I knew that even a sharp intake of air would sound judgmental at this point. Boats sounded like a bad idea to me, a really bad idea, but I was willing to withhold judgment for a while. I trusted Sam, even if I didn't understand him at the moment.

"Okay," I said.

Sam turned his head over and looked at me. "Okay what?"

"Okay, I heard what you were saying and I promise not to be critical and to think it through the way you asked me to."

"Great," Sam said, closing his eyes. "You think I'm an idiot."

My father was in the kitchen reading a John le Carré novel. His arms were spread out over the table. I came in just as it was time to turn a page. He pushed the book out with the tip of the metal halo until it was down near his fingertips, then, using the slightest amount of touch possible, he maneuvered one page over and slid the book back toward the edge of the table again until it was close enough to read. "It breaks up the narrative flow, I'll tell you," he said, not looking up. "But I'm using my fingers."

"Dad, I've got to talk to you."

"I'm a captive audience."

"You can't keep hounding Sam to discover himself. He needs to get a job, to get back to his regular life. That's what's going to make him happy."

"That's what will make you happy," my father said.

"We have bills. Wyatt's in college, we're still paying off Camille's braces, this house isn't paid for. Don't you ever think about those things? Shoes, insurance, school trips, the auto club? Doesn't any of that stuff occur to you?"

"Not anymore, really. I've lived my whole life outside the box. People feel so bound down to their possessions, their responsibilities, that they wind up not even living their lives. I know you have your worries, I just think that Sam deserves to think about Sam for a change."

I picked up his hand and started to rotate his fingers, first in one direction and then the other. Florence was coming back today and I wanted him to be limber. Still, I will admit there was a part of me that felt like giving one a little bit of a twist until he agreed to see things my way. "Do you know," I said, starting with his index finger, "that he's thinking about buying a boat?"

My father looked down at his spy novel. "I don't know anything."

"Okay, just for the sake of conversation, forget about the fact that we are in real financial straits, did you ever stop to think that he could be hurt on a boat?" I took another finger and went five times to the right and then five times to the left in circles that were slow and no larger than quarters.

"Gently now," my father said. He was always nervous when we touched his hands.

"He could drown."

"Oh hell, Ruthie, don't give me that. Sam can swim."

Sam could swim, but from where? The middle of the Atlantic? The doorbell rang. "That's Mrs. Allen," I said. "Try to behave yourself."

"Behaving. There's more to life than behaving. I never should have left you with your mother. That was my mistake. I should have taken you with me. Then maybe you'd be able to see some version of the world other than the one that's presented to you on the ABC nightly news."

I walked away from him, the old adage "Saved by the bell" ringing in my head. Florence Allen stood at the door in her white lab coat, smiling. For the first time in my life I understood the idea behind medical professionals wearing white. Before it had always just struck me as terribly impractical, what with all the mess they had to deal with on any given day. But now I could see that the white was a message. It said order, it said the calm inside the storm. It stood out like a beacon, a brightness you turned toward in your confusion.

"How's he doing today?" she said.

"Which one?"

She laughed as if I had made some sort of joke. "Your father."

I sighed and stepped away from the door. "Come in and see for yourself."

When we walked into the kitchen my father stood up. "Mrs. Allen," he said. "How nice of you to come back. On your way to work?"

"On my way home from work, actually. I'm not in such a rush today. How have you been feeling?"

"Fortunate, mostly. A man with such a fine family to take care of him would have to feel fortunate."

"Are you having much pain?"

"Nothing that isn't manageable. Ruth very kindly moves my fingers around three times a day just the way you told her."

As if it were a piece of good advice, she picked up his hand and started moving his first finger in circles. I noticed her circles were bigger than mine.

Sam must have heard us. When he came into the kitchen he was wearing a pressed shirt and his hair was combed. I hadn't noticed it before he had made the effort to straighten up, but Sam had been getting a little disheveled lately. "Florence, I thought that would be you."

She looked up from the work of my father's hands. "How've you been, Sam?"

"I can't complain," he said.

"He should complain," my father said. "Everyone in this family conspires against this man."

Sam gave a halfhearted smile. "Guy likes to exaggerate."

"Don't pretend it isn't true! This is a sensible woman here. I feel it. Everything about her says that she has some insight into the human condition."

Florence put her chin down slightly and stared first at my husband and then my father. "Have I come at a bad time?"

"No," Sam said. "Listen, Guy. Let's not tie Florence up here. She's doing us a favor coming by. Speaking of which, I have a call in to the doctor. I'm hoping that we'll be able to come and see you," he said to Florence, "as a regular paying patient instead of having you make free house calls."

"Do you have any interest in sailing, Mrs. Allen?"

It was at that point my mother walked past the kitchen. She did her level best to stay out of any room my father was in, but then she saw that we had company and she stopped and backed up a few steps.

"You're the woman who took the cake," my mother said by way of introduction.

"Mother, this is Florence Allen. She's helping us with Dad's therapy."

"Well, I can see that."

"I took the cake," she said. "It was a wonderful cake."

"We're supposed to call her Mrs. Allen," my father told my mother.

"I don't mean *took* the cake, of course. I don't mean that you stole the cake. My daughter said she gave it to you. I guess I didn't say that right. My name is Hollis. May I call you Florence?"

"Of course," Florence said. I thought there was the slightest edge of nervousness in her voice. Run! I wanted to say to her. Run as fast as you can.

"Now wait a minute here," my father said.

"Okay," Sam said. "It's time to let Florence get to work."

"He calls you Florence and she calls you Florence and I'm supposed to call you Mrs. Allen?"

"With my patients I find it's better if—"

"But I'm *not* your patient, exactly. We don't come to the hospital. We don't pay you anything."

"I'm working on that," Sam said.

"For heaven's sake, Guy, just listen to Florence and do what she tells you." My mother crossed her arms snugly across her chest. She was glowing with self-satisfaction. "You think he's bad now, you should have seen him when I was married to him."

"Can you hold a fork, Mr. Nash?" Florence said. She put down his hand. With that question she regained complete authority. The room settled down to listen.

"In my hand?" my father said.

My mother started to say something—one imagines not something very helpful—but she decided to keep it to herself when Florence took a fork out of her bag whose sky blue handle was as big around as a small apple. The little silver tines were bright and shiny. It looked like a cartoon fork, something Sylvester the cat would use to try to eat the little yellow bird. She put it down on the table in front of my father. "I want you to just rest your fingers on top of the fork. Don't try to pick it up yet. Just curve them around the side."

He watched the fork for a while. "I have a perfectly good system of eating," he said finally.

"Ruth spooning in your breakfast cereal is not a perfectly good system of eating," my mother said.

"I'm not asking you to pick it up." Florence looked at my mother while she spoke. "This might be easier without an audience."

Sam put his hand on my mother's shoulder. "Come on, Hollis. Let's you and me go to the grocery store."

But my mother shook him off. "He knows perfectly well he can pick up the fork," she said. Then she took off her glasses, wiped them on the bottom of her blouse, and put them back on just to say she didn't plan to miss a minute of it.

My father took a deep breath and set his hand on top of the fork, then he curled his fingers around the side and left them there for a minute. "The thing is," he said to no one in particular, "I've been doing things for myself my whole life. You want to know what independent means, there will be a little picture of me next to the word in the dictionary. But once you can't do something, it's like you forget how to do everything."

"You're doing fine," Florence said. "You're doing exactly what I wanted you to do."

Camille breezed into the kitchen wearing a long-sleeved cropped top and a pair of corduroy pants. If it was cold enough outside to wear sleeves, wouldn't you want your stomach covered as well? "Hey, Grandpa's got a fork. That's great."

And with that my father circled his fingers to the best of his ability around the chubby handle and lifted it into the air. He held it aloft for a good five seconds before he dropped it back on the table.

"Look at you!" my mother said proudly, and put her hand on the back of his neck. In a fraction of the time he had held the fork, she remembered herself and pulled away.

"Hey, you dropped it," Camille said, then she smiled. "But at least you've got a fork now."

We were all enormously impressed. I introduced Florence to Camille, who shook her hand and was exceedingly polite. I was never sure how a person could have such good manners for strangers and such bad ones for the people she saw every day, but probably if I had to choose, I would want it to be this way instead of the other way around.

Florence moved the fork over to the other side of the table, turning the tines faceup again. "That fork isn't just a way to eat. That's the way you play the piano. So if you're feeling like you don't want to be bothered with the fork, like maybe you'd just as soon have someone else feed you, you remember that. I want you to pick it up with both hands."

"Both hands," my father said obediently.

After that, we left them alone. Sam did in fact convince my mother to ride to the store with him and Camille went back to the private world of her bedroom where she was headed in the first place. I sat for a minute in the quiet den and looked at cookbooks, trying to get inspired for a great strawberry frosting, while Florence worked with my father in the kitchen, telling him to press down, to roll his shoulders, to curl his fingers. I listened to the steady instruction of her voice while my eyes scanned over familiar measurements of sugar and cream of tartar. I hoped it seemed as comforting to him as it did to me.

"Enough?" I heard her say finally.

"Enough," my father said. He sounded beat. As angry as I could get with my father, my heart always went out to him where his wrists were concerned.

"That's a lot of work."

"Ruthie!" my father called out. I got up and went back into the kitchen. "Let's invite Mrs. Allen to stay for dinner, shall we?"

I remembered stories my mother used to tell about my father swinging through the front door after practice, the whole brass section of the band trailing him like the tail of a kite. "Hollis!" he would say as she looked up from the stove. "I've invited a few of the boys for dinner!"

"You'd be very welcome." In this case, I was glad for my father's inclusive nature, but I was wishing there was something more exciting on the menu than stuffed bell peppers.

Florence shook her head. "I think my family would be awfully disappointed if I got dinner and they didn't."

"So call up and invite your family too," my father said.

"Thank you," Florence said. "I really can't."

"Then you should at least stay for some of Ruthie's cake. My daughter is a fine cook, you know."

"Oh, I know that," she said with great authority. "Don't tell me you have a cake today too."

Actually, I had two cakes, a lemon poppy seed cake, which was my favorite casual cake and was for anyone to eat, and then the elaborate scarlet empress, which had occupied my time so completely the day before. It was sitting under a glass dome in the pantry waiting like a present waits under a tree. That was for Florence to take home.

"Ruthie always has cake. Even if you don't see any out on the counter, you just ask. She's always got something squirreled away in the freezer."

I cut us each a slice of the poppy seed cake and put on some coffee.

"None for me," my father said. "I'm pretty tired."

"I won't make you use the fork," Florence said.

He shook his head. "It looks good," he said kindly. "I'll have a piece when I get up." My father stood but paused at the edge of the table to give the cake a long, hard look. For a minute I thought he was going to change his mind. "You should stop asking Sam when he's going to get a job and start thinking about getting one yourself." He seemed to be speaking to the slice of lemon poppy seed cake. He made a special effort to lower three of his fingers down a half inch so that he was, in a fashion, pointing at my cake. "You should go into the baking business. That's something you could do."

My father didn't think I could do much. I suppose I should have been grateful that he liked my baking. "Thanks for the advice," I said lightly. "Come on. I'll help you get the bed turned down."

I took my father into his room and folded back the bedspread. I closed the blinds to block out some of the sunlight in the room, but it was still brighter than he would have liked it. He sat down on the bed and held his feet out so I could pull off his shoes. He could have done that himself. It is quite possible to remove shoes without using your hands. I knelt on the floor in front of him and pulled them off. "I wish you'd stop putting all your efforts into protecting Sam," I said in a low voice.

"Sam's a good man." My father flexed his toes up and down. "Leave the socks on. My feet get cold."

"I know Sam's a good man. I'm not saying he isn't, but I'm not so bad, you know, and I'm your daughter. Doesn't that count for something?"

My father lay on his back, one encased arm straight out to either side, and slid his legs neatly between the sheets. I pulled the covers up to his chin and tried to better arrange the pillow under his head.

"Darling girl, you're confusing the issue. Just because I'm rooting for Sam doesn't mean I'm rooting against you. I love you. I'm always going to be behind you. But look at the way the deck is stacked. You've got both of your parents living here, two people who always think you're the best. It wouldn't hurt if someone took up for Sam once in a while."

It seemed wonderfully crazy to me that my father would think I was the lucky one for having both of my parents living with us. "But *I* take up for Sam," I said to him. Didn't I? I thought about the boat magazines. Maybe he didn't feel like he could confide in me anymore.

I sat down on the edge of the bed and my father grimaced a little. "How about a pain pill? You haven't had one all day."

But he shook his head. "I'm cutting back. I'll be fine once I go to sleep," he said. "That Mrs. Allen's a devil with that fork." His voice was so tired. My father was back in school now and he'd made good marks for the day. Suddenly I felt as though I was picking a fight with a tired old man who had two broken wrists.

"Get some rest." I kissed the top of his head and turned off the light.

"Don't worry too much about Sam," he said. "You've just got to have a little faith in a person. If your mother had had even a little bit of faith in what I could do, I bet we would have stayed together."

"You have no idea what you're saying. You'll be more clear-headed after you've had some rest."

"When I wake up I plan to saw my way through a steak, with a fork *and* knife. You'll see." He gave me a chuckle and I softly closed the door.

"Sorry about that," I said to Florence when I came back in the room. "My father has a lot of opinions."

"I'm used to men with opinions." She took her first bite of cake. She'd been waiting for me. "My pound cake always gets a little rubbery strip near the bottom. I bet you've never even had a rubbery strip. Yours is absolutely perfect all the way through."

"You might need to check the oven temperature. I have an oven thermometer if you ever want to borrow it. "

She nodded her head. "That might be exactly what I need." She cut off another bite but she didn't eat it. "So is Sam having problems finding a job? I don't mean to be nosy. It's just when your father said that about him looking for work, I was wondering."

"Sam is having problems finding himself. He thinks he needs to find himself before he can find a job. I think he should find a job and then the rest of it will fall into place. My father and I are in different camps on this particular issue."

"I just can't imagine it. Sam was the very best. I would think there would be hospitals beating down his door. The whole place has fallen apart without him."

"I'm not so sure he wants a hospital anymore. Sometimes I wonder what would have happened if my father hadn't been staying with us. Maybe Sam would have gone out and gotten a job the next day. Then again, it may not have anything to do with my father." I shook my head. "I used to think I knew Sam better than anybody in the world. Now I'm not so sure."

"What does Sam think he wants to do?"

I looked around behind me. The door to my father's room was closed. Camille was too far away to hear us. There wasn't anyone around but still I was afraid to even say it, as if saying it would make it true. "He says he wants to rebuild wooden boats," I whispered.

"Build boats?"

"Build them, sail them, sell them. All of it."

"That's why your father asked me about sailing."

"Exactly."

"Boats." Florence closed her eyes and shook her head. "That's a bad sign."

I thought so too but it frightened me to hear her say it.

"I used to call it the Mode of Transportation Crisis. My husband had a terrible one when our girls were young. I think the pressure got to him, you know, having to be responsible for a family. One day he'd come home talking about how important it was to see America by train, and then the next day he'd tell me he was going to take flying lessons. Do you have any idea how expensive that is? We were barely making the rent back then and he wanted to take flying lessons! And cars, it was all the time about cars." She took another bite of cake and smiled, not at her story but at the sweetness in her own mouth. "He just wanted to go, that was the bottom line. Everything he dreamed about featured leaving us behind."

"What happened?" My fingers turned cold around my fork.

She shrugged. "He left. He was gone for about six months." She paused, as if she were counting up the days in her head. "Then it took another six months after that for me to let him back in the house. But we got over it. That was a long time ago. I like to keep the past in the past. We've got a good marriage. He doesn't talk about going anyplace now except maybe the grocery store."

I couldn't eat the cake. I felt like the room was spinning. I could see my husband untying the line from the dock, using a slender oar to push himself away. It was a bright blue day, a few puffy clouds in the eastern corner of the sky for decoration. Everywhere there was the slap of waves and the plangent cry of seagulls. "I don't want to lose Sam."

Florence took another bite of cake. "You know, this cake is every bit as good as the other one. It's just not as flashy. That other one took my breath away, but now that I'm really getting through this slice, I can see that it has a lot of character. That lemon glaze, it just has so much lemon to it. Usually a lemon glaze is just a sugar icing that a lemon has passed over."

"I always use three times as much lemon juice as the recipes call for," I said. I could barely make the words. There went Sam's little boat. The sail was swelling up with wind. The sun was shining in his hair. "You just have to cook it down longer." Why were we talking about the glaze? I was going to lose my husband, and while he was what I really cared about, I would have been lying if I said that the attending issues did not cross my mind, such as how I was going to pay for things, school and the house and the health insurance.

"So what if your father is right?" Florence said.

"And he shouldn't be forced to feed himself?"

She sighed and started over again, using her most patient tone of voice. "What if your father is right and the answer to your problems is sitting on that plate in front of you?"

I looked down at my plate. My slice of lemon poppy seed cake was untouched.

"You think I should bake cakes for a living?"

"You have a whole lot of things you're worried about, emotional things like who's happy and who's fulfilled, and practical things, like how to make money and who's supposed to work. So maybe you should try to find an answer for yourself instead of waiting around to see what Sam's going to do. Doing something is always easier than waiting. Besides, what if it worked out? Then Sam wouldn't have to worry about finding a job. You could give him a job working for you, sifting flour or something. You could give him such a good salary he could buy himself a boat."

"It's a lovely thought, but it's crazy. So I can bake. Everybody can bake."

She tapped her fork against my plate. "Not like this, they can't. I may not know you very well, but you seem to spend a lot of your energy holding things together. Why not put that energy into doing something big?"

"Cake isn't big enough to pull us out of this mess."

Florence smiled at me. She had absolute confidence in what she was saying. "Take a bite of that cake and tell me that everyone in this country wouldn't like to have a piece of it."

She looked at me hard until I realized that she was not being rhetorical. I took a bite of my own cake. I had to admit, she had a point. The cake was crunchy and sweet and all pulled together by the tart edge of lemon.

It was good.

Chapter Seven

MY FIRST MEMORY OF CAKE IS NOT OF EATING ONE, although in this memory I am five or nearly five and so certainly I must have had plenty of cake by this time just from birthdays alone. In my first memory of a cake it is summer and my mother is standing in the kitchen of our apartment with the windows open and the sun shining off the side of her metal mixing bowl. She is young and straight-backed and beautiful in a serious sort of way. She is measuring the flour she had sifted, holding the cup up to the abundant light to make sure she has exactly the right amount. My mother did not believe in cake mixes, not because she was a purist, but because she was poor, and the cake mix was a relatively new invention of luxury meant to free up more time for the modern homemaker. My mother, who always had tests to grade and rehearsals to attend, didn't see herself as much of a homemaker.

On the morning of the cake, I am standing on a stool beside her, which puts me at a comfortable height to see everything that is going on. My mother pours the flour into a fine-mesh colander that sits over her mixing bowl, and into that colander she adds one tablespoon plus one teaspoon of baking powder from a bright red tin with an Indian on the label, and three quarters of a teaspoon of salt. The precision of it all appeals to me, and I love the teaspoons, but especially the quarter teaspoon, as children love things that are small. They are held together by a single silver ring and the ones that aren't being used at the moment make a music like bells when she picks up the one that she wants. My mother was a teacher, and when I say that, I don't simply mean it was the way she made her living. She was a teacher in her soul and found that inside every action there was the opportunity for instruction. I used to wonder if she would have talked the same way if I wasn't there, if she would have tried to teach the cat how to bake a cake instead.

"Always take the time to double-check your measurements. I read one teaspoon, I measure one teaspoon, and then I go back to the book and check again. It's easy enough to beat an egg into the batter but it's a lot harder to pull one out." She runs her fork inside the colander and then shakes it gently into the bowl until the flour and salt and leavening all fall together like a light snow. "This resifts it." She shakes again and the last of the powder wafts down. "There. All the dry ingredients are ready to go." Next she unwraps the butter and scrapes a stick and a half from the paper into another bowl. "Always soften the butter. I put it out this morning first thing when I woke up. If you try to beat sugar into cold butter, you're not going to get anywhere. You have to follow the rules, Ruth. It's all in the book. If a person can read, they can cook."

I find that I am taking in every word of what she is saying. Even as a small child I didn't always listen to my mother, but everything she has to say about cake is something I want to hear.

She pours a cup of bright sugar on top of the butter and hands me the bowl with a wooden spoon. "Mix," she says. "Put your back into it."

And so I begin to beat the butter and sugar together. My mother stops me a couple of times to help me get a better grasp on the spoon or to demonstrate the vigor she is expecting. I love the work. Maybe that's what I'm remembering: It was the first time I ever had a real job that was more than setting the table. Then my mother shows me how to separate an egg so that the whites slide out into a bowl and the bright yellow yolk stays nestled in a half shell. She drops the yolk onto a waiting saucer. The whole thing seems like a brilliant magic act to me, so when she hands me a whole egg and suggests I do it by myself, you would have thought she was letting me drive the car.

"Someday, when you're very good at this, you can break them directly into the bowl, but for now you have to check yourself and make sure that none of the shell falls in. Nobody wants a cake with shell in it," she says with sharp authority.

"What about the whites?" I want to know.

"We'll think of something later," my mother says. And she will. She is not a woman to let a perfectly good egg white go down the drain.

I crack each egg into the saucer and then slide the yolk carefully into the batter one at a time, beating in every trace of yellow before going on to the next. Six eggs in all! It seems inconceivable that one cake could take in so many eggs yolks. I beat and beat until I feel like my arm might disengage from my shoulder. My mother looks into the bowl from time to time but she never says, I think that's about got it. She just nods at me and smiles. "We've got to get the air to stay in there," she says. "It's no trouble at all to make a cake that tastes like a brick, but no one will enjoy it. Making a light cake takes a lot of work, and that's the kind we make because that's the kind people like."

She goes to the highest shelf of the pantry and brings down a brown bottle so small I would have given it to my dolls to play with had I ever been able to reach it myself. "Vanilla," she says. She unscrews the cap and holds it down to nose level so that I can take a sniff. "This is the secret ingredient and it's very expensive. This is what makes a cake a cake." She measures out a careful teaspoon, going all the way to the top without spending a drop more than she has to. It is a skill she would use when making screwdrivers years later. She pours it into my batter and I continue to beat. Now with every stroke there is a soft wave of vanilla in the air, and I can for the first time imagine how the cake will taste. In the most fundamental way I have my first glimpse of how ingredients come together, how each is nothing in particular by itself but once they are joined they can make something miraculous. My mother adds part of the flour and then some milk, taking those two ingredients back and forth while I work. She butters the pans using her fingers and then sprinkles in some flour and knocks it from side to side until the pans are evenly coated. Then she pours the batter into each pan in a way that strikes me as completely even and therefore fair. There is a system, an order to everything she does, in much the same way there is order to the notes she plays on the piano. The light on our oven is broken and so to see the cakes I have to open the door a crack to peek inside.

My mother tells me to cut it out. I am compromising the temperature with my curiosity.

The measuring cups, the round pans, the wire cooling racks that looked like a section of delicate fencing—all of these things amaze me. While the cakes are cooling, my mother beats up a pan of dark and glossy frosting, her wooden spoon attacking the mixture with such ferocity that I realize I've been doing next to nothing all this time. Once the cakes are completely, unquestionably cool, she lets me help her spread the frosting on, sweet and stiff across the layers. When we stack one cake on top of the other, we have made something miraculous, a building, a piece of art. She lets me smooth down the top with a wide spatula and does nothing to correct my work when I'm finished.

"You made a cake," my mother says, and gives me a kiss on the top of my head.

I ask her if we can have a piece. I imagine the two of us sitting at the little table in the kitchen and eating the entire thing, slice by slice. "It's for the school," she says, and tells me to go and get my jacket. The cake that we have made is bigger than the two of us. It has places to go.

Do I remember any other day from my childhood so clearly? Maybe a minute, a particular dress, some praise or punishment in class, a girlfriend with whom I traded sandwiches, but I don't remember any of it with the detail, the breathing Technicolor with which I remember that day. The cake, as it turns out, was to be taken to the school, where the band was raising money for new instruments at a carnival. My mother and I go to the same school. I am in preschool and she is a teacher in the high school. At this particular carnival there is an event called a Cake Walk, in which people buy tickets for the right to walk in circles over numbers written in chalk on the ground. They go around and around while someone plays a song, and when the song is over, the person who is standing on the lucky number (called out by a man wearing a red-striped coat) gets to go to the cake booth and pick out any cake he or she wants.

The cake booth has as much to do with my education as helping my mother bake the cake. When we come to the carnival I believe that the cake my mother carries in is as beautiful and perfect as anything I have ever seen. But when we set our cake down on the long wooden table, I know it is only in the middle of the pack. There are towering white cakes buried beneath an avalanche of coconut, delicate golden cakes rimmed in strawberries. There are cakes with roses the size of hens' eggs made out of frosting and a sculpted Bundt cake that looks like the base of an elaborate fountain. There must be fifty cakes on the table when the Cake Walk begins and I stand in front of each one of them for a minute and wonder about their ingredients. Did they all have vanilla? One smells like oranges. My mother talks to her students who cluster around her, wanting her attention. Other parents come and put their cakes down on the table. I judge each one against ours, deciding if it is lesser or greater. While our cake doesn't look particularly special, I know that the six egg yolks are our secret strength.

Every trip around the ring costs a dime, which means that if you win you can have one of these beauties for ten cents. My mother lets me go around twice and then says enough is enough, and while it is thrilling to be out there in the game, stepping from number to number and wondering when the song might finish up, I don't mind not winning. I don't want to have to choose. I want them all, not to eat but to study. I want to take them apart, unmake them until I understand every component. There is a cake at the end of the row that has four layers.

Looking over my life, I can remember certain cakes the way other people remember particularly happy birthdays. When I was eleven my mother let me go to Chicago to see my father for a weekend. He was playing at the Drake, an impossibly fancy hotel with heavy carpets over polished floors. There were flower arrangements throughout the hotel that were twice as tall as I was. I could only imagine they were put together by people standing on ladders. I sat at a little table in the lobby so small it could barely hold the slice of golden genoise and the glass of milk the waitress brought me out from the kitchen. She leaned over the piano and whispered to my father, who laughed and whispered something back to her, all the while playing a song he wasn't even thinking about. I ate my cake, which was light and dry and wouldn't have been sweet at all except for the gorgeous puddle of syrup that surrounded it. I could barely stand to swallow each bite, I was trying so hard to figure out what had gone into it. It was a very special and rare occasion that I was allowed to visit my father alone, and he had solemnly promised my mother that I would be asleep by nine, but it was a quarter till eleven before he took a break and walked me up to the room. By that time I'd had two petits fours and a flourless chocolate torte and called it dinner. He said good-night and left me alone to go back to his work. I was alone in a hotel room, something that I knew would have sent my mother into an uncontrollable frenzy. I slept on a roll-away cot at the foot of my father's bed. He didn't come in until after four in the morning. When he flipped on the light switch he absolutely gasped to see me there. I had no idea if he was playing a joke or not. When he got up the next afternoon (I spent the morning in the bathroom reading magazines from the stack on the dresser, mostly things about where to eat in Chicago) he took me to the bus station, gave me a kiss, and sent me home a day early with a book of matches and a bottle of shampoo that said "The Drake" on the front. I kept them for years.

In high school I saved up my baby-sitting money and sent away to a cooking supply store in New York City to buy a madeleine pan and a bottle of lemon flower water so that I could make the little shell-shaped tea cakes for my French teacher. She was a tremendously kind woman from a small town on the Upper Peninsula of Michigan who was patient with my mistakes. She told me it was very important to keep up with my studies because the French were the best cooks in the world. I asked her what she had eaten when she was in France and she confided in me (and none of the other students) that she had never actually had the chance to go, but she still hoped that someday she might. The idea of a French teacher who hadn't been to France struck me as the saddest thing in the world when I was fifteen, and that's when I set out to make madeleines. When I gave them to her, tears welled up in her eyes. "Everything began with a madeleine in Proust," she said to me. Further proof that cake could take you places you might not be able to get to on your own.

All my life, cakes have won me affection. I baked them for boyfriends and for boyfriends' mothers. Early on, my mother told me I was running up too much of a bill and would be expected to buy my own ingredients. "I'm not saying you have to buy your *food*," she said. "But five pounds of sugar a week? I can't be responsible for that."

I baked cakes for church sales and the volleyball team and the birthday of anyone I was even slightly fond of. I baked for the families I baby-sat for, often using their sugar while I was at their house. I taught their children how to neatly crack an egg and let them lick the beaters and scrape out the bowls with their fingers. I left them the cake and always got an extra dollar for my efforts.

I baked a cake for Sam, of course, a gingerbread cake cut into thin layers and stacked with applesauce I had made. It was on our second date, because on our first date he bought me dinner in a nice restaurant. I was living in my own apartment then, a tiny studio whose kitchen floor consisted in total of twelve ten-inch tiles. The oven was smaller than the play oven I had as a child and I had to cook every layer of the cake separately. I kept my pots and pans in a box under my bed. There was a little courtyard in back of the building that residents were allowed to use, so I served dinner outside on some old lawn furniture that someone had mercifully left behind and prayed for good weather. Otherwise we would have had to have eaten the way I ate, sitting on the end of my bed. Sam told me later he was ready to marry me on the second bite of cake. "It wasn't that I wanted to marry you for your cooking," he said on our honeymoon. "I mean, I thought it was wonderful that you could cook, but it was more than that. It was just such a smart cake. I'd never tasted anything like it. I thought, The person who made this cake has a soul. Have you ever thought that a cake could convey soul?"

I, in fact, believed that a cake was the best way to convey soul. I was also sure at that moment I had married the right man because I knew not everyone could see the soul in a cake.

Our wedding cake, like our wedding, was modest but lovely. I covered it in generous flowers, blues and pinks and yellows, a fistful of spring-green leaves spiraling down the sides. The photographer thought it was the most interesting thing at the party, and so there are many more pictures of the cake than there are of Sam and me on our wedding day.

The cakes I made for my children, especially before they were old enough to ask me to tone it down a little, were tributes to the architectural abilities of frosting. Any mother who brought her child to one of our parties must have left our house shaking her head. Poor, bored woman, they must have thought. That was the height of my frosting phase. I made trains and pine trees, tracks that spelled out *Happy Birthday, Wyatt*. Ballerinas pirouetted over *Happy Birthday,*

Camille. The bigger the sheet cake, the bigger the canvas. Mine were enormous. I would work on them for days, tucking them into the freezer at night to hold my place.

This is not to say that my life consisted of nothing but cakes. I had a full life. I raised a family, had a good marriage, volunteered at the Red Cross, played the piano. But it's true that if I were watching my life flash in front of my eyes, there would have been a lot of people holding up empty plates and asking for seconds in the really good parts. Which leads me to wonder why it never even registered with me that what my father was saying might be a good idea, or why, when Florence pointed out the logic of it all, my first impulse was to laugh.

"Really," Florence said on the phone later that night. "I've been thinking about it."

"I don't know anything about business."

"Don't worry about business right now. If you get into so much money that you have to start worrying about business, then you can hire someone to do the books for you."

"So what do I do, put a sign up in my yard that says 'Cakes Sold Here'?"

"You're going to have to start thinking, Ruth. You spend all your time putting out fires. That's a different way of going at life. Now you have to make something happen. You have to start a fire."

"With a cake?"

"Listen, there are a lot of highbrow restaurants in this town. Make up a dozen of your best cakes and give them to the owners as gifts. If they don't like them, they don't call you back."

"And what if they do call me back?"

"Then we go on to the next phase."

"Which is?"

Florence sighed. "Stop getting ahead of me. What's the worst you'll be out? A hundred dollars for ingredients if you make something really fancy. Probably not even that. I bet you've already got just about everything you need in the house. It's not like I'm telling you to go out and spend money on pans."

I thought about some candied orange peel I'd ordered from a specialty store in Luxembourg a few months ago. I hadn't been exactly sure what to do with it, I only knew that sooner or later it would be exactly what I needed. "I don't know," I said. I felt that old familiar queasiness, like I was going to have to play the piano in front of people.

"Somebody is going to have to save your family," Florence said in a serious voice. "Maybe your father is right. Maybe it's just going to have to be you."

It was impossible not to take Florence seriously. I think it had something to do with her height. "Can you save a family with cake?"

"That cake you sent home with me today, the scarlet empress? That's a cake that can save people. That's a cake that could lift up the country on its shoulders and redeem it."

After I hung up the phone I sat and stared at it for a long time. Maybe it would ring again and it would be Florence or a telemarketer or anybody who would give me more advice. Sam came into the kitchen with a copy of *Classic Yachting* in his hand. Since we had our talk he didn't try to hide them anymore. "Who was that?"

"Florence," I said, not looking up.

"Tell her she doesn't need to drive all the way over here to see Guy. I can take him to the hospital."

"It wasn't about Dad." I could hear the weight in my voice but I had no idea how to get rid of it. Suddenly it felt as though the responsibility for everything was about to move onto my shoulders. I would go from worrying about Sam finding a job to actually having to find a job myself. Maybe my father was right. Maybe I was a total prefeminist wimp who expected to be taken care of by a man. But how could I have come to feel that way? I certainly never had role models who said the man worked and the woman stayed home.

"Are you talking to yourself?" Sam sat down in the chair across from me. He looked concerned.

"Am I?" I put my head in my hands. "There's a horrifying thought."

"What did Florence say?"

I would just tell him, put it right out on the table. He had told me about the boats after all. "She said I should bake cakes."

"Aren't you always baking cakes?"

Sam didn't look like a man who was folding under the weight of stress. In fact, Sam looked more relaxed than I had seen him in a while. I was the one who was folding. "Florence thinks I should sell cakes."

Sam seemed puzzled. "Is she having a fund-raiser for something?"

I shook my head, took a deep breath, and started over from the top. "No, we're having a fund-raiser. We need to make some money. I don't mean to harp on this but we're going broke. She thought I should sell cakes as like, you know, a job."

Sam shrugged. "Sure, if you want to. I don't see how it could hurt anything to try."

"No, I'm really serious."

He stood up and stretched, came up to the balls of his toes and bounced a couple of times. "If you can sell some cakes, that's great," he said. He rolled up his magazine and tapped me lightly on the head. "Nobody makes better cakes than you. Is your dad back in his room? The Timberwolves are playing."

I nodded. "He'd like nothing better."

"Call us when dinner's ready," he said, and then he was gone. I sat there feeling completely stunned. Sam didn't think I could do it. Maybe that's what I deserved for thinking that he couldn't make a living working on boats, but as soon as I saw that he thought the cakes were a lark, I knew I was going to take them seriously. I was going to save my family through the sheer force of my mixer. In the other room I heard the television click on and then came the roar of the happy basketball crowd. I got up and went to my cookbooks.

There was a lot I didn't know: which restaurants to go to, who to ask for, how much to charge if in fact they wanted to buy. When I thought about those aspects I wanted to just forget about it and go take a nap. But I kept Florence's voice in my head. I was to take things one at a time, stick to what I knew. I knew how to bake. The first thing I was sure of was that this was all about cake. Pies, tarts and tartlets, a dozen different kinds of gorgeous cookies, soufflés— they all spun through my head and I dismissed them all. I was going to specialize. It also seemed to me that there was no single cake that could really represent what I could do. I got on my hands and knees and emptied out a low cupboard until I found a set of six-inch cake pans. With these it would be reasonable to take every restaurant three different kinds of cakes, one chocolate, one fruit, and one wild card, like the sweet potato cake or the scarlet empress.

I had a Bundt pan that held about three cups of batter, and I thought of an almond cake surrounded by little marzipan birds, tiny yellow buntings asleep at the base. I was a fool for marzipan.

"Sam and your father are going to be deaf within a month if they don't learn to keep the volume down." My mother was standing over me in the kitchen.

"I don't even hear it anymore."

"That could be a bad sign. Maybe you're going deaf too. Why are you cleaning out the cabinets before dinner?" After all, I was sitting on the floor with pans going out in every direction.

"I was just looking for something." I held up the pretty little Bundt pan to show her. I had had this pan for years. Camille used to love to balance it on her head like a crown.

"Dear God, Ruth, you aren't going to bake another cake, are you?" My mother had changed since my father had moved home. She had gone from someone who seemed scattered and a little foggy to someone who was, well, overly sharp. I wasn't sure which way I liked her better.

"I am going to bake another cake," I said. "In fact, I'm going to bake a lot of cakes. I'm going to bake until every surface of this kitchen is covered in cakes."

My mother looked at me as if she thought I had lost my mind. "We're supposed to eat that much cake?"

I crawled back into the cabinet and pulled out a few more pans. It was shocking to see how many of them I had. They not only represented a lifetime of what I had bought for myself, they represented years of gifts, from Sam, from the children, from my mother, from anyone who had no idea what to buy me for Christmas or my birthday or an anniversary. I found five springform pans. I was like one of those people who collected salt and pepper shakers and snow globes so that all they ever got were salt and pepper shakers and snow globes, except now I was going to need all these things, the cookbooks and the nutmeg graters and the industrial-size Cuisinart. I was going to be able to use them all.

"Ruth, get out from under there."

There they were, all the way in the back. Four-inch pans. Six of them. "Do you have any idea how difficult it was to find a set of heavy four-inch pans?" There was dust in the bottom and I blew in them. I hadn't made a really small cake in years.

"I'm glad you found them. You're worrying me."

Having tried the idea out on Sam, I wasn't so inclined to tell anyone else in my family about my plan. It was very new and felt about as vulnerable as a day-old mouse, its eyelids still sealed shut. On the other hand, people tended to congregate in the kitchen and I didn't know how long I was going to be able to keep it from them, either. "I've decided to try and sell some cakes to restaurants. It's just an experiment. I want to see if I can make some money."

My mother studied the scene and thought this over. She looked at the little four-inch pans in my lap. "You're going to sell them little cakes?"

"I'm going to *give* them little cakes, to see if they like them. If they like them, I'll have some work, if they don't—"

"Then all you're out is a few little cakes. You bake too much anyway. You might as well give them to people." My mother leaned over and picked up a huge iron Bundt pan. She strained a little at the weight. "This was mine, wasn't it?"

"For as long as I can remember."

"You really do hold on to things."

"So you don't think it's a terrible idea?"

My mother sat down on the floor. The way she was cradling that pan, I was wondering if she was planning on taking it back to her bedroom with her. "When I was a girl there was only one thing in the world I was any good at at all and that was playing the piano," she said. "I knew I was never going to be a soloist, but I was good enough to teach, so I went to school and worked hard and that's what I did. I might not have been Nadia Boulanger, but I kept us out of the poorhouse, I can tell you that much. I think if you have something that you really love to do, you're already ahead of ninety-nine percent of the people out there in the world. Look at poor Sam. That's what his problem is, you know. He doesn't have anything that he really loves. At least you've got cake. I never thought of it as a moneymaker, but I guess it's possible. People eat fancy cakes all the time and I suspect they pay good money for them. Why shouldn't you be the one making the money? As far as cakes are concerned, you are definitely a soloist. You could be baking cakes in Carnegie Hall, if you get my point."

I felt a lump the size of a walnut come up in my throat. "Thanks, Mom."

"It doesn't hurt to try, as long as you're not going to be too disappointed if things don't work out. You go out into the business world, you have to be tough. Do you know if you're tough?"

"Florence says I should just take it one step at a time."

"Fair enough." My mother put the pan down and stood up again. She brushed the wrinkles out of her pants. "So, what about packaging?"

"Packaging?"

"Well, you aren't just going to show up at the restaurants holding a bunch of little cakes, are you? You need something that makes a statement, something they'll remember you by."

"I was kind of thinking they would remember me by the cake."

My mother shook her head. "Cover all your bases. There's no sense leaving things to chance. I'll make you some nice boxes. Nothing expensive. I'll be in charge of presentation."

My father walked into the kitchen, his arms hanging down to his sides in their silver cages. I was trying to remember if I'd checked his pin sites today. "What's she in charge of?" he said loudly. I wondered how he could hear us over the game. I guess my mother was wrong. He wasn't going deaf after all.

"Presentation," my mother said. She put a snap in the word, as if to say that she had a job and he didn't.

"Why does she get to do presentation?"

"Do you even know what we're talking about?" my mother said. "Ruth, did you already discuss this with your father?"

"No," I said. "I just discussed it with Florence. It was her idea."

"Mrs. Allen is my therapist," he said. "I don't see why I can't do a presentation."

"It isn't *a* presentation. Are you telling me you're going to make fabric-covered boxes?" my mother said.

"I could. How hard could that be?"

"You don't have *hands*," my mother said, her voice rising. "You have to have *hands* if you're going to make boxes."

"Don't tell me I don't have hands. You can say I can't use my hands. That would be true. But they're not gone. They're right here." He lifted them up as best he could but the right one came up much higher. His left shoulder was still bothering him.

My mother closed her eyes. "You don't even know what we're talking about."

"Ruth!" my father barked. "What are we talking about?"

"I'm going to bake some cakes and try to sell them to restaurants, that's all."

Suddenly my father smiled and nodded, halfway raising up his arm again toward my mother in a gesture that this time meant something along the lines of *See?* "Well, that was my idea. I was the one who told her to do that."

My mother glared at me, utterly betrayed. "This is your father's idea?"

Ah, yes, well. I suppose if you broke it down. "He mentioned it."

"Fine," my mother said, throwing up her hands to show my father how it was supposed to be done. "The two of you work on your little project, then. Guy, you can make the boxes. You can market the cakes. You can lick the goddamn beaters for all I care."

This stopped us. My mother was not one for swearing. Sam came in from the den. "What are we yelling about now?"

"Nothing," my mother said. "Ruth and her father are going into business together. There's nothing to talk about."

"What kind of business are you going into?" It had not been a half hour since we had spoken but Sam seemed to have forgotten.

"Cakes!" my father said in triumph. "Ruthie is going to bake cakes just like I told her to."

"Oh, that," Sam said, turning back to the den. "I knew about that."

"Everybody knew about it except for me," my mother said.

I lay down on the floor, stacking the four-inch pans on my stomach. "Look," I said softly. Sam was already gone. I spoke to my parents. "The two of you may not realize it, but this ship is sinking fast. We're nearly out of money and we have no clear prospects that I can think of except for cake. Now, cake might not be much to work with, but until someone else comes up with a plan, I think it's all we've got. I don't know what I'm doing, but at least I'm going to try and do something. If you want to help that would be brilliant. I need some help. You want to go at it like a couple of gang members from warring tribes, then please, love me enough to take it outside."

My parents were both silent for a while.

"Really almost out of money?" my mother asked. "Because I have my pension and my Social Security. It isn't a lot of money, but no one's going to go hungry."

"I appreciate that."

"So where are you going to sell the cakes?" my father asked. His tone was breathtakingly reasonable.

"First I give them away."

"I like that. I got a lot of jobs in my life that way, walk in and tell them I'd work a set just for tips. Everybody loves a freebie. So where are you going to give them away?"

I looked at the light in the kitchen ceiling and noticed there were a few dead bugs caught in the glass fixture. You never really know what's going on with your ceiling until you just give up and lie down on the floor. "I don't know."

"I'm thinking you might as well go for the best, if money is the object here. You make cakes that are works of art, you might as well sell them for the price of art, which means you don't want them going to some home-style joint. You need to find the very classiest restaurants and then you need to find out which ones have good desserts and which ones just fired their pastry chef."

"That would be helpful," I said.

"So I will defer to your mother for presentation. She always wrapped up a pretty Christmas box, I will give her that."

Out of the corner of my eye I saw my mother give a curt nod of agreement.

"I, therefore, will take marketing."

"How will you take marketing?" my mother said.

"I know every concierge at every good hotel in this city, and most of them owe me a favor of one sort or another. I'll make a few phone calls and put together a list. I'll get you the names of the owners, the chefs, the managers, right on down the line to the busboys if you want them. I'll find out who needs you and who would take your cakes and never call you again."

I sat up and put the pans on the floor. "That would be really helpful."

"But your mother is absolutely right. It isn't enough to just show up with cakes. The whole thing has to be stylish. She'll make them stylish and I'll find out where they have to go. The only thing is I'm going to need some help with the phone. I might be able to push the buttons but I can't pick up the receiver."

"Certainly if I can take you to the bathroom I can hold the phone for you," my mother said.

"Good," my father said, and smiled. "Then we're in business."

Chapter Eight

SOMEWHERE IN MY LIFE I GOT THE NOTION THAT if you tried to make a business out of the thing you loved, then that thing would become a job, like standing in a factory all day putting beans into bags, and the love would be ruined forever. Maybe it was the fact that my mother, who had to play the piano for hours a day in order to make a living, so rarely sat down to pick out a song that she liked when she had a minute to herself. My father, of course, was an example of another way of looking at things. Every minute he wasn't playing the piano he was hoping to get back to the piano. Even now I saw him standing in the living room running the tips of his fingers over the tops of the keys like a prisoner pushing his face through the bars hoping to feel sunlight on his nose. Maybe I was going to turn out to be like my father in this way, because the thought of having to bake cakes morning, noon, and night filled my heart with inestimable joy. I stayed up half the night pouring over cookbooks, making notes. Which cake served into the neatest slices and looked best on the plate? Which frosting was both delicious and strong enough to stand up to decorating? What surprises could I put inside, thin slices of apricots or a layer of chocolate shavings on the bottom? My head was full of promise and possibility. Even my trip to the grocery store the next morning was met with real enthusiasm. I shouldn't have gone until I picked out exactly which cakes I would bake, but I couldn't help myself. Anyway, there were certain things you were always going to need. I piled my cart full of all-natural eggs laid by happy, free-range chickens. I hefted in ten-pound bags of King Arthur flour. I cut no corners. I bought Plugrá butter and Dutch-processed cocoa and the most expensive nuts in every variety, everything first rate. I bought heavy whipping cream in quart containers and nestled it down between enormous bags of sugar. I found myself smiling at everyone who peered suspiciously into my cart. *I'm starting my own business!* I wanted to sing to them.

"Somebody's doing some baking," the dark-eyed check-out girl said to me as she ran the almond extract over the scanner, her twenty silver bracelets ringing over her wrist.

"A little," I said innocently. I thought that if this all went well I would give up the local grocery store completely. I would start shopping at members-only wholesale clubs, where the flour came in fifty-pound sacks. I would leave the small time behind.

I stopped by the mall to pick up a few bottles of Madagascar Bourbon vanilla at Williams-Sonoma, something I had once considered an enormous luxury now seeming like an absolute necessity. I looked at every baking pan they had to see if there was anything I needed but found that, short of a couple extra cooling racks, I was better stocked than the store.

The day was sunny and clear with just the slightest touch of warmth in the air. I whistled that song about whistling from *The King and I.* When I brought my first load of groceries into the house, I found my parents sitting close together at the kitchen table in a strange configuration. My mother was holding the phone to my father's ear with her left hand and holding a pen on top of a pad of paper with her right hand.

"It was the damnedest thing you ever saw, Lenny," my father was saying. "I thought I was going to the john and I opened the wrong door and went right down the stairs to the basement. Smashed up both my arms in a dozen places. . . . No, I'm not kidding, *both* of them. You should see me now. I can't do a thing. . . . No, I'm serious, I'm not even holding the phone right now. My wife's holding the phone. . . . Sure I have a wife, an ex-wife, whatever. They all hold the phone just the same regardless of whether or not you're still married to them."

My mother snatched the phone away and clamped her hand over the receiver. "Will you just *get* to the *point*?" She shoved the phone back against his ear, making a little clunk against the side of his head, which caused him to turn and give her a dirty look.

"Sure I can still play the piano! Of course, I'm not playing right now, but the doctor said I'll be back one hundred percent. He even thinks my hand is going to be able to spread out wider when this is over. . . . That's right. I'll be playing things nobody else will be able to do. My plan is to try some dual piano stuff with me playing both parts. Wouldn't that be wild? We'd have to do a show with two seatings every night, hundred bucks a ticket, just like Bobby Short."

My mother took the phone again and hit my father soundly on the top of the head and then put it back to his ear.

My father glowered at her. "That?" he said to the phone. "No, that's just the call waiting. Ignore it. It's probably my agent again. The guy's driving me nuts trying to get me back to work. He understands nothing about the healing process. . . . That's right.

But let me tell you why I'm calling, Len. My daughter . . . Yeah, I've got a daughter and a wife. You never know what's going to come out in the wash, right? My daughter, she's a big-time pastry chef, been living out in L.A. all these years making cakes for the stars. She's come out to Minneapolis now, you know, trying to settle down, clean up her act a little."

Now I was reaching for the phone, but my father wrinkled his forehead and shook his head.

"I want to set her up with some restaurants, the best of the best. She's going to be sending some cakes around and I wanted to call you first. You're going to know what would be good enough for my kid. Can you give me a list? . . . Brilliant. There's a cake in it for you. . . . No kidding. You've got a wife, don't you? Wives love cakes. . . . Sure I'll come down and see you. Who've you got playing down there now? . . . That moron? You've got to be kidding me. The guy only plays about a third of the keys. I always thought he must have taken his lessons on an abridged piano. . . . Well, you've got to make do. I'll be back on the circuit soon enough. You can buy me a drink when I bring the cake down. Listen, I'm going to put my girl on. This is Hollis. You can tell her anything. Buddy, I owe you. I'm not going to forget this. . . . Perfect. Here's Hollis." Then he nodded to my mother.

"Hello, Lenny?" my mother said, her pen up and ready to go.

"Rub my head," my father said to me. "Right there in the middle where she hit me. It hurts like hell."

"You're telling people I'm a drug addict?" I said to my father.

"Hush," my mother said. "No, Lenny, not you, I'm sorry. Would you give me that number again?"

I motioned for my father to follow me out into the mud room.

"I didn't tell him you were a drug addict," my father said.

"No, you said I was in Los Angeles, worked for movie stars, and was coming to the Midwest to try and clean up my act. Excuse me if I've misinterpreted you."

My father shook his sore head at my ignorance. "Everybody's got a problem. Certainly everybody in the restaurant business. If I tell the concierge at a ritzy hotel that my daughter is a middle-aged housewife who likes to bake, he isn't going to set us up at Aquavit."

"I could do without the middle-aged part too, if you're trying to make amends."

"I'm trying to help you. I'm not trying to make amends."

Then my mother was in the mud room. "If you ever refer to me as your wife or your girl again, I'm going to take your teeth out with the handset of the telephone, is that perfectly clear?"

"She hit me!" my father said to me in a plaintive voice.

"'She hit me'? Are you serious? My children are grown and I'm back to dealing with 'She hit me'?"

"Why do you always take her side?" my father said. "Somebody rub my head. I really think she broke something."

"I don't take her side," I said. "If I took Mother's side you'd be in a convalescent home in Des Moines."

"You're impossible. How am I supposed to work with the two of you?" My father walked away from us and back into the kitchen.

"Stop acting like you're Louis B. Mayer for starters," my mother said, following him.

"Look, I never told you how to teach school," he said to my mother. "And you, I never told you how to raise your kids. We've all got our own areas of expertise. Well, I've spent the last sixty years of my life on the working end of fancy hotels and good restaurants. I know something about the way things operate. I might not be able to bail you out financially, but don't underestimate what I'm bringing to the table here. I'm the guy who can get you in the door, or at least I can connect you to the guy who can get you in the door."

My mother sighed in defeat and held up her piece of paper. "Lenny gave me a list, all top-notch places. He said he'd call ahead and put in a good word. His list more or less coincides with the lists of the other two men we talked to this morning, who also said they'd put in a good word."

"See?" my father said.

"Did Dad tell them I was a drug addict?"

"He implied that you were an alcoholic the first time but I kicked him pretty hard under the table. He's been a little more vague since then."

"She damn near broke my leg."

"Speaking of which," my mother said. "You told that guy you fell down the stairs."

"So what? I fell down the stairs."

"I thought you said you slipped on the floor."

"I slipped on the floor, then I fell down the stairs. There was a real nice order to it. You would have been pleased."

"I don't believe you." My mother crossed her arms in front of her chest.

"You don't *believe* me?" He held up his caged arms. "You think I pounded these little pins into the bone myself?"

"I don't know what you did," she said.

"Okay, Hollis." My father suddenly looked pale. His shoulders slumped forward. "You want to hear it? I opened the door to go to the men's room. I was talking to the guy standing behind me at the bar. I was making a joke and then I stepped forward. I thought I'd gone right into the mouth of hell. It was pitch-black dark. I had no idea what was going on. I just fell and fell and fell and I thought there were guys kicking me but they turned out to be the stairs. Is this what you want to hear? The whole story? I kept trying to catch myself and I could feel my arms smashing up like glass. The whole thing felt like it took a half an hour. When I was at the bottom of the stairs my left arm was through the banister. I couldn't pull it out. I thought I must have broken my neck. I could hear all the people upstairs, the music, everybody having a good time. You don't believe me? Is there some part of this you think I'm not telling you?"

The room was so quiet I could hear the hum of the electric clock on the oven. My mother looked stricken. She put her hand on my father's good shoulder. "I'm sorry."

"You don't have to be sorry," my father said. "Just don't think I did this for fun."

I realized then what a good job my father had done making sure we didn't worry about him. We all stood there looking at each other for a minute. I couldn't stop thinking about him falling.

"Okay," my father said. "Snap out of it. This is why I didn't tell you two this story in the first place."

"Did I miss the funeral?" Sam came in the kitchen with a copy of the want ads folded under his arm. My heart nearly leapt into my throat. Maybe he was finally looking for a job. Maybe I wouldn't have to go through with this cake thing after all. "Are you two finished with the phone?" he asked my parents.

"They're finished," I said.

"We still have two more guys to call," my father said defensively.

Sam shrugged. "This can wait. I don't believe you'll make it through two more calls anyway. You should have heard them when you were at the store," he said to me. "It was a regular bloodbath around here. I had to come in and break it up a couple of times."

"You did not," my mother said sullenly.

"Well, I thought about it," Sam said, smiling.

"They don't have to use the phone now," I said. "They're just doing a favor for me. You use the phone. We'll all be quiet. Do you want to use the phone in the kitchen? We could go in the other room."

Sam tilted his head and looked at me. "It doesn't matter which phone I use."

"I thought you might want to spread your paper out on the table. Maybe you'd like to have some privacy." I made "privacy" sound like a very cheerful word, something that I was happy to give.

"There are only a couple of ads I'm interested in," Sam said. "I've got them all marked. It isn't going to take that long unless I get some really rabid broker on the phone. Some of these guys are not going to let you off the line until you've sworn to buy a boat. I'll tell you, I used to think I could be a boat broker, but the whole sales thing seems a little desperate to me."

"Boat ads?" I said. I put my hand on the back of a chair for support.

"Don't worry. I'm just getting some prices, making up a few lists. I'm still just thinking about things."

"You have to think things through," my father said in his knee-jerk support of Sam.

Camille buzzed through the kitchen dressed in black jeans, blacks boots, a black sweater and jacket. Her pale hair shone like a Roman candle knotted on top of her head. "Going out," she said.

"Going out!" Sam said. "What is she doing home? It's past ten o'clock! Why aren't you in school, young lady?"

Camille turned, her hand on the door. I had a brief flash of insight into how hard it must be for someone as cool as she was to be trapped in a house with her insane grandparents and her insane parents. Everyone around her was aging, nutty, bickering. "Hello? It's *Sun*day. I'm going to the mall with Tricia. Somebody in this house needs to get a job or buy a calendar or something." She did not wait for the satisfaction of a reply. She simply hit her palm against the back screen door and was gone.

"Sunday?" Sam said as he watched her go. He looked at the tiny date on his watch. "I wonder if yacht brokers are even open on Sunday."

"I have no idea," I said, and went outside to unload the rest of the groceries from the car. I was no longer whistling.

That night I used my insomnia to weigh out my options. I did my very best to put the boats and my parents and everything in the world that wasn't dessert out of my mind. Standing at the kitchen counter, I reviewed my options: I could make a series of test cakes and try them out with Florence and my family and pick which ones seemed best for the restaurants; I could make thirty different cakes and send out a completely unique combination to every restaurant on the list, making careful notes of what cake went where to track their success or failure; or I could pick three cakes, make them each ten times, and just go with it. In short, I could, for the first time in maybe thirty years, make my own decision, trust it, and move forward. After a great deal of culinary soul-searching I picked the almond apricot pound cake with Amaretto, a black chocolate espresso cake with a burnt-orange frosting, and the beloved sweet potato cake with rum-soaked raisins. I could either make it in a Bundt pan with a spiked glaze or I could make it in three layers with a cream-cheese frosting. In the end I settled on the latter because I knew my cream cheese was one of my greatest strengths (the secret being to substitute *fiori di Sicilia* for the vanilla). It made me slightly crazy to think of leaving out the lemon cake with lemon-curd frosting—everyone died over that cake—but the frosting was very wet and the layers had a tendency to slide when transported. I loved the little lime-soaked coconut cakes but so many people took issue with coconut. A genoise was perfect for showing off, but if I wasn't there to serve it myself, I couldn't trust that it would be completely understood and I didn't think there would be any point in sending a container of syrup on the side with written instructions. And what about the sticky toffee pudding with its stewed dates and caramel sauce? That was as much a cake as anything else if you were willing to expand your boundaries a little. I wasn't sure about the chocolate. It was my best chocolate cake but I didn't absolutely love chocolate. Still, I knew other people did. I felt I needed an almond cake and this one worked in the apricots, but I wasn't so sure about not having a frosting. Would it seem too plain? And the sweet potato cake, I had to have that. That was the cake from which everything had started. I had to make a commitment. I had to bake.

The next day I started early. I put Chet Baker on the little tape player in the kitchen to help me remember to keep the cakes soulful and individual. Every cake must stand alone. No mass production. I took out the butter and the eggs to come to room temperature. My mother was in her room starting plans for the boxes. My father had followed her to oversee her work despite her loud protestations. Chet was singing "Let's Get Lost." I was ready.

The doorbell rang as I tore open my first bag of flour. I waited for a minute, fooling myself into thinking I wasn't the only one who was capable of opening a door, and then I went to open it.

"Big day for you," the handsome FedEx man said. He was tan, which seemed so exotic in Minnesota in the spring, even though I knew there was a tanning bed on every corner. He handed me four large envelopes and I signed four times. "You starting a business or something?"

"I am," I said. Could he tell? Would people be FedExing me so soon?

"Have a good one," he said as he swung up into his truck. Everything felt like an omen, even his generic good wishes. Why not have a good one?

But the envelopes were all for Sam. They were from Newport, Fort Lauderdale, New York, and, perhaps most troubling, Italy. They were all from yacht brokerage houses.

"Sam?" I said in a weak voice.

He came to the door. "Was that FedEx?" he said nervously. "I should have answered the door. I didn't think they came until afternoon."

"We must be well situated on the route. These are all for you."

He took them quickly without looking at the return addresses, which made it clear he knew what they were. "Thanks."

"Sam, are you buying a boat?"

Was this jealousy I was feeling? How could I be jealous of boats? Why did I feel as if he had sent off to Singapore for information about mail-order brides? Inside these envelopes would be four pretty young Asian women who wanted a chance at a life in America and in return would take care of his every need.

"I'm looking at a lot of things. You know that. We've talked about that. I'm looking at jobs and I'm looking at boats. You said you thought it was a good idea for me to look around."

I had said that. I had also said he should take some time off and go sailing. I had practically pushed him into the arms of some gorgeous sloop.

"Ruth, there's a boat here that is worth three hundred fifty thousand dollars and they're asking a hundred thirty. The broker says that absolutely means I can get it for ninety-five."

"If he's absolutely sure they'll sell it for ninety-five, then why are they asking one-thirty?"

Sam smiled as if I were making a joke. Then, what I found most unnerving was he picked out the envelope that contained pictures of the boat in question without looking down at the stack. He tore it open and walked into the kitchen. "Here, look at this. Isn't she a beautiful boat? That's a fifty-three-foot Nevins-built Sparkman & Stephens yawl. That is not a boat you're going to see every day."

"It's in a shed," I said, holding up the first picture. It was more a picture of a giant shed than the boat. Was the shed included in the price? "Is it supposed to be in a shed?"

"That's where they're storing her. See, there she is in the water." He handed me another picture. It was a good-looking boat, something that Aristotle Onassis might have used on the weekends when he wanted to get away from the *Christina*. It was not, to my way of thinking, an appropriate boat for working people in Minnesota. "That picture is a couple of years old, but isn't she gorgeous? Will you take a look at those lines?"

"So why can you buy a three-hundred-fifty-thousand-dollar boat for ninety-five thousand dollars?" If a person had an extra ninety-five thousand dollars in the first place.

"Because she needs some work. It's the same thing as buying a house and fixing it up and selling it. You remember the Hobarts used to do that. They made a fortune. He quit his job. They had a wonderful time."

"He quit his job as a contractor to remodel old houses. He didn't quit his job as a hospital administrator to fix old boats."

"I didn't quit my job," Sam said darkly.

I put down the pictures. "Oh, Sam, I'm sorry. I want to be with you on this. I really do. But we can't afford to buy a boat. Even if it's the thing that would help you more than anything else in the world, we just don't have the money for it."

"I'm not saying I'm going to buy this, I'm saying I'm thinking about it. There are a lot of boats here." He held up the other FedEx packages as an example. "Some of them are very inexpensive. Look at this one." He tore open another envelope, again without appearing to know which one it was. It was like a magic trick. "Here's a thirty-six-foot Hinckley sloop. They're asking fifty but I know I can get it for thirty-five or forty."

"Doesn't anyone ask a price they plan to get?"

"This is a much more practical boat. It's much smaller. You could single-hand this boat."

"*I* could single-hand a thirty-six-foot sailboat?"

"You know what I mean."

"So you could fix this one up and sell it for fifty?"

Sam checked the papers that were clipped onto the back of the picture. "No, actually, it looks like this one is in pretty good shape."

"So what would the point of buying it be?"

Sam looked like he didn't understand where I was going with the question. "To sail it."

"So the forty-thousand-dollar thirty-six-foot sailboat is just for our personal use. The first one is the moneymaker and this one is for fun?"

Sam stuffed all the pictures back in the envelopes and I immediately felt like a shrew. I was a shrew. Why couldn't we just talk to one another? How had everything become so tense? I felt like I was keeping him from his dream, but what about our bank account? Wasn't that keeping him from his dream too? "Listen, I'm sorry I said that."

"I'm just thinking, Ruth. You can't tell me I shouldn't even be able to think about something."

I nodded and sat down in a chair. "Okay," I said. "You're right."

"I know it must not seem this way to you but I do know a lot about boats. I was working in a boatyard every summer when I was in college."

"It's not that I don't think you understand anything about boats, *I* don't understand anything about boats. I need to stick with what I know. I'm just going to work on my cakes for a while. You look at your boats and I'll bake my cakes."

"Are you making a cake for dinner?"

Do you want to leave me? I wanted to ask him. Or have you so completely forgotten that I'm here that you don't even realize what you're doing? But instead of saying what was in my heart I only nodded and told him I was making a cake for dinner.

In the stress-reduction class I learned to go to the cake inside my mind, but these were darker days. To escape the level of stress in my house, I had to go inside a much more literal cake. I had to sur-round myself with cake, build a foxhole out of cake in which I could hide. Whether or not it was healthy no longer concerned me. It was all I was capable of doing. I pretended I was Martha Stewart. I put all the ingredients into glass bowls of different sizes and poured them in as needed. It gave me a feeling that life had a tremendous sense of order. Because the pans were small I could make two cakes out of one recipe, but I only mixed up one batch at a time for reasons of quality control. Maybe in the future when business was booming and I was making a hundred cakes a day I would come up with a different system, but for the time being I thought I would be better off sticking with what I knew. I had started with the sweet potato cakes. I was running my sweet pota-toes through a ricer when my parents came in.

"We're going out," my mother said.

"Both of you?" My mother hated to drive and my father couldn't drive and they couldn't stand one another's company. Now they were going out.

"She wants to make the boxes herself. Make a cardboard box? Stupidest damn thing I've ever heard of."

"You want one that's exactly the right size. We're making a quality product from the best ingredients. You don't see Ruth using margarine, do you? We aren't going to stuff a piece of news-paper in the side of the box if it's too big. I'm going to take one of each of the pans for now so that I know what I'm dealing with."

"Sure," I said. My father seemed grumpy and my mother seemed insane and I was perfectly happy to see them taking up each other's energy.

"You'd think there weren't enough cardboard boxes in the world already. These are *modern times,* Hollis. You don't have to make everything yourself. Look at Ruthie here. You don't see her building a mill in the backyard to grind down her own flour. Where are the chickens? Where is the cow? I thought you said everything has to be from scratch."

"Shut up and get in the car," my mother said. "Do you have to go to the bathroom again before we leave?"

"I went to the bathroom five minutes ago and you know it. Stop showing so much interest in my bathroom habits."

My mother shook her car keys to indicate that the wagon train was pulling out and then they were gone.

As completely overwhelming as my parents were, it was a real novelty for me to see them like this: together. Before my father came I had looked forward to getting to see my father. Despite the viciousness of their fighting, I hadn't thought that there might be some very peculiar pleasure in seeing the two of them together.

By the time Camille came home from school I had amassed ten cakes in different stages of readiness. Every one of them was perfect except for one that seemed to have lost its spring when touched. I held it back for our dinner.

"What's going on?" Camille said. She put down her backpack and made one slow circle around the kitchen. Her pink lips parted in disbelief. "Have you completely lost your mind? Do you really think we're going to eat all of these?"

I turned off the KitchenAid. If I had it to do over again I would have assembled my entire family together and told them about my plans all at once. "I'm trying to start a little business. I thought that maybe I could sell cakes."

Camille leaned over and inhaled deeply from an almond apricot loaf. "You want to be a baker?"

"Bad idea," I said. I was tired.

"I think it's genius," she said.

I wiped my hands off on the dish towel tied around my waist. I never was one for aprons. "You really think so?"

"Well, face it, you have all this, like, cooking energy, and you are always unleashing it on your family but it's too much for us. It's just too *big*. So if you could take that energy and put it off on some other people, things might be easier on everyone."

It was the greatest number of sentences Camille had spoken directly to me without shouting for years. I felt timid and hopeful. "I hadn't thought of it that way."

"So are you going to incorporate? What's your company called?"

"Called?"

"Well, you have to have a name, don't you? I mean, you're going to have business cards, right?"

"I don't have business cards."

"You can't just write your number on the bottom of the box. Oh my God, you do have boxes, don't you?"

"Grandma is doing that."

"Good, then I'll make the cards on the computer. You need a great name. Something catchy and to the point."

I mulled it over. I looked around the kitchen for inspiration. "Cakes by Ruth?"

Camille rolled her eyes. "Didn't you ever take a marketing class in school?"

"You take marketing?"

"You need something that just hits you, bang! And then everybody will remember you. It's like the Taco Bell Chihuahua. What is it you want to say?"

"Please buy these cakes."

I was making a joke but she shook her head with great

seriousness. "Not buy. You don't want to ask people to buy something so up-front like that. It's too, I don't know, desperate."

"Please eat these cakes."

"That's closer. That's on the right track." Camille bent down
until her nose was parallel with a cake. She looked at it very hard.
She seemed to be in conversation with the cake, then suddenly she
yelped and clapped her hands together. "Eat Cake!" she cried.
"That's what the company will be called. It's very classical, its got
the whole Marie Antoinette thing, except of course you know she
never actually said that. It's hip, it's funny, it's memorable, it's in
your face. Eat Cake."

"Eat Cake," I said. I might have wanted something a little
fancier but that certainly summed up the goals of the project.

"Mom, it's great. You'll make so much money you can rent
some kitchen someplace and stop cooking at home all the time.
You can get out on your own."

"Do you think I'm ready?"

"It's time," she said solemnly.

How I wished I had an ounce of Camille's confidence and
bravado. She so rarely showed any enthusiasm about anything that
when she did she practically lit up the room.

"I have to say, I find these cakes much more attractive now that
I know they're leaving home."

"Sort of like the way boys get better looking when they're
going off to war."

"Or junior year abroad."

"Exactly. I have a slightly bum cake here, if you want a piece."

She peered over to the cake in the corner, the one that had
been shunned by the more perfect cakes. She was thinking it over.
"Sure," she said finally. "A little piece."

I was cutting two little pieces when the phone rang. It was my mother.

"I wanted to tell you, we're eating out."

There was an enormous amount of racket in the background, music, laughing. "Are you in a bar?"

"We're in the mall, we're going to get some dinner. There's a Friday's in the mall. If you need us you can call the Friday's."

"For Christ's sake, we are not fifteen years old," I heard my father say in the background. "We do not have to tell her where we are and where we're going."

"She makes us dinner every night, Guy. Have you not noticed that? Do you think it's fair to let her set two places for us at the table and then just not show up?" My mother had obviously turned her face away from the phone but the conversation was remarkably clear, along with all the screaming children and high-pitched laughs, the call and reply of shopping teenagers.

"Who is that?" Camille said. She could hear the noise in the background but she couldn't make out the voices.

"Your grandparents," I said.

She pointed her fork at me. "Your parents."

"So you called her. Great. Hang up the phone." My father.

"Thanks for calling, Mom."

"We should be in by eight."

"Give me the phone!" he said.

"Here, take it. What's wrong? Can't hold the phone?"

"We have no idea what time we'll be in! We're adults. Adults go out to dinner." I could hear him shouting but I knew that the phone was nowhere near his mouth.

"Cakes going okay?" my mother asked.

"Oh sure, everything's fine. You two have fun."

Jeanne Ray

"Did you get a chance to see Oprah? I walked right out and missed her today."

"Mom, you're just doing this to make him crazy. Say good-bye and hang up the phone."

"Hang up the goddamn phone or I'm going to go to dinner without you."

"I don't care if you go to dinner without me," I heard my mother say. And then the line went dead. I was grateful. I couldn't stand the thought of hanging up on someone.

"So none of this is genetic, right?" Camille said.

"My parents adopted me and then your father and I adopted you. I was just waiting for the right time to tell you."

"Thanks," Camille said. "It's a relief."

For the first time since my mother moved in with us more than a year ago, Sam and Camille and I ate dinner together alone that night. We were oddly shy around each other, no one really knowing what to say and all of us wanting to say, Gosh, this is kind of nice. We were thrilled to have them gone and yet they were the only thing we could talk about.

"So I'm kinda getting used to the whole pin-through-the-bone thing," Camille said. "At first, I didn't think I was going to be able to stand it. Now I hardly notice it at all."

"And he's getting more flexibility in his fingers," Sam said. "Those exercises that Florence gave him have really been working. You've got to hand it to the old guy. He's doing really well."

"I'm surprised at how well my mother is doing, really. I know she despises him but they seem to be doing okay. I mean, they fight constantly but at first I didn't even think she was going to speak to him."

"Oh, that first night when Grandpa came? I thought she was going to go the whole time without saying anything."

And then we pretty much ran out of things to say. I had thawed out some frozen vegetable soup I found, some frozen French bread. It wasn't bad. There was cake for dessert. I started to wonder how the family was going to be reconfigured in the future. Wyatt was in college and might not ever live at home again except for summer vacations. In all probability, one, if not both, of my parents would still be in the house until Camille went off to college, making this evening the rarest thing in the world. Would one—and God, please, not both—of my parents live with us until they died? I didn't want them to die and yet I wondered what the time line was we were talking about. Would they live to be a hundred? Would I be taking care of my parents when I was nearly eighty? And then there was the biggest question of all: Would Sam always be here, or was he really thinking about sailing off and leaving his responsibilities behind him? I felt a terrible sadness come over me. I knew there was no sense in trying to hold on to anything in life, and yet I wanted to keep everything just like this. Just the way it used to be. I would be better this time. I had learned how to appreciate what I had.

That's when my parents came in, my mother's arms full of cardboard boxes and various packages, my father trailing behind her with empty arms.

"Behold, the wanderers," Sam said, and raised his water glass to meet them.

"Did you have a good time?" I asked.

"I'm just going to put these things down in my room," my mother said.

"You've got two minutes," my father said. "I don't want you in there cheating."

"What do you think? I've got sheet music stuffed under the mattress?"

"You're tricky," my father said. "And you're cheap. You'd do anything to win your bet."

"*I'm* cheap? Who paid for dinner?"

"You picked a cheap restaurant."

"Mom told me today that I was adopted," Camille told my father.

"That's great, sweetheart, but your grandma and I have a little bet going. There's money involved. It's a very serious business."

My mother came back into the kitchen with her jacket off. She was curling and uncurling her fingers the way I had seen her do a million times when I was little, the way she always made me do before I sat down to play the piano.

"What's the bet?" Sam said.

"Your father thinks I can't play 'Rhapsody in Blue' without sheet music."

"Now, let me tell you, in all fairness, the second half is her fault. What I said was that she couldn't play 'Rhapsody in Blue' if her life depended on it. She threw in the no-sheet-music part herself."

I was a little concerned about this one because I had no memory of my mother ever playing "Rhapsody in Blue" and I certainly had no memory of her ever playing anything without sheet music.

"Okay," she said without a care in the world. "Let's do it."

"I'll warn you," my father said. "She had a drink."

"I had a glass of white zinfandel. That hardly means I'm impaired."

We all filed into the living room, where really no one ever went unless it was to play the piano. My mother's baby grand Steinway, which she had brought with her from Michigan, had

taken the place of my upright, which had been squeezed uncom-
fortably into the den. We did not need two pianos in the house, but
neither of us wanted to be the one to give ours up.

"Take a seat. Everybody take a seat," my father said, dropping
himself down into the most comfortable chair. Sam and I sat
together on the sofa and Camille lay down on the rug even though
there were plenty of seats left. My mother took her place on the
piano bench.

"I used to play this piece two or three times a night," my father
said. "It was my opener. I remember there was one night back in
Denver—"

But my mother had no interest in the story. *Dum-dum-dum-
dum . . . dum-dum-dum,* she flew into the keyboard, her hands
springing up higher than her shoulders. She attacked the Gershwin.
She got so much energy out of that piano you would have thought
there was an entire orchestra in the room. Her back stretched and
flexed with the power of a sixteen-year-old Olympic swim champion. She tore the keyboard apart, evoking Manhattan at night, the
sweeping skylines of brightly lit windows, the syncopated energy of
the crowds in the streets. I had seen my mother play all my life and I
had never seen her play like that before. Camille rose up on her
elbows. Sam and I leaned forward. My father, speechless at last, had
tears in his eyes. It was no abridged version, either. She knew the
whole thing, every surprise turn, every crescendo. When she roared
through the final notes we were clapping like crazy, my father was
stamping his feet and whistling, his poor useless arms immobilized
and envious. My mother stood up and made a light comic bow
from the waist.

"Ten bucks!" she said.

"I had no idea you could do that," Camille said.

"Anybody can do that if they practice long enough," she said casually.

"You never told me you could play like that," my father said. "I think you're a ringer."

My mother crowed. "I've been telling you I could play like that all night. You-never-listen-to-me." She smacked the back of her left hand into her open right palm to punctuate each word. "That was always the problem. He never listened."

"I would have listened if you had played like that," my father said.

"Where did you learn that?" I asked her. "I don't remember you playing that at all."

"Play it? I played that thing so much that when I'm in my casket you'll be able to pull me out and set me in front of a piano and I'll still be able to play it."

"But where was I?" I asked.

My mother sat down backward on the piano bench and relaxed. "Oh, you were a little girl. You were only two. Even at two I'm surprised you don't remember it. It was right after your father and I broke up and I took on a bunch of extra piano students. There was this boy, Jimmy Depriest. He was a mediocre piano student until one day he heard Gershwin on the radio. He was so obsessed with Gershwin his parents came to talk to me. They thought there was something wrong with him, like he wouldn't be a regular kid again until he learned this music and could shut up about it. They wanted me to teach him Gershwin, which was more than a little bit out of his league. But they were insistent. Well, you can't teach what you don't know, so I learned the piece. I played it a hundred times. Then I started teaching it to Jimmy and I played it about a thousand times more. He wanted to come for a lesson every day and his folks paid, so what was I going to say? It drove the neighbors batty. They would bang on the walls every time we started. That song got so stuck in my head I couldn't have gotten rid of it with shock treatments. After a while I wanted to run screaming from the room every time it came on the radio. I was never so sick of a piece of music."

"And you're telling me you hadn't played it in all that time?" my father said.

"Why would I have to? I know it."

"But you always have to have sheet music," I said, trying to make sense of what I knew and what I had seen.

"That was an old habit. I never look at sheet music anymore."

It was a piece of music I have always loved, and now I knew why. It was the theme song of my childhood.

"Well, you would think this would be the moment when I would say that if I had two good wrists I would get up and show you how it's done, but that's exactly how it's done. I couldn't do any better than that, Hollis. My hat's off to you."

"That's awful sweet talk," my mother said. "But you still have to pay me the money."

That night Sam and I lay down beside each other in the bed, not talking about cakes and not talking about boats. "Your mother," he said. "Who would have thought it?"

"Amazing," I said.

We rolled toward each other and kissed in the dark, sweetly, chastely. No matter what happened there was always that kiss at the end of the day, and I wondered what it would be like to try to go to sleep without it, not like I went to sleep without it when Sam was out of town. I was thinking of sleeping without it as in never again. I wanted to turn to him and grab him in the dark, but I didn't know if I wanted to pull him to me or smother him with my pillow, so I stayed on my side of the bed and went to sleep.

While I was asleep, I dreamed of all my little cakes in the water, buoyant as ducks. To every cake there was attached a small sail, every one a different and beautiful color. It was a regatta of cakes, and they left the dock and the rocky shore of the lake and headed out toward open water, which I worried was dangerous. But the cakes seemed to be having a wonderful time. They were finally going someplace. Their sails puffed out with the wind. They picked up some speed. I thought, This is it, I've lost my husband and my cakes. And I stood alone on the dock and I cried.

When I woke up it was four o'clock in the morning but I knew that I was finished sleeping for the night. I watched Sam for a while. He was probably dreaming of boats too. I remembered the day we met at the library, our first awkward dinner, the second date in my courtyard, where we ate cake and knew we were in love. I thought of our marriage and the birth of our children and I loved him. I loved him so much that for a minute I wondered if I could sell everything so that he could have a boat.

I picked up my bathrobe and headed to the kitchen. All of the cakes from the day before were tightly wrapped, unfrosted, and sitting in a row. They looked so beautiful, golden and full of promise. I would bake another dozen this morning, and then when they were frosted and glazed and tweaked with powdered sugar and scattered raspberries, I would take them out on the road. I was measuring out the flour for the day when I heard the creak of a door. It was then that I realized I hadn't turned the kitchen light on. I was working by the back porch light and the little light put out from various glowing kitchen clocks. My mother came down the hall from the direction of my father's room, robe unbelted, smiling to herself. When she saw me she let out a little scream.

"Ruth! Heavens! Are you trying to kill me?" She had her hand over her heart.

I held out my measuring cup. "Do I look like I'm trying to kill you?"

From down the hall I heard a door creak open. "Hollis!" my father called in a stage whisper. "Are you all right?"

"I'm fine," she whispered back loudly. "Go back to sleep." My mother turned around to look at me. It was as if I were the one sneaking around at four in the morning and she wanted an explanation.

"I'm sorry I scared you," I said. "I couldn't sleep. I wanted to do some baking." I held up the bag of flour to show my good intentions.

"You don't need to bake twenty-four hours a day," she snapped.

I looked down the hall. The light was off. "Is Dad okay?"

She pulled the belt on her bathrobe tight and then knotted it. "He's absolutely fine. He had to use the bathroom."

I started to ask her how she knew that at four o'clock in the morning, and then suddenly thought better of it. "Oh," I said.

"Good-night," she said.

And I said good-night.

Chapter Nine

WHEN SAM WALKED IN THE KITCHEN THAT MORNING
he turned around three times and whistled. "Will you look at all
these cakes!" He was wearing a suit.

"It's a lot of cake," I admitted. "What's with the suit?"

"I have a meeting this morning. Not exactly a job interview,
but I don't know, maybe a job interview." He picked up a small
chocolate espresso cake by its cardboard cake round and whistled
again. "This is gorgeous. I mean, even by your incredibly high
standards this is a work of art."

I had put two rings of chocolate-covered espresso beans
around the rim. It practically vibrated with caffeine. It wasn't a
cake you'd want to eat at bedtime. A job? "Thanks."

He put the cake down and dipped his finger into a bowl of
cream-cheese frosting. "*Fiori di Sicilia*. God, I love that stuff." He
closed his eyes and shook his head. "I didn't get it, Ruth."

"Get what?"

"I didn't get the *industry* of what you wanted to do. I thought
you were talking about a couple of cakes. I didn't know you had
such big plans."

"I didn't try very hard to explain it."

"I should have asked some questions. I should have known that if you had plans they'd be big."

"I haven't exactly been a fountain of understanding myself. I feel terrible about the boats."

"The boats look very suspicious. Even I can see that."

"So we can both try a little harder to understand what the other one is doing?" I felt so hopeful.

"Starting now," Sam said. "What can I do to be helpful? Could I drive you around, anything?"

"Not in that suit."

"I can change the meeting."

I shook my head. "I've got everything under control. Who knows, maybe we'll both land a job today."

Sam kissed me. "Don't get your hopes up about me. Just get your hopes up about yourself."

Camille walked in the kitchen and made a brief inspection of the cakes.

"Have you ever seen anything like it?" Sam asked her.

"Even by the standards of our house this is a lot of cake."

Sam looked at his watch. "I'm going to be late." He kissed us both good-bye. "Are you sure you don't need me?"

"I'm going to be fine," I said. But as soon as he left I wished I had said it another way. Yes. I need you.

"Good luck today," Camille said. The timer rang and I went to take two more sweet potato cakes out of the oven. There was a pot of sweet potatoes simmering on the stove. The kitchen was a warm and steamy place that smelled of cinnamon and nutmeg. A tropical rain forest of baking.

"Thanks a lot."

"Remember, nobody out there bakes a better cake than you."
She held out her hand and gave me a thick stack of small cards.

Eat Cake
Fine Desserts by
Ruth Hopson

Beneath that was our address and phone number and Camille's
e-mail address. I wiped off my hands and then I touched the little
cards with the tip of my finger. "Oh, Camille. They're so beautiful." I had never had a card in my life. I had always watched other
people exchanging cards and wondered what mine would say if
I had one. Now I knew. I was getting a little teary and Camille held
up her hand to indicate that these were only business cards and I
should pull it together.

"I thought we should keep it elegant," she said. "Less is more."

"I agree. You did these yourself?"

"Actually, the computer did them. It's nothing once you understand the program. I really am going to be late if I don't leave right
now." She leaned forward to give me the briefest of kisses on the
cheek. "You're going to do great." She waved to me and was out
the door. I ran after her and gave her an apple and the cucumber-
and-herb-cheese sandwich I had made for her lunch, and for once,
she took it.

Two minutes later my mother zipped through the kitchen,
avoiding eye contact.

"How are the boxes going?"

"Fine, fine," she said. "I worked on them all night. I should
have started a month ago. Of course, a month ago Sam still
had a job and you didn't know it was going to come to this. It

smells great in here, by the way. I'm just going to check on your father."

I thought of how overwhelmed I would have been by so many mixed messages a mere twenty years ago. I was glad that I was finally old enough to deal with my mother.

She was down the hall and back again not five minutes later. I only had time to butter and flour the next set of pans. "Back to work!" she said. "Lots to get done."

"Dad's okay?"

"Fine, fine. Everybody likes to go to the bathroom in the morning. I was only brushing his teeth."

I wondered if my mother wasn't protesting a little too much.

Gently boiling potatoes make a sound not unlike a small stream moving quickly over rocks. I thought it would be perfect for one of those ambient-noise tapes: The Ocean; Wind in the Pine Trees; Boiling Potatoes. It was very soothing. I measured baking powder to its dulcet tones.

When the doorbell rang I thought it was probably another delivery for Sam, but when I opened the door it was not to the roaring engine of the idling FedEx truck. It was Florence, her dear and immaculate self, coming by on her way to work to wish me luck. I brought her back to the kitchen to show her the production line.

"They're darling," she said, picking up one of the wrapped chocolate layers. "The little cakes were a great idea."

"Oh, wait. This is even better. Here, have a card." I handed her one of my new business cards. "Not only are you the first person I've given one to, that was the first time I ever got to say that sentence."

"This is very classy." Florence slipped the card into the pocket of her uniform. "So if you have cakes and you have cards, why don't you look any happier than you do?"

I put down my measuring spoons. There are some things that all the cinnamon and boiling sweet potatoes in the world cannot hide. I poured us each a little of the espresso I'd made for the chocolate cakes. "Sam's been getting FedEx packages from boat dealers. He even showed me some pictures of boats. We talked it over and I know we're okay, but every time the doorbell rings my heart stops. Do you think they ever just deliver a boat to the house?"

"I used to wonder about that," Florence said, putting her coffee cup down on the table. Her face was stricken with the memory.

"That isn't all. My father has arranged appointments at fancy restaurants today by telling them I am a recovering drug addict. So I'm a little nervous about going over to meet the managers."

"I can see that."

"And on top of everything else, I have the distinct impression that my parents are having sex."

"Sex?" Florence raised her eyebrows. "Sex isn't bad."

"Don't get me wrong. I have nothing against sex. I just think that if someone is having sex in this house it should be me." I shook my head. "It's more than that. My parents hate each other. I mean they despise each other. If they're having sex, then, I don't know, it's like there's no order in the world anymore."

"Oh, there's order in the world all right. It just might not be the order you want."

I got up to flip the last set of cakes out of their pans. If you left them in too long, the crust got tough and they ran the risk of sticking. "Maybe you're right. There are so many things I should be worrying about now that it's hard to hold them all in my head."

Florence nodded. "I know what you mean."

I cut her a piece off the almond apricot loaf. There was always time to make another one. As long as cake didn't have two inches of frosting on it, I thought it was perfectly reasonable breakfast food. "Are things getting any better at the hospital?"

"Things are getting so much worse. I'm eight years away from retirement and I have no idea how I'm going to make it."

"Well, it hasn't been very long since the takeover. Don't you think it could get better once everything settles down?"

"It's a whole new mentality over there. It's all about money. Nobody cares how you do your job just as long as you're doing it faster." Florence sighed and looked down at her own perfectly operational hands. "It seems like overnight we have half the staff and twice the patients. I never wanted to work in a factory. I just feel like I don't want to do this anymore."

"Can you go to work someplace else?"

"All the hospitals are going to be the same. It's the wave of the future. I'd need to figure out a whole new career for myself and I am too old to do that. When I tell my husband about it, it just makes him feel bad. He thinks he should be making more money so I don't have to work, and that's not it at all. I don't want somebody to take care of me, I just want to be working someplace that makes a little more sense." She took a bite of her cake, thought it over, and then smiled at me. "Have I mentioned to you how good these cakes are?"

"Don't change the subject. Why do you get to tell me that I should be willing to change everything in my life if you're not willing to change everything in yours? That doesn't seem fair."

"Nothing's fair," Florence said. "Anyway, it's different. You needed a job. I already have a job."

"But not one you like."

"Well," she said, cutting herself another bite. "My cakes aren't as good as yours. Maybe I still haven't figured out what I'm supposed to be doing with my life."

My father shuffled down the hall in his bathrobe, his hair sticking up in a hundred different directions. He needed a shave. "Hey, good morning, Mrs. Allen. Is it time for us to work so early?"

"I'm not here for you this morning, Mr. Nash. I was just stopping by to check on your daughter and her cakes."

"Aren't they something?" my father said. "Her mother and I are so proud of her. We're thinking this is going to be a booming business."

I was too old to be going over the major issues of my childhood, but the phrase "Her mother and I are so proud of her" meant a great deal to me.

"Are you working your fingers?" Florence asked him.

"All the time. I do it every hour. I wake up in the night and stretch them. You were right about that. Look at this." He held out his hands to her and very carefully spread his fingers to the side. That wasn't something I had seen before.

"Wonderful work," Florence said. She managed to sound genuinely impressed. From here she would go to work and teach people how to pick up cups and hold forks and all day long she would find it in herself to sound impressed when they managed to do what she had asked. That's the kind of person Florence was.

"I've been working on that as a little surprise. I'm thinking I'm going to get back to the piano soon."

"Why not now?" Florence said. She polished off the end of her espresso.

"Now? I don't know if I could do it yet. I haven't even tried. I haven't even had a cup of coffee."

"You didn't think you were ready to pick up the fork, either."

"A fork is not a piano."

"Well, I'm here for about—" She looked at her watch. "Another seven minutes. You couldn't wear yourself out too much in seven minutes, right?"

I reached over and combed my father's hair down with my fingers. "Why don't you give it a try?"

My father shrugged, pushed up from his chair, and walked into the living room as if he were going to the gallows. Florence and I followed him. There it was, my mother's piano on which she had played so brilliantly the night before. He sat down on the bench and gave an enormous sigh. "It's not going to work," he said. "I can't get my right elbow to bend."

"Try it standing up," Florence said.

I pulled the stool away and my father stood in front of the piano. They seemed to be squaring off for a fight.

"Don't try to play something," Florence said. "That's not what this is about. Just press some keys. Get the feel of it."

For all the times I'd seen my father brushing over the tops of the keys, I hadn't heard him push one down. He put a finger on C sharp. He pressed. The note rang out clearly on his command. My father winced as if the sound hurt him. "Oh," he said sadly.

"That's great. Try again," Florence said.

He tapped at a few more keys. It wasn't a tune, but there was an order to what he was doing. He closed his eyes.

"Try to use all your fingers," Florence said. "Try to play scales."

"I've never played scales in my life." He kept on hitting keys. I could almost make out the sense of it. It was almost like a melody.

The sound of the piano, however disjointed, was enough to bring my mother out of her room. She stood in the doorway and watched quietly. Suddenly I could follow the tune: "What'll I do—when you—are far away?"

"Go away," my father said, his eyes still closed. How was it he always knew where she was?

"You're doing fine," my mother said.

"Says the woman who plays Gershwin."

"Just play," my mother said. "It's good for your hands."

But at that my father's hands slipped off the keys. He walked past all of us without saying a word and went back to his room, kicking the door closed behind him.

We just stood there, the piano so helpless and silent. Finally my mother exhaled, a long, slow breath. "Poor Guy. Can you imagine how terrible it would be not to be able to play the piano?"

"I can't play the piano," Florence said.

My mother looked at her with inestimable sadness. "I'm so sorry," she said. "I had no idea."

"Maybe I'll learn later," Florence said.

"If you ever need some help, call me. After all you've done for us, the least I could do would be to give you some lessons." My mother looked at her watch and shook her head. "I need to get back to work. Thank heavens your father insisted on me buying the boxes ready made. I'm barely going to be able to finish them as it is. If I were in there cutting cardboard, I'd never make the deadline."

"Are you going to go talk to Dad?"

"If it were me I'd just want to be alone for a little while," my mother said. Then she said good-bye to Florence and left.

"Don't worry too much about your dad," Florence told me. "He doesn't believe it but he's coming along right on schedule. This stuff is hard on everybody. You'd think it would be harder on him being a pianist and all, but the truth is we're all awfully fond of our hands."

"Maybe that's what's so hard about it. I think of what I would feel like if I were him. I don't imagine I'd hold up very well."

Florence looked down at her own hands for a minute, wondering what they were capable of. "Maybe I should take your mother up on her offer," Florence said. "Do you think it would be too late for me to learn to play the piano?"

"At this point I don't think it's too late for anything."

I wrapped up the rest of the almond apricot cake and sent it along with Florence. I tried to go back to work after she left, but I couldn't help worrying about my father. My mother may have wanted to be alone in such a circumstance, but if it were me, I would hope that someone would come and find me. I went and tapped on his door.

"No," he said.

"Just for a second."

"Well, I can't turn the damn lock, so I guess I can't keep you out."

He was sitting on the edge of his bed, still in his bathrobe and pajamas. Of course he was. No one had come in to get him dressed. His eyes were watery and red. His arms were resting in his lap. He looked at me blankly. "So I'm sitting here feeling sorry for myself and you've come to talk me out of it. Okay, I feel better. Thanks."

I went and sat down beside him on the bed. "I don't want to talk you out of anything. If you want to feel lousy, then be my guest."

"Is this the pep talk then? 'Don't worry, Dad, I know it looks bleak now but in time things are going to be a whole lot better'?"

I tilted my head to one side and then the other. "That sounds pretty good." I reached over and took a Kleenex out of the box on the nightstand. "I don't know that I'd use the word 'bleak' in a pep talk, though. 'Bleak' is a very depressing word." I dabbed at his eyes and then held it up and told him to blow. He blew.

"You know what I am, Ruthie? I'm a one-trick pony. In all my life I have known how to do exactly one thing. I was a crappy husband. I was a rotten father. I never owned a home. And none of that bothered me because I was a really good piano player. I may not have been Glenn Gould, but for a guy in a bar, you weren't going to find any better. I guess I thought that I'd just keep playing and then one night I'd have a couple of drinks and be going to the men's room but instead I would fall down the basement stairs and break my neck and that would be that."

For a minute I thought my father was saying this was all some sort of botched attempt at taking his life. "Are you telling me you threw yourself down the stairs?"

At least that got a laugh out of him. "I'm not that inept. What I'm saying is I didn't think about the past and I didn't think about the future. All I ever cared about was the night I was living, the piano that was in front of me and whether or not it was in tune. And now I can't play and the strangest thing is I'm not sitting around feeling all chewed up over that. I'm feeling all chewed up over all the other stuff. I mean, I feel good about all the pianos I played, it's the other things I'm feeling bad about."

"You're feeling bad about Mom?"

"About your mother, about you, about these kids of yours that I never saw. What kind of insane man would miss his own kid growing up and then miss his grandkids growing up on top of that?"

"Maybe one who was a great piano player?"

My father rubbed his slipper against my ankle in lieu of squeezing my arm. "Yeah, but I'm not a great piano player anymore. That means I've got to face up to everything."

"You're on the injured list, that's all. Florence thinks you're coming back and I'd take Florence's word on anything."

"She does seem to know what she's talking about. Something tells me if I had known her when I was younger I wouldn't have made so many mistakes. That's a woman who could have kept a fellow on the right path." He tapped my foot. "Enough of this. See, you did cheer me up. Now you need to go back out there and bake your cakes."

"Sure," I said. I kissed his head and went to the door. "You know, Dad, everything is changing around here. I wasn't crazy about it at first, but maybe it's all going to turn out okay. Maybe there are certain times in a person's life when everything can suddenly be different. Maybe this is one of those times, so if you want to be different, you can be."

"It's a sweet thought," he said.

"No," I said. "I think it really might be true."

At one o'clock my mother emerged from her room looking exhausted and triumphant. In her hands she held a box the likes of which I had never seen before.

"You made that?"

"I made it ten times." She set it down on the kitchen table. It was somehow lightly padded and covered in a pale green silk organza on the bottom with a darker green tapestry on the lid. It looked artistic, professional, and extremely important. There was a covered button on the top and the inside was lined in pale pink silk.

"Did you use all your remnants?"

"What was I saving them for? I had to use them for something eventually."

My mother's remnant collection right there in my hands. I sat down and turned the box over. It was perfect and I told her so.

"Good," she said. "Because I'm planning on making about a hundred more. We need to take a cake to all the hotel concierges we talked to, and I want to make a box for Florence, and there are some people at church I'd like to give cakes to if you wouldn't mind making a few extra."

"Of course. And look at the cards Camille made."

My mother took a card and smiled, then she went back into her room and returned with a pearl-studded hat pin. She pinned the card on top of the box. "All it needs now are some cakes."

The cakes were ready, and together my mother and I nestled three inside each box. We added a few berries, a couple of tiny marzipan birds. My father came out of his room and looked at the production. "It couldn't be nicer," he said appreciatively. "It tastes good, it looks good, and it has the right connections. If these cakes don't fly, then this town just doesn't eat cake."

It was done. All of the measuring and sifting and frosting, the creaming and dusting. It was behind me now. I had made something that I loved. I had put my name on them. It was the best work I had ever done. I hugged both of my parents. They had helped me, really helped me, at exactly the moment I had needed them. Nothing could have made me prouder.

The birds, so recently returned from their long southern vacations, were back in Minnesota and singing up a storm in my yard. The sky was blue and the grass had turned a shade of bright green I hadn't seen since before the first snow last autumn. I loaded the cakes in the back of the station wagon and pulled out of the driveway feeling like a woman with a product. I had taken control of the situation. I had potentially saved my family from disaster and ruin. I was ready. I drove away from my house with a list in my hand and a heart full of confidence. I was going to distribute the cakes.

Then I got lost.

Not terribly lost, but I missed the turn for parking and fell into a maze of one-way streets that took me farther and farther away from my destination. Once I got myself back on track, I was feeling less certain. Were my cakes any good anyway? Were they better than anybody else's cakes? Were they really any better than a mix cake? Suddenly I was seized with doubt. I had picked the wrong recipes, the wrong outfit. I no longer liked my hair. Maybe what I told my father was wrong. Maybe things don't change. I pulled up to the restaurant and got a good parking place. It was three in the afternoon. It was the quiet time in between the lunch and dinner crowd, when a handful of people sat at the bar and smoked cigarettes and talked. The manager, whose name was Bill, would be expecting me. All I had to do was walk the cake inside. Easy. I opened up the hatchback and slid out a box. I closed the hatchback. I stood there. I stood there for a long time. The sky had clouded over and it started to sprinkle a little. Then the sprinkling turned to snow. It was light at first and then it came down in wet clumps. The box was getting wet and so I got back in the car to think things through. My name was on the box. It was a beautiful box. Inside there were three beautiful cakes. All I needed to do now was to walk it inside. A short trip. I found that I was clutching the box too hard, wrinkling the fabric a little bit, and so I put it beside me on the passenger seat. I could go in and not speak to the manager. I could just ask the bartender to give it to the manager for me, unless the manager was behind the bar, in which case I could tell him I was not Ruth Hopson but a friend of Ruth Hopson's who had volunteered to drop off the cakes because she was at home, very busy baking or kicking her drug habit or whatever. My hands started to shake. I was ten years old and being forced to play "Clair de Lune" on a small stage in the auditorium of my grade school for an audience of people I knew. I sat on my hands. I felt sweaty and vaguely nauseated. I put my head down on the steering wheel. What if the manager was just coming in now? What if he saw me, sweating and half-collapsed in his parking lot? Those drug addicts from Los Angeles, he would think. They never change. You give them a chance and they blow it every time. I put my seat belt back on. I put the car in reverse.

All the way home I cried. Cried because I had wasted all that money on ingredients and all my time and, more important, my mother's time and my father's connections and Florence's good advice and Camille's beautiful cards, which now I would never be able to use. "That's my name and phone number," I would say, giving my pretty card to another parent at school who asked me to drive hook-up for swim practice. "Just scratch out the part about the cake. I don't do that anymore." I thought that if I had tried to just get a regular job, if I had put in for substitute teaching and had an anxiety attack before going into the classroom and wound up on a cot in the nurse's office, it wouldn't be so bad. I did not love substitute teaching. But the worst of it was that on some essential level I felt I'd let the cakes down. And I loved the cakes. I was so proud of them.

When I turned into the driveway I just stayed in the car. I couldn't pull it together and I didn't know what I was going to say anyway. My mother would give me that awful concerned expression she gave me when I failed at playing the piano in public after having done so well in practice. They would be so sad for me, all the while saying to themselves that they never really thought I would come through. They would tell me I could try again tomorrow. But there wasn't going to be a tomorrow. Tomorrow the cakes would not be exactly stale but they would no longer be perfect. I had had a chance and I had missed it.

After ten minutes or so Camille tapped on my window. When I looked up I saw the snow had stopped. "Mom?" She opened the door. She looked at the cake box sitting next to me and then she looked into the back of the station wagon and quickly tallied up the full load.

"You didn't do it."

I shook my head.

She sighed, her old exhausted sigh of disbelief that she could have been saddled with such a ridiculous parent. "Okay," she said. "Wait here a minute."

Five minutes later she came back to the car wearing low fitted gray pants, high-heeled black boots, a white T-shirt, and a long black nylon coat that flapped behind her like a graceful set of wings. She had on eyeliner and her hair was pulled back into a severe ponytail. She looked like a rock star or a publicist for rock stars. She opened my door again. "You'd better let me drive."

"Where are we going?"

"Go get in on the other side. We need to get moving. We're going to hit traffic as it is."

Being despondent can bring out a sense of obedience. I got out of the car and got back in on the passenger side, holding the box of cakes in my lap.

"You're going to have to navigate," she said. "I hate driving downtown."

Camille had had her license for less than six months and I had a hard time remembering that she drove at all, or I should say, I knew perfectly well that she drove, but I tried to block it out as much as possible because the thought of it made me a nervous wreck. There was not a stop sign or a streetlight that did not involve the slamming on of brakes, and when she started up again the car leapt forward like a greyhound at a freshly opened gate. I held on to the box tightly. I was glad I hadn't made the lemon cakes with lemon curd frosting that were so inclined to slide. Another time I might have mentioned these errors in Camille's driving, but I knew instinctively that now was not the time.

"So you didn't go in anywhere?"

"No. Turn left at the next light."

"Well, that's probably better. They didn't see you. It would be strange if the cakes came in, went out, and then came back in again later."

"I can't go in there."

"Why do you think I'm here?"

"Left again. You're going to take the cakes inside?"

Camille nodded. "We should have thought about it in the first place. I don't think you're cut out for sales. Speaking of which, what are you charging for the cakes?"

I looked at her. She was such a beautiful girl. I never ceased to be amazed by it. She had a profile that would have done very nicely on a cameo. "I never thought about it."

"You don't have a price sheet?"

I shook my head again. Wouldn't it have been sensible to think this over? It occurred to me that there had been a scant forty-eight hours between the idea of cakes and the cakes themselves.

"Mom, Mom, Mom," she said. She sighed. "Okay, how much do they cost you to make? I'm talking about a full-size cake."

"I have no idea."

"Ballpark?"

"Well, I already have a lot of flour and sugar. The chocolate is kind of expensive, but per cake?"

She shook her head. She started again, speaking slowly, as if I had recently immigrated from Paraguay. "Let's go at this from another direction. How many people would the chocolate cake serve, restaurant-size slices?"

"Twelve."

"Good, so let's say the house charges six dollars a slice. That's seventy-two dollars."

"They wouldn't charge six. That's too much."

"Stop sounding like Grandma. Six is shooting for rock-bottom low. It could easily be nine. So, out of seventy-two dollars, what do you think your take is worth, figuring in ingredients and a profit?"

"Twenty?" I said. It could not possibly cost more than eight dollars to make a cake.

Camille smiled, keeping her eyes on the road. "You want twenty dollars a cake?"

"It's right here. I missed the parking lot last time. Do you think that's too much?"

"No," she said. "I think that's perfect."

We pulled up to the same restaurant, the same parking place. Camille glanced at my list for the name of the manager. "Bill," she said. "Okay, give me the box."

"You're just going in there?"

She sighed one more time for good measure, this time dropping her head back slightly and closing her eyes. "Give. Me. The. Box."

I gave it to her and she was gone.

I sat in the car and waited for my daughter to come back. I was nervous but nowhere near as nervous as I had been the last time I sat in this space. Nobody likes to think they need to be rescued and everybody is grateful when it happens. I got out and got back into the driver's seat. Even if I wasn't ready to meet the public, I was ready to resume my role as the principal driver. After about ten minutes Camille came back. All smiles.

She pulled on her seat belt. I started the car up and put it in reverse. I waited and waited but she said nothing. She was not used to talking things over with me, even when the information was actually about me. "So you're not going to tell?"

She looked out the window and gently bit her thumb. "Bill was very nice. He liked the way the cakes looked. He was impressed with the packaging. He said he'd give them a try and then he'd call." She pulled down the visor and checked her lipstick in the little mirror. "Actually, he said he'd call anyway. He said he'd like to take me out to dinner."

"Did you mention that you were a high school junior whose mother was waiting in the car?"

"I told him I was seeing someone."

"Are you seeing someone?"

Camille glanced over in my direction and made it clear that that was not a conversation we would be having.

"What did he say about the price?"

"He said he thought it was high."

"I knew twenty was too high."

"I told him the cakes were forty."

"Forty dollars! Are you kidding me? That's robbery! No one is going to pay forty dollars for a cake."

"They will if they can turn around and sell it for seventy-two. Anyway, forty is where we started. I'd do it for thirty-five."

"So you're the accountant now too?"

"I'm the booking agent. You're never going to get what you're worth if you don't shoot high."

"Where did you get all this confidence? Really, I couldn't even walk in the place. Where did you come from?"

"You forget," Camille said. "I'm adopted."

We delivered the cakes. Toward the end I got up enough nerve to stand at the side of the window just so I could see her walk in. She kept her shoulders back, her head up. There was no one in the world she was afraid to talk to. I wondered if I had been self-confident at sixteen and then somehow life had taken it out of me, but it wasn't true. I was never like Camille. She knew she was special and she had no problem at all with that. I was crazy about her.

Well after dark we returned home in triumph. Everyone was waiting for us in the kitchen. "How did it go?" my father said. "Did you kill them?"

"We killed them," Camille said.

Sam was back in his jeans and a sweatshirt, looking like his best true self. "I knew you'd kill them," he said proudly.

"You should have seen Camille. She handled all the business. She just walked in there, gave them the cakes, and told them what she wanted."

"Everybody in the family has a job in Mom's business except for Dad," Camille said. "You're going to have to give Dad a job."

Her heart was in the right place but I felt terrible that she'd said it. The only person who didn't seem to mind was Sam. "I'm trying to get on the payroll," he said.

That night in bed I asked Sam about the job interview.

"It wasn't really an interview," he said. "I just met with another administrator I know. I was putting some feelers out. I didn't think there was going to be a job for me."

"Did he say if anything looked good?"

"There are a lot of people in the same boat I'm in right now." Sam waited for a minute. In the darkness he reached out and held my hand. "He said it wasn't such a good time to be looking."

"You're going to find something," I said.

"And you've already found something. I'm so proud of you, Ruth."

As happy as I was about how the cakes had turned out, I didn't like the idea that Sam was now in one boat and I was in another. I liked it better when we were both in the water, swimming.

Chapter Ten

FOR THE SECOND MORNING IN A ROW I WAS UP AT four o'clock. Yesterday I couldn't sleep because I was too nervous about getting the cakes off. This morning I couldn't sleep because I was worried about how they were doing. Did the manager take them home and eat them? Did he feed them to his wife and kids, throw the box away, and consider all the unseen perks of being a restaurant manager? Or were the cakes eaten at a conference table, the owner, the manager, the sommelier, and the head chef all sitting down for a serious slice? Did they discuss the body of the cake, the crumb? Did they analyze the icing? Choose a nice Sauternes to complement it, or did they drink a little water between slices to clear their palates?

Sam rolled over, sighed, and pushed down deeper into his pillow to dream of sloops and yawls. I got up and put my bathrobe on and headed to the kitchen. I turned on the light over the stove and set the oven to three-fifty. I was just going to take the butter out of the refrigerator when, for the second morning in a row, I met my mother coming down the hall from the wrong direction.

"Don't you sleep anymore?" She was very nearly shouting.

"Keep your voice down. Somebody in this house is probably still asleep. I'm tense, okay? I'm worried about the cakes."

"Why can't you be tense in your own bedroom?"

"Mom, I'm not asking you what you're doing wandering around at four in the morning, why do you care what I'm doing? Why can't we both walk through the kitchen whenever we want to?"

"There's no privacy in this house."

"There hasn't been in a long time."

We both folded our arms across our bathrobes and stared at each other.

"What *are* you doing anyway?" she said.

"I'm going to bake some cakes."

My mother looked at me as if I had told her I was going to move to Memphis and join an Elvis cult. "All you've done is bake! You have to stop this."

"I didn't make the cakes for the concierges that Dad called. And you said yourself you wanted some cakes for people at church."

"I didn't say I wanted them at four in the morning."

"Well, you don't get to set the schedule."

"Fine!" she said. "Then I'll just go back to work on the boxes. I wasn't planning on sleeping anymore anyway."

My mother had on her same old pink chenille bathrobe and her hair was a little out of whack, but there was something different about her. "You look different," I said. I couldn't place what it was.

She gave me a very nasty look, as if I was referring to whatever was going on down the hall, which I was not. "I look exactly like I always do at four in the morning."

"No, there's something . . ." I smiled. "You don't have your glasses on."

My mother reached up and touched her face and then the top of her head as if she didn't believe me. Then she turned around without a word and went back to my father's room. By the time she came out again I had two cakes in the ovens and was working on my third. It was seven o'clock in the morning.

At noon my father got up and I poured him a bowl of cereal, which he ate by himself using a large-handled spoon. It was as magnificent as seeing a man walk on the moon.

"Are you going to issue a press release? Stop staring at me. I've been feeding myself my whole life," he said.

"Well, I have a short memory."

He put the spoon in the bowl, picked up a napkin, and wiped the corners of his mouth. It wasn't fast, but it was perfect. "You know, I've got a doctor's appointment this afternoon. Why don't we throw those cakes in the back and I'll go with you to drop them off at the hotels. It would be good to see those guys again. Some of them, man, it's been years."

My mother came in with a new set of boxes. Each one was so beautiful, such a deeply realized piece of art, that I didn't want to let any of them out of the house. Who knew she had it in her? "If you gave me a little more time, you'd be impressed with what I could do."

"I'm impressed anyway," I said. "They're wonderful."

"Hey, Hollis, Ruth and I are going to take these cakes to the hotels. Why don't you fix yourself up a little and come along for the ride? You can help carry the boxes."

"If I'm going to be the porter, then I don't have to fix up," my mother said. "Is that a spoon you've got in your hand?"

"I'm almost grown," he said, smiling. "Before you know it I'm going to be out of the nest."

He meant it as a joke, but a dark cloud passed over my mother's face. She turned back to her room and walked away. "Let me know when you're ready to go."

It didn't take long for my mother to get herself ready, but she put a special effort into getting my father bathed and dressed. It was no small task. He went out of the house so rarely that we didn't have to deal with the issue of his clothes very often. At home he wore ratty button-down flannel shirts with half of the sleeves cut off, things that were easy to take off and on. But today he wore pressed pants and a white short-sleeved dress shirt that made him look like he had retired to Miami. My mother had cut open the sleeves of a cardigan sweater partway and hemmed up the edges so that they covered the steel halos nicely. She had shaved him and combed his hair and, in short, made him look more like the man I had known before he fell down the basement stairs of a nightclub.

"Look at you," I said approvingly.

"I have people to see," my father said.

"Don't you think he should wear a tie to go to the doctor?" my mother said. "He won't wear a tie."

"I remember when you used to tie my ties. You always tried to choke me."

Our first stop was Sam's old hospital, where we went to see the surgeon who had taken over my father's case. When we entered the front lobby I felt a little like I was betraying my husband, going to see a building that had done him wrong. I thought of all the times Sam had forgotten a file and I had brought it over to him, all the times I'd run over for lunch in the cafeteria when he had a break, the countless Christmas parties, punch cups, and buffet lines. Sam had given an awful lot to this place. It should have ended better for him. We rode the elevator to the fourth floor and went to sign in. A little while after we'd taken our seats in the waiting room, a nurse came to take my father away for X-rays. "Don't you want one of us to come?" I asked him.

"I don't think they're going to ask me to operate the machine. I only have to show them my arms."

"I'll take that as a no," I said.

"Family," my father whispered to the pretty nurse as they walked away. "They think I can't even feed myself."

"I liked him better when he was helpless," my mother said, picking up a two-year-old issue of *Ladies' Home Journal*. She was watching the door he had disappeared through. I could tell she had been planning on going back with him.

"Are you falling for him?" I said. I don't know why I felt I could ask her that in a crowded waiting room of a doctor's office when I couldn't say it when we were alone in my kitchen at four in the morning.

My mother kept her voice even and her eyes on the magazine. "You know I can't stand your father."

"And you probably couldn't stand him when you married him, either. That's not my question."

"No, then, to answer your question, I am not falling for your father. Now, there's an article here I want to read if you don't mind."

I picked up a *People* magazine that had a picture of Diana's two boys on the cover. "No, I don't mind." I tried to figure out whether or not I cared if my parents were having sex or falling in love or fighting like badgers or playing gin rummy in the small hours of the morning. I was clear on the fact that it was none of my business and also clear on the fact that it certainly bumped up against my life both past and present. The problem was this: My mother and I had a hard time when I was young. There was a great deal of scraping by and doing without. I was led to believe that the reason we were scraping by was because my father was gone and the reason he was gone was that he and my mother absolutely could not abide the sight of one another, a fact that was supported in the few times I ever saw them in the same room over the years. These are the things that shaped every aspect of our lives. So what if the central fact of your life turns out not to be true? What if my parents, in fact, actually loved one another? I'm not saying it would be a bad thing, but it would be a little bit like finding out that the early Spaniards were right: The earth was flat and it was quite possible to sail off the edge of the map and plummet down into the nothingness below.

When the nurse came back for me and my mother, we had been waiting for nearly forty-five minutes and neither of us had turned a single page of our ancient magazines, both of us sitting side by side, lost in what I would bet were exactly the same thoughts.

A different nurse led us back to a small office with a desk and a few chairs. My father was waiting for us. "Have you ever seen so many framed pieces of paper in your life?" he said. "I bet this guy frames his Reader's Digest Sweepstakes entries."

I was about to answer him when the doctor came in. He was friendly and hurried and suspiciously young. He said a quick hello to everyone and then stuck some film of pinned-up bones on a light board and clicked it on.

"You see there, these little lines? That's everything healing up nicely. The doctor who put you together in Des Moines did a fine job, Mr. Nash. I'd say you've got at least another month in the braces, but you're going to do fine."

"A month?" my father said.

"Could be three weeks, could be six weeks." He clicked off the light with an authoritative snap. "I don't know the exact time schedule your particular bones are going to heal on."

"I've been working on my flexibility," my father said. He held out his hands and bent his fingers down and then straightened them out again.

The doctor looked up from his notes, but he had already missed the show. "That's great," he said. "Are you doing that, Mrs. Nash?"

"I'm working with him," my mother said.

"That's just great." He slapped my father's file closed to indicate that our audience was terminated. He had never sat down. He was shaking my hand. "The pin sites look great. Keep them clean. Come back in four weeks."

"You said it could be three," my father said.

"Right you are. Make it three. The nurse will make an appointment for you on the way out."

Bang, just like that he was gone. The man should have been a bank robber. Nothing, and I mean nothing, could have held him down.

We all went back to the car feeling an overwhelming sense of neglect. "You should have told him you were a pianist," my mother said. "I'm not even sure he knows."

"When was I going to fit it into the conversation?" my father said.

"You've always found a way in the past," my mother said.

"He wouldn't have cared anyway."

"It was good news, though." I tried to make my voice sound cheerful. "He said the bones looked good. So he didn't have any bedside manner. It would have been nice, but at least he didn't say you were going to spend the rest of your life with pins in your arms. Something tells me if the news had been bad, this guy would not have hesitated to break it to you."

"It's true." My father got into the front seat of the car and held up his arms while my mother reached around him and buckled up his seat belt. "Thanks, Hollis," he said.

"The last thing we need is to have you go flying through the windshield," she said.

"Let's go have a little fun, shall we?" my father said. "There's nothing like a really good hotel." My father had called on three concierges he knew and told us our first stop should be to see Sid at the Marquette.

"Just pull up front," my father said once we arrived there. He pointed to the front of the hotel with his head.

"Don't you want to go in?" I asked.

"Right there."

I pulled in front of the hotel, right into the middle of the loading zone, and rolled down my window. A man in a complicated black suit and top hat that made him look like a wealthy character from a Dickens novel swept up to the driver's side. There must have been eighty buttons on his jacket. "Good evening, madame. Will you be checking in?"

"No, we're just—"

"Hey, Wexler. You trying to hit on my daughter?"

The doorman stuck his head in the window and then leaned across to my father. "Guy? Where the hell have you been?"

"I'm having my arms copied so that they can be preserved for future study. All for the good of science!" He held up his cages.

"What the hell happened to you?"

"Sharks! Get us out of this car and I'll tell you the whole sordid story."

Wexler came around and opened my door and let my mother out of the back. "Should I go park?" I said.

He shook his head discreetly. "Leave the keys," he whispered. "All taken care of."

While my mother and I got a cake box out of the back, Dad caught up with the doorman and a handful of bellboys. As we stepped into the gleaming marble lobby, everyone was on us. "Guy, where have you been?" "Guy, what did you do to yourself?" My father spun stories of fistfights, bionic arms, and a deadly case of carpal tunnel syndrome from playing too damn beautifully for too long. "It catches up with you," he told the pretty Korean girl at the front desk.

"How do you *know* all these people?" I said. I was starting to wonder if my father had actually lived in Minneapolis for a while and just never called to tell me.

"I've played here from time to time over the years."

"So have a lot of people, I would think. Do they treat all returning piano players like Frank Sinatra?"

"Only the really good ones," my father whispered to me.

Then Sid caught sight of us and crossed the lobby with long steps and open arms. "I thought you were making it up," he said, kissing my father on each cheek and then, after proper introductions were made, kissing my mother and finally me. "I thought you had just gotten too big to play here and you were trying to spare my feelings."

"I'd never spare your feelings, Sid."

"Come in the bar and I'll make you a drink."

"First take your cake." He turned to me with a flourish and let me know it was time for me to fulfill my part of the ceremony. I set the box in Sid's hands.

"I appreciate your help," I said.

"Your help!" my father said. "Ruthie, this man didn't help us. He made us! We're going to be in business, thanks to you."

Sid politely demurred. "Au contraire. I've had four calls already this morning, people telling me how brilliant I am to have found the best cakes in the city."

"Who called?" my mother said.

"You're going to be busy, busy," Sid said to me, wagging his finger. "Everybody loves what you do. And now I have a cake. I can see what the fuss is all about. Of course, I told them I had been eating your cakes for years, that everyone on the inside had them shipped in from L.A. for the big parties."

"Sid, you're an operator."

"I owe you a favor or three. Surely you haven't forgotten that."

We sat down beside a piano in a dark bar and Sid went off to get our drinks without asking us what we wanted. I tried to call him back but he was gone.

"That piano," my father said wistfully, "is one of the greatest pianos I've ever had the pleasure of knowing."

My mother looked over her shoulder. "Really."

"A profoundly beautiful tone. And the acoustics in this room . . ." He shook his head. "Heavenly."

Sid came back with a tray. "Something soft for the lady who is driving and had every intention of turning down a drink." He sat a tall glass on the table in front of me. "And something with a little more bite for the two people I suspect will join me in a drink." He set a tall water glass upside down on the table and topped it with a short highball glass into which he placed a straw for my father.

I was somewhere between impressed and amazed by Sid's preternatural sense of what people wanted. I guess that is the hallmark of a good concierge. We toasted my father's health and the luck of the cakes.

"Hollis here is going to play you a little something on the piano," my father said to Sid.

"No, she is not," my mother said.

"You've got to hear this piano and I can't play it and you know good and well Ruth isn't going to play."

"You've got that right," I said. I sipped my drink, which was a cross between a lime and a cucumber with a lot of sparkling water thrown in. It was perfect.

"I don't play piano in bars," my mother said.

"That's only because no one has ever asked you to and you know it." My father gave her a hard stare. "Come on, Hollis, be a sport about this."

Sid looked at my mother as if he loved her. "Nothing would make me happier," he said.

She took a healthy sip of her own drink. "One song."

I waited for her to ask for some sheet music. Maybe she was going to play the Gershwin again, but she sat down and started playing "Stardust," a loose and rambling interpretation that went perfectly with the surroundings. Maybe my mother didn't need sheet music after all, maybe she just put it out as a sort of habit, the way I looked at cookbooks when I knew the recipe backward and upside down. My mother was finding a way to break with her routines. It wasn't such a bad thing.

"Oh, this *is* a nice piano," she said.

My father closed his eyes and smiled.

The people who were in the bar, and there weren't many of them, stopped their conversations and turned to face my mother. They watched a seventy-three-year-old woman in mint-green slacks and an overly colorful patchwork sweater play her heart out. She didn't mind the attention at all. For all the timidity she had shown in the past year, she never was afraid of a piano or a spotlight.

She looked over her shoulder. "Come sing this, Guy."

My father got up without a word and sat down backward next to my mother on the piano bench. It took him just a minute to find his place in the song and when he saw his opening he stepped inside, his voice effortless and sweet.

"Beside the garden walls, when stars are bright—you are in my arms . . ."

It was worth everything, that moment, that song. It did the very thing that music can do when it is at its best: It elevated us and healed us and showed us how to be our better selves. My parents were happy together and they made something so heartbreaking and beautiful that no one in the room so much as touched a glass for fear of disturbing it. When they came to the end of their song the room demanded they do another, and then another. They did four songs together and then got up at the same moment and said good-bye.

Sid was wiping tears from his eyes. "I'll hire you on the spot. Right now, the two of you just as you are."

"As we are?" My mother laughed. "My dear, you have no idea what you're saying."

We were thanked for the cake and returned to our car with promises extracted to come back and sing immediately, maybe tomorrow. I was so included in Sid's praise that I felt as if I'd been at the piano too. When we went outside the sun was weak but still shining. I couldn't believe it. I felt like it had to be after midnight.

My father fell into his seat, exhausted, and my mother buckled him up. "This may have been too big a day for me."

"You're not used to being out," I said.

"I'm not used to being out," my father said. "That's a laugh. My problem has always been that I wasn't used to being in."

"We'll just drop the other cakes off at the front," my mother said. "We'll have the bellboys take them inside. Then if you want to go back another day, that would be nice."

"Who knew you played so beautifully?" My father closed his eyes and rested his head back against his seat.

"You used to know," my mother said. "You've just forgotten."

When we got back to the house Camille was beside herself. "Don't you people ever leave a note when you go out? Where have you been?"

"We've spent the afternoon in a piano bar," my father said.

"Well, that's nice for you but meanwhile I'm home fielding phone calls."

Sam came in the kitchen with a handful of notepaper. "The phone has been ringing off the hook around here. We may have to get call waiting."

"What did they say?" I asked. I was afraid to hear it, even though it was good news. I could see good news written all over Camille's face. I never knew that people could be afraid of good news too. I realized that good news took you places you didn't know anything about. It changed everything as much as bad news did.

"Ten restaurants, ten orders!" She threw her arms around my neck and screamed the kind of scream that was reserved for best girlfriends telling secrets about boys and class elections.

"Ten cakes!" I said.

"Ten cakes from the first one, that's over a week." Camille started flipping through her notes. "Then eight cakes from the second place. The third one wants fifteen, they're having some sort of massive party."

Sam hugged me and kissed my neck with an enormous smack. "I think my new job is going to be as the booking agent," he said.

I felt dizzy, but I didn't know if it was from business or pleasure. "How many cakes the first week?"

"Um, let me see. Dad, where are your numbers?" Sam gave Camille his sheets of paper and she ran through the numbers. She tapped the papers with her fingertip. "One hundred twenty-eight cakes this week."

"They all want you to call them back too," Sam said. "They need to talk about kinds of cakes."

"One hundred twenty-eight cakes?" my mother said. "Full-sized cakes?"

"This week," Camille said cryptically.

"And money?"

Camille raised her eyebrows at me. "Don't you think I held the line?"

"Forty?" I sat down in the kitchen chair.

"Five thousand one hundred twenty dollars, gross," Camille said.

"Forty dollars a cake!" my mother said. "That's robbery!"

"I heard that already," Camille said.

In a moment of sheer bluff my daughter had doubled our earnings.

"I love this girl," Sam said, and kissed Camille, who didn't even flinch.

"I can't make that many boxes," my mother said. "I'd need to buy a factory. I'd need to hire every child in Camille's school."

"The boxes are what pulled them in," my father said. "The cakes are what keep them. You need to make new boxes for new clients. I've got some ideas for some other people I can call. There's no reason why we have to stay local. We can target a few cities nearby, places we could drive to in a couple of hours. Then we hire a few teenaged kids and get a delivery service going."

"I don't have a plan," I said. "I don't have the ingredients. I don't have enough pans. I'm going to need more ovens. Where are we going to put extra ovens?" For a second I closed my eyes and took a deep breath. I put myself inside the cake.

It was good.

When we got into bed that night I put my head on Sam's shoulder. "Big surprise," I said.

"No surprise at all," he said. "Once I saw all those cakes, I knew there would be no stopping you."

"I don't know what I'm doing."

"You'll figure it out. Look how smart you are, getting all of this going."

"It just happened, you know that. It's like all these years we've been living in a house full of cakes not knowing what to do with them and now, all of the sudden, there aren't nearly enough cakes to go around. It's crazy. I never thought the day would come when I wouldn't have enough cakes."

Sam kissed the top of my head. "You're going to be great."

I wanted to tell him I was scared and absolutely thrilled to death. I wanted to talk about what a wonderful job Camille had done, how proud I was of her. I wanted to tell him about my parents at the piano and about Sid and how they could go back any time they wanted and play at that club and probably make a fortune, but I didn't say any of it. I was afraid it would only seem like I was doing well when Sam wasn't. I wanted to be closer to him and yet all the things I could think of to say were things I was afraid would drive us apart. I didn't know how I had let things come to this and I didn't know how to get out of it.

"I was thinking of flying out to Newport, just for a day or two. I want to talk to some people, look around." Sam's voice was tentative. I knew somehow he had been trying to find the right time to tell me this for days. "Ever since I talked to that guy about the state that hospitals are in, I've thought I should go and look at boats. I could get a better idea about whether or not I have any chance trying to do something with this if I could talk to some people face-to-face."

I was determined to sound supportive. "Sure, that makes sense."

"I thought I'd check out some hospitals too. Just to see. Maybe I could do some sort of combination of the two things. Something practical, something impractical. That way both of your parents would be happy."

"Do you think you might want us to move to Newport?" Now? When I might have a chance at something big?

He patted my shoulder in the dark. "I'm sure it won't wind up that way, but I just thought it wouldn't hurt to look."

"Sure. It's like you said, you have to think things through. When would you go?"

"Maybe soon. Maybe even in the next day or two. I got a really good ticket on the Internet."

"When would you go?"

"Tomorrow," he said.

There was so much I had to tell Sam. I need you to stay. I want you to stay and help me mix batter and deliver cakes. I have to have you stay so that you can help me and be proud of me. Please, I thought. Please stay. But what I said was, "I can drive you to the airport."

"You're going to be so busy tomorrow you won't even know I'm gone. I'll just leave my car at the airport. It's only going to be a night or two."

It was then, on one of the best days of my life, that I started to cry, but not so anyone would notice.

Chapter Eleven

THIS TIME WHEN SAM CAME THROUGH THE KITCHEN in the morning carrying an overnight bag my mother didn't even blink.

"Did you pack your sunglasses?" I asked him.

"They're in the car."

"And a life jacket. I don't want you falling overboard without a life jacket."

"I'm not going sailing. I'm just going to look at some boats."

"Someone might ask you to go sailing. I want you to be careful." I want you to stay home.

"I promise to be careful."

There was no other way to drag it out. The time had come and I had to let him go. "Have a good time." I gave him a kiss. "I'm going to miss you."

"You'll be up to your neck in cakes. It's probably better that I won't be underfoot."

"Sam," my mother said, reading over the order lists for the eighteenth time. "Could you pick up some things at the grocery store while you're out? Not the big list, just enough to keep us going for today."

"I'm not coming right back," Sam said.

My mother didn't look up. "No problem. We should probably just do it all at once anyway."

Sam kissed the top of my head and was gone. For a minute I thought I should cancel every cake and go with him.

"I don't see how we're going to do this," my mother said. I was standing at the back door watching my husband drive away. It wasn't that I thought he wasn't coming back, but just seeing him drive away with so much left unsaid made me inestimably sad. "We're going to need to start buying things, that's for sure, and you're going to have to get on the phone and talk to these people about what they want and when. We're going to have to hire somebody, at the very least a driver to make deliveries. We can't have you out driving around the city when you should be home, baking."

"I know," I said. All my life, whenever I had had a crisis I had turned to cakes, so at least I knew what I had to do. I felt like my heart was breaking and so I turned on both ovens and tied a dish towel around my waist.

"Don't you think you should call the restaurants first?" my mother said.

"It's too early for that. I just need to bake for a while."

There were a lot of lemons in the house and so I started there. I went to work on a batch of lemon cakes. I got out the electric juicer Sam had given me three Christmases ago and felt a pang of gratitude every time I pushed a lemon half down and watched it spin out lemon juice into a cup. I had thought it was such a silly extravagance at the time. I never minded squeezing lemons by hand, but Sam said he thought it would be so efficient. We vowed to drink fresh-squeezed orange juice every morning and then gave it up by New Year's.

As I started to cream the day's first butter into the day's first sugar, I realized that cakes really could solve a lot of problems. Maybe this could be a real business. Maybe cakes could make tuition payments and mortgage payments. I didn't mind the thought of working hard. I had been working hard all along. But what I found to be so scary was accepting the responsibility of taking care of people financially. What if the cakes sold really well for a couple of months and then everyone got tired of them? What then? I had had this job for a few hours and already I was wondering how I would feel if I lost it. Suddenly I understood what my father had been saying to Sam about taking some time off and figuring out what he wanted to do. There was a lot of pressure being the person who took care of the children and made the meals and kept the house running, but there was also a lot of pressure if you were the one who had to come up with the money. I wished that Sam had stayed around so I could tell him that. I wasn't sure I had ever made it clear how much I appreciated all that he had done.

When the phone rang, I thought that maybe it would be Sam calling from the airport. I turned off the mixer and dried my hands.

It was a man's voice, but not my man. "Ruth, dear, it's Sid."

"Sid? Oh, Sid." The beautiful hotel lobby, the sparkling green drink. Was that only yesterday? "Thank you for being so kind to my parents."

"Your parents were wonderful."

"I thought they were. Do you want to talk to my father? I could have him call you in just a minute." I didn't think my father was up but I could get him up quick enough.

"I always want to talk to your father but actually it's you I'm calling for."

"Me?"

"I loved the cake. I had to tell you. As soon as I had a piece I took it into the restaurant, and as soon as our chef had a piece he called the president of the hotel. We had some very good luck on that one. He's here this week. The chef called him and said, 'Come downstairs and have the best piece of cake you've ever had in your life.' It melts, Ruth. It's like magic. I've never even imagined cake like this."

"I'm glad you liked it." I felt nervous. I had a terrible suspicion there was more good news on the way.

"Liked it? No, I *loved* it."

I realized this was one essential difference between raising a family and having a job: the praise factor. "I'm glad you loved it."

"So, of course we want the cakes for the restaurant. We'll start them out as specials, and once we get a feel for which ones are doing the best, I'm sure that the chef is going to want to add them to the menu. I should have brought you in to meet Azar yesterday. He says you are extremely gifted."

"That's wonderful." I was feeling a little sick.

"Wonderful, yes, but that's not even the wonderful news. Mr. Sanders, the top man, the president, he's very interested in your cakes. He's wondering if you can get that sweet potato cake into the mail. He likes the whole package—the cake, the box. He's thinking about using them as gifts."

"For his family?" I asked hopefully.

"Corporate gifts, V.I.P. guests. He thinks they're completely unique. This could mean a lot of cakes."

I put the phone against my chest for a minute and took one good deep breath. I was going to try for a version of honesty. At this point it was my only hope. "Sid? I think this is all great. I'm really appreciative, but I'm going to need to talk to the girl who's managing the business. I want to find out how many cakes a day we can handle right now, realistically."

"Of course. Give yourself a couple of weeks to get the whole thing up and running and then we'll talk corporate. In the meantime I want to put you in touch with Azar. I want you to come up with something that's just uniquely us, a cake that we're not going to see anyplace else in town."

"Sure, I can do that."

"And you'll bring your parents back?"

"Absolutely."

"I'd like to see your whole family working here. I think you're geniuses, all of you."

After I hung up the phone I sat at the kitchen table and held my head in my hands. Two seconds later the phone began to ring again and I got up and switched on the answering machine.

No one is here to take your call right now, Camille's voice said. *But if you leave your name and number—*

I knew that the call was going to be somebody wanting more cake and right now I didn't want to talk to them.

My father walked into the kitchen just at the sound of the beep. "Guy," a man's voice said. "It's Lenny. I've called to talk to your daughter about this cake."

"It's Lenny from the Four Seasons!" my father said. "Pick up the phone."

I held my finger up to my lips, as if maybe Lenny could hear us on his end.

"I don't know why I told you to go to restaurants. We want her cooking here. At the very least we want to buy these cakes. Guy, I want a lot of these cakes."

"Why aren't we picking up the phone?" my father whispered.

"Too much cake," I whispered back. I looked over my kitchen. It was covered in cooling racks and half-empty cartons of eggs. I was already out of baking powder and I hadn't even started on what needed to be done. I didn't even understand what needed to be done.

Lenny finished his message, leaving his phone number and an emphatic request for a return call. When he hung up the phone it rang again. I went to turn off the volume on the answering machine.

"What's wrong? Are you suddenly afraid of success?"

"I don't think I'm afraid of success but I have no idea how to bake that many cakes. Don't worry, I'm going to call everyone back. I just need a second to think."

"What's there to think about?" my father said. "All you've got to do is cook."

"Sam," I said. "I'm thinking about Sam."

"Is he having a problem with the cakes?"

I shook my head. My father sat down at the table and rested his arms on top of the newspaper. "I don't think so. I don't know. We haven't exactly talked about it. We haven't talked about anything. Something's happened. He's in his world dealing with his problems and I'm in my world dealing with mine and I feel like we just keep getting farther and farther apart."

My father leaned over to look behind me. "So talk to him. Where is he?"

"He went to Newport this morning to look at a boat. He wants to sail. I want to bake cakes."

"And you want to be married to Sam?" my father said.

"Of course I do. Don't you think I can have a business and be married?"

"Sure you can. You have to remember, I'm the one who suggested this business in the first place, and you're always getting your nose bent out of shape because I like Sam so much, so I must think that they're both good ideas, the business and the marriage."

"I don't get my nose out of shape."

"You do too. Listen, Ruthie, your mother and I both played piano. We had everything in the world in common, but when I stopped teaching school and started playing in clubs, it was a big change for us. Somehow, I don't know why, we never really talked about it. We had this nice new baby and I thought I could make more money if I traveled and she thought I was gone too much and the next thing you know we'd had some terrible fights and then we weren't together anymore. I look back on that now and I think, What, were we crazy? All we had to do was try and work it out. If we had each said what we wanted to do, what we wanted the other one to do, I think we could have sailed right through it. When you get older you see what real trouble is. You look back on what you thought was trouble before and it all seems so small. You've just got to give it a little bit of effort."

"I'm just so afraid of hurting Sam's feelings. I don't want him to think he can't get a job and everything's going great for me."

"You'd hurt Sam's feelings a lot more if you wound up divorcing him down the line. He's a good guy. You know he's happy for you. But don't forget all that's happened: He lost his job, you have these crazy old people living with you, his wife turns out to be some kind of superstar cake baker. It's a lot for a fellow to digest."

"You're right," I said. "I just need to talk to him when he gets home."

"That's not what I'm saying at all. I think you should get on a plane and go to Newport. Talk things over with him now."

"He's coming back in a day or two."

"Yeah, well, I was going to come back from Chicago in a day or two and then I was going to come back from New York in a week and then the next thing I knew I was back out in California."

"I can't leave now. You forget that I have a couple hundred cakes to bake."

The phone rang again.

"You're starting a new job. If you start today or if you start three days from now, it isn't going to make any difference, the good people of Minneapolis will still have food. You took a big chance sending those cakes out there. Take another chance. You were the one who told me that this was the time that everything could change."

"What about all those phone calls?"

"Your mother and I will call everyone back. We'll take the orders and set up a schedule. You can be home by tomorrow. What's going to happen before tomorrow?"

"I have no idea."

My father came over and kissed the top of my head. "Do as I say, daughter, not as I did. Now I'm going to go talk to your mother. We're going to come up with a plan. You go and get yourself on an airplane."

In my life I had never gone on a trip that hadn't been planned at least three months in advance. Buying tickets the day of travel to express your love for someone who already knows you love them was something that people did in movies. Then again, the people in movies had bigger lives than I did, and suddenly my life had become a whole lot bigger.

Sam had left me the name of the hotel where he'd be staying. I went back to our bedroom and looked through the trash can. I found the empty FedEx envelopes. Now I had the name of a hotel and the name of the yacht broker in Newport. I had as much information as anyone needed to get something done.

I called the airport and booked myself on the four o'clock flight to Providence, then I put a couple of things in a bag. When I came back out I found both of my parents in the kitchen listening to messages on the answering machine.

"All three of the hotels called!" my father said. "It's a jackpot!"

"He tells me you're going to see Sam," my mother said.

"Dad thought it was a good idea."

My mother put her hands on my shoulders and squeezed. "Always listen to your father," she said to me. "Isn't that what I told you when you were growing up?"

I kissed my parents good-bye. I told them to take good care of Camille.

I still had an hour before I had to be at the airport and so I decided to stop by the hospital and see Florence. I gave one of my cards to the receptionist in the rehab unit and told her I was there for Mrs. Allen.

"Let me guess. Everybody loved their cakes," Florence said when she came down the hall dressed in white. "You wanted to tell me so in person."

"Something like that."

She took me into an office that was full of big-handled spoons and various cups and balls. The sign on the door said OCCUPA-TIONAL THERAPY.

"If it's occupational therapy it seems like you should be finding people occupations."

"I found you an occupation," she said. "After a fashion."

"So maybe I can return the favor. Listen to me, I have no idea if this is something you could do or something you'd want to do, but how would you feel about taking a leave of absence and coming to work for me?"

"The cake business?"

"It's booming. It's more than I'm going to be able to handle. I think I'm going to have to rent a kitchen, if such a thing is even possible, either that or put stoves in all the bedrooms."

"How many cakes are we talking about?"

"Right now, probably two hundred a week, but I have a feeling that if we could figure out a way to really move them, we could do even more business than that."

"But I wouldn't know what I was doing." Florence picked up a red rubber ball and squeezed it.

"You'd know as much as I know. I'm not saying this is what I think you should do with your life, but if you just wanted a little switch, who knows? At the end of a couple of weeks you might feel really great about occupational therapy again. Plus, there's no one else I'd rather spend a day in the kitchen with."

Florence looked around the room; posters of hands in different positions lined the walls. "It would be nice to take a break."

"Think it over. I'm on my way to Newport now. I'll probably be back tomorrow. We can talk then."

"Newport?"

"I'm going to go and see Sam."

"Sam went to Newport?"

I nodded my head.

"He's fallen for some boat, hasn't he?"

"It's not just about the boats. I just realized that I really wanted to be married to my husband. I thought I should go and tell him that."

There was a tap on the door and then a nurse stuck her head inside. "Florence, you're backing up out here."

"I need to go anyway," I said.

Florence stood up and gave me a hug. "Cake sounds pretty good right about now. We'll talk tomorrow," she said. "You tell Sam I said hi."

Everything changes. Sometimes when your life has been going along the same way for a long time you can forget that. You think that every day is going to be the same, that everyone will come home for dinner, that we will be safe, that life will roll along. Sometimes the changes are the kind you can't do anything about: Someone gets sick, someone dies, and you look back on the past and think, Those were the days of my happy life. But other times things change and all you have to do is find a way to change with them. It's when you stay in exactly the same spot when everything around you is moving that you really get into trouble. You still have a chance if you're willing to run fast enough, if you're willing to forget everything that you were absolutely positive was true and learn to see the world in a different way. So I was not the kind of person who would start a business or fly halfway across the country to declare my love for the man I had been in love with since I was twenty-five. I did not rent cars and find my way alone to seaside towns, but now I did, because I was someone else, because the circumstances changed and I decided to follow my father's advice and try to change with them.

I had never before set foot in the state of Rhode Island, but Newport is not such a big town. I only had to ask at one gas station to find out where I was going. It was after dark when I got in and the hotel was lit up bright, as if every guest had gone to turn on the lights in their room just to help me find them. It was nowhere near as grand as the hotels I had been to with my parents the day before, but in a way it was better, more romantic. I went to the young man at the front desk and told him I was Mrs. Hopson looking for Mr. Hopson. I held up my bag as if it were proof that I was who I said I was.

"Room three fifty-seven," he said, and smiled at me. He looked like a college student. He probably decided to go to school here so he could sail in his spare time. "Do you need a key?"

"That would be nice," I said, though what I wanted to say was, Is that all it takes to get a key to someone else's room? People seemed to me to be very trusting in Rhode Island.

I went up to 357 feeling oddly nervous. I stood in the hall and tapped a few times on the door. When no one answered I slipped the key in the lock. There was a double bed with a striped bed-spread and a couple of old prints of sailboats on the walls. Sam's bag was sitting on the dresser and his extra pair of pants was hang-ing in the closet, the same pants that had been hanging in our closet this morning. I ran my hand along the leg and felt the broken-in smoothness of the fabric.

I called the yacht broker's office, but it was after six o'clock. A friendly voice on the answering machine encouraged me to leave a message and my number but I didn't do it. Sam was probably com-ing back soon, unless he was going out to dinner. If he was going out to dinner he could be a couple of hours. I sat down on the edge of the bed and it occurred to me how little I had slept in the past few days. I kicked off my shoes and turned off the light on the bedside table. It had been my intention to just close my eyes for a minute but instead I fell into a deep sleep. For the first time in a while I slept without dreaming of cakes.

When Sam told me the story later he said he thought he had opened the door to the wrong room. He glanced inside, saw a woman asleep on the bed, and shut the door. After he checked the room number and the number on the key, he went downstairs to tell the desk clerk that they had put another guest in his room and that that guest was now asleep in his bed.

"It's your wife," the college boy said, and gave Sam the kind of smile one guy gives to another in those circumstances.

So Sam came back upstairs and looked again. He had to say my name three times and shake my shoulder before I woke up.

"Ruth," he said. "What happened?" He was panicked, because why would I fly all that way unless something terrible had happened, something I couldn't tell him about on the phone?

"I missed you," I said, and as soon as I said it I knew that missing Sam was exactly what I had been doing. I had been missing him for a long time.

"You saw me this morning."

I yawned and shook my head. I couldn't believe how deeply I had slept. "No," I said. "It's bigger than that. I mean I've really been missing you. I love you."

"You flew to Newport to tell me that?" He looked somewhere between pleased and confused.

"There are so many things I've been wanting to tell you," I said. "Things about working and not working and family. A million crazy little things that I haven't been saying. I feel like we've been right next to each other this whole time but we haven't really been together. I want us to be together. I want to hear everything you've been thinking about or worrying about. I want to hear all about the boats. I want to get up in the morning and see the boats that you're interested in."

"I can show you the boats, but I don't want you to worry about them. I've been a little crazy myself lately. I walked around the docks all day and wondered what I was thinking."

"You were thinking you loved boats. You probably do love boats. There's nothing wrong with that."

"Do you really want to see them?"

"I just want to be together."

"Don't you have a lot of cakes to bake?"

I reached up and kissed his left eyebrow. "I have so many cakes to bake I think that I'm in serious trouble, but we can talk about cakes another time."

"While we're looking at boats maybe?"

"Maybe we could take turns. You could show me a boat, I could tell you about some cakes. I need your help, Sam. If the whole thought of the cake business leaves you cold, I understand it, but I'm asking you, at least for a little while, please help me."

"What are you talking about? You know I'd do anything in the world for you. I want to be helpful. I just didn't want you to feel like you had to give me a job."

"I'm dying to give you a job!" It would seem to me that administrating cakes would be pretty simple after administrating a hospital.

Sam kissed me. We kissed. "That would mean I was in bed with my boss."

"You're in bed with your partner," I said, and even though there was still so much more we had to say, we decided at that point to stop talking for a while. I fell back onto the bed with my partner of twenty-six years.

Epilogue

AFTER SIX MONTHS IN THE RESTAURANT BUSINESS it became clear to everyone at Eat Cake that the real money was in cakes as gifts. The corporate offices of the Marquette Hotel had shown us the tip of the iceberg when they ordered seventy-five cakes in boxes and mailed them to people who all wanted to send cakes in boxes to other people. My father said it was a regular pyramid scheme. Camille doubled the price for mailed cakes. We said she was insane, but she explained that by cutting out the middleman, we could essentially charge restaurant prices. Then she said this was her part of the business and so we should leave her alone. She hired a boy in her class who she said was not her boyfriend and together they designed a website that gave buyers everything they needed to place an order except for an actual bite of cake. My mother wound up having to make her own cardboard boxes after all. Every time we thought she had perfected the art of the covered box, she came up with something new. The boxes were round now, satin, padded, and beaded until they looked like throw pillows in the Taj Mahal. Eat the cake, keep the box—that was the principle we operated on.

But Mom wound up passing the box division onto Florence, who was as good with a bolt of fabric and some scissors as she was at the ovens. After spending her life working on other people's hands, she discovered there was nothing she couldn't do with her own. Dad's hands were getting better all the time. He worked on his piano every day, but he was still tentative, slow. He said the best part of being out of the braces was being able to wear cuff shirts again. Still, he thought it would probably be another year before he was playing in public, which is where my mother stepped in.

"It's not that I'm bailing out on you," she told me. "Florence makes better boxes than I do and we both know it. Your father really needs me now. I can't play the piano all night and then get up and go to work in the morning. Plus there's all the rehearsing. I'm too old for that. I've got to pick one or the other."

I told her I understood.

And so my mother played the piano and my father sang. That way, she reasoned, when he was ready to go back to playing again, people wouldn't have forgotten about him. "It's a very fickle business," she said. But if the business was fickle, they were the flavor of the month. They appeared almost every weekend at a club or hotel and turned down more offers to sing than I turned down cakes to bake. They were putting together quite a following. My father wanted them to start traveling. He said they could make more money if they took their act out on the road. But my mother said that's how they got into trouble in the first place.

"Except maybe we'll do a couple of cruise ships. Your father wants to book us on cruise ships."

My parents got their own apartment in the summer when Wyatt came home from college. My father said, and it was true, there were just too many of us in the house. Of course, they still had terrible fights, and one or the other of them would wind up in what was once again the guest room sometimes, but never for more than a night.

"Why don't the two of you just give up and get married?" Sam said to them last week when my father came by to pick up my mother. "You have an act now. You have to stay together."

"We are married," my mother said.

I was with Sam on this one. "Well then, remarried. Why not get married again?"

"We never got divorced," my father said.

I squinted at them, my parents standing side by side, looking like an advertisement for happy senior living. "What do you mean, you never got divorced?"

"That's not such a hard sentence to figure out, is it?" my father said.

"We certainly meant to divorce," my mother said. "It was on the top of my to-do list for years. But there was never any money for the lawyer and we didn't have anything to split up anyway. Divorce was so much more complicated back then. You had to come up with a reason. None of this irreconcilable differences nonsense."

"I always thought we'd get divorced when one of us decided to remarry," my father said. "And then, I don't know . . ."

"I just sort of forgot about it," my mother said.

My parents were married?

"But you always said you were divorced," Sam said.

"Well, what are you going to say? It's easier than explaining the whole thing to everyone."

"You could have explained it to me," I said.

"You were two," my mother said. "What can you explain to a two-year-old?"

Contrary to what I may have believed, I was not a child of divorce after all. I was merely a child of a long estrangement that was now almost completely patched over.

"Maybe you'd want to have a little ceremony anyway," I said. "It's been a long time."

"What?" my father said. "Like a commitment ceremony? People only do that on soap operas. You just want an excuse to bake a wedding cake."

"The last thing we need around here is another cake," my mother said, and patted her stomach.

We employed Wyatt for the summer doing packing and shipping. He was good to have around. He could carry anything and he liked to eat any cakes that didn't turn out to our standards. He had been gone for the birth of the company. He was the only one of us who could still get excited over a slice of cake.

Camille took a job as a counselor at a vegetarian camp in Maine for the summer. She said she had to get away from the smell of baking, but it turns out the camp did a lot of baking, mostly with turbinado sugar, carob, and whole wheat flour. She came back for her senior year in high school with a much kinder attitude toward my cakes, even though she still begs us to rent a proper kitchen and move out of the house.

We still haven't moved out of the house. We took out the breakfast table and put in three extra ovens and some more counter space. We had to have the kitchen rewired to bring it up to code and we eat all our meals in the dining room now, but there's nothing wrong with that. Sam says he left the house every day for his entire working life and now he wants to spend some time at home.

Sam hasn't bought a boat yet, but he's still looking. He says with business going the way it is, there wouldn't be time to sail it. I tell him he should have a boat. You only go around once, after all, you've got to live out your dreams.

"I used to pretend I was standing inside a giant cake," I told him. "Whenever I got upset about something I would close my eyes and imagine that I was surrounded by cake. It always made me feel better."

"I bet you don't do that anymore," he said. "Now you're surrounded by cake all the time."

"Exactly. Now when I feel stressed I see myself on a boat. You and I are sailing in a beautiful wooden boat, and there's wind but not too much wind, and the water is clear and blue. I can see the fish underneath us and the birds over us. I just put myself on that boat and I feel better."

"So you've gone from being in the middle of a dark cake to being out in the open water on a boat," Sam said. "That sounds like progress."

"I've gone from being alone inside a cake to being with you on a boat," I said. I kissed him, but just as I did, a timer went off. In this house timers are always going off. After a while you come to realize the cakes can wait.

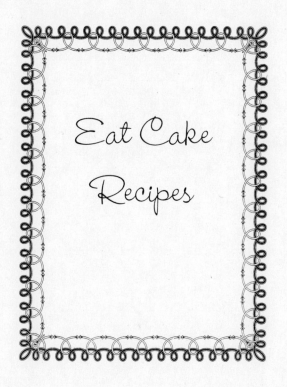

Eat Cake

Recipes

Almond Apricot Pound Cake with Amaretto

Serves 16 to 20

   1½ cups blanched almonds, lightly toasted
   3 cups plus 3 tablespoons granulated sugar
   1 cup unsalted butter, at room temperature
   4 oz. good-quality soft marzipan, at room temperature
   6 large eggs, at room temperature
   2 teaspoons pure almond extract
   1½ teaspoons pure vanilla extract
   ¼ cup Amaretto or other almond liqueur
   ¼ cup apricot or orange brandy
   2½ cups all-purpose flour
   ½ cup cake flour, sifted
   ¾ tablespoon salt
   ½ teaspoon baking soda
   1 cup full-fat sour cream
   ⅔ cup chopped dried apricots, preferably unsulphered

1. Preheat oven to 325°. Grease and flour a 10-inch tube pan and
    tap out the excess flour, holding the center tube if it is
    a removable bottomed pan. Process the almonds and 3 table-
    spoons of the sugar in a food processor until finely ground,
    then set aside.

2. In a large bowl, or the bowl of a stand mixer fitted with the
    paddle attachment, cream the butter and remaining 3 cups
    of sugar together for 3 to 4 minutes, or until the mixture is
    very fluffy and pale. Add the marzipan and cream until well

blended. There may be a few little pieces of marzipan that don't break up in the batter—this will add a little texture and pockets of flavor to the finished cake. (If the marzipan is not soft enough to cream, grind it in a food processor with the almonds and add it to the batter when the nuts are added.) Scrape down the sides of the bowl and do so frequently from now on—this is a large batter, and you want to ensure everything is properly distributed. Add the eggs, one at a time, beating well between each addition. Beat in the almond and vanilla extracts, Amaretto, and apricot brandy.

3. Sift together the flours, salt, and baking soda. Add the flour mixture to the creamed batter in three additions, alternately with the sour cream in two additions, beginning and ending with the dry ingredients so the batter never gets too dry, causing the flour to become overworked. Fold in the chopped apricots and ground nuts and scrape the batter into the prepared pan, smoothing the surface with a rubber spatula.

4. Bake the cake in the center of the oven for 1½ hours to 1¾ hours, or until a wooden skewer inserted into the center of the cake comes out clean and the cake is beginning to pull away from the sides of the pan. Cool the cake in the pan on a wire rack for 15 minutes. Run a thin-bladed knife around the outside of the cake and the center tube. If the pan has a removable bottom, lift the tube out, freeing the cake. Invert the cake onto a wire rack and pull out the tube and bottom. If the pan does not have a removable bottom, simply invert the cake onto the rack. Allow the cake to cool completely before serving or storing. It keeps very well at room temperature for up to 4 days, stored in an airtight cake dome or well-wrapped

in plastic, and it may also be frozen for up to 2 months, wrapped securely, and thawed, without disturbing the wrapping, at room temperature. This wonderful cake really doesn't need any embellishment.

In the Sweet Kitchen by Regan Daley. Artisan/Workman Publishers, 2001

Black Espresso Cake with Bittersweet Glaze

Serves 12 to 16

Cake

- 1½ cups unsalted butter, in small pieces
- 7 oz. unsweetened chocolate, the best you can afford, coarsely chopped
- 3 oz. bittersweet chocolate, coarsely chopped
- 2½ tablespoons instant espresso powder dissolved in 2 cups boiling water, cooled (or 2 cups strong black coffee)
- 3 cups granulated sugar
- 10 tablespoons (5 oz.) Kahlúa or other coffee liqueur
- 1½ teaspoons pure vanilla extract
- 3 large eggs, lightly beaten
- 2¼ cups all-purpose flour
- ½ cup cake flour, not self-rising
- 1½ teaspoons baking soda
- ½ teaspoon salt

Glaze

- 10 oz. bittersweet or semisweet chocolate, chopped
- 7 tablespoons unsalted butter in small pieces

Additional unsalted butter, at room temperature, for
    greasing the pan
Dark chocolate-covered espresso beans or chocolate
    coffee bean-shaped candies, for garnish
Lightly sweetened whipped cream, optional

1.   Preheat the oven to 325°. Grease a 10-inch springform pan, line with a circle of parchment paper and lightly grease the paper. Combine the butter, both chocolates, and coffee in the top of a double boiler or a stainless steel or glass bowl. Set the bowl or insert over a pot of barely simmering water and stir frequently with a wooden spoon until melted. If the melted mixture appears somewhat speckled with what looks like unmelted chocolate, don't be concerned. (Different chocolates have different cocoa butter and cocoa solids content and when melted with such a large quantity of liquid may seem to separate.) Place the sugar in the bottom of a large mixing bowl, or the bowl of an electric mixer. Remove the chocolate mixture from the heat and pour over the sugar. Stir to blend and dissolve the sugar, and then allow to cool for 10 minutes.

2.   With a wire whisk or the paddle attachment of an electric mixer, add the Kahlúa and the vanilla extract to the cooled chocolate mixture and blend well. Blend in the lightly beaten eggs, making sure they are thoroughly incorporated. The batter at this point will be extremely thin; don't worry, just make sure to work each added ingredient in carefully.

3.   Sift the flours, baking soda, and salt together. Add dry ingredients to the chocolate mixture in two additions, scraping down the sides of the bowl several times. Beat on medium

speed for one minute. The batter may have little lumps, but they won't affect the finished cake.

4. Place the prepared pan on a baking sheet to catch any leaks and pour the batter into the pan. Bake in the middle of the oven for 1¾ hours to 2 hours, rotating the pan several times during that time to ensure even baking. The cake bakes slowly and stays beautifully moist. A crust will form on the top of the cake and may crack. Test for doneness by inserting a wooden skewer in a fault of the crust, poking near the center of the cake. It should come out clean, or with only a very few moist crumbs clinging to it. Remove the cake from the oven and cool completely in the pan set on a rack. (The cake may be made up to 2 days ahead of time and kept in the pan at room temperature, covered tightly with plastic wrap.)

5. To prepare the glaze, combine the chopped chocolate and butter in the top of a double boiler or a bowl set over barely simmering water. Stir frequently until the chocolate is melted, then remove from the heat and cool slightly, stirring occasionally. Run a thin-bladed knife around the cake and loosen and remove the sides of the pan. Using a long-bladed serrated knife, carefully even out the top of the cake, slicing off any domed or uneven part of the crust. Use long, slow strokes of the knife, keeping the blade perfectly parallel with the counter.

6. Place a dab of the chocolate glaze on a 10-inch cardboard cake circle and invert the cake onto the board. Remove the pan bottom and the parchment paper. (If you haven't got a cake circle or other piece of cardboard cut to 10 inches round, invert the cake onto a plate and remove the pan bottom but

leave the paper. Re-invert the cake onto a second plate and place the pan bottom on the top of the cake. Invert the cake a third time, ending up with the bottom-side up, top-side down on the metal pan bottom, and peel off the paper.) Brush any crumbs from the cake and pour the warm glaze onto the center. Using a metal spatula or palette knife, coax the glaze to the edges of the cake and over the sides; quickly spread the overflow evenly onto the sides. Garnish with the chocolate-covered espresso beans. Give the glaze an hour or so to set, then serve the cake with lightly sweetened whipped cream, if desired.

In the Sweet Kitchen by Regan Daley. Artisan/Workman Publishers, 2001

Coconut Pineapple Cake

Serves 8

ACTIVE TIME: 1 HR   START TO FINISH: 3 HR

For cake

    1 cup cake flour (not self-rising)

    ½ teaspoon salt

    6 large eggs at room temperature

    1 cup sugar

    2 teaspoons vanilla

    ¾ stick (6 tablespoons) unsalted butter, melted
       and cooled

For pineapple filling
    1 (20-oz.) can crushed pineapple, including juice
    2 tablespoons sugar
    1 tablespoon cornstarch
    1 teaspoon fresh lemon juice

For rum syrup
    ⅔ cup water
    ¼ cup sugar
    3 tablespoons light rum

For assembly
    Coconut buttercream (recipe follows)
    3½ cups fresh coconut shavings or 2⅔ cups sweetened
        flaked coconut (7-oz. package)

MAKE CAKES: Preheat oven to 350° and butter 2 (8-inch) square cake pans (2 inches deep).

Sift flour with salt into a bowl.

Heat eggs and sugar in large metal bowl set over a pot of simmering water, gently whisking constantly, until lukewarm.

Remove bowl from heat and add vanilla, then beat with an electric mixer at medium-high speed until thick and pale and tripled in volume (about 5 minutes with a standing mixer or 10 minutes with a handheld). Sift flour and salt over eggs in 2 batches, folding gently but thoroughly after each batch. Fold in melted butter until combined. Divide batter evenly between cake pans, smoothing tops.

Bake cakes in middle of oven until a tester comes out clean and cakes are golden, about 15 minutes. Cool in pans on racks 5 minutes, then invert onto racks to cool completely.

MAKE PINEAPPLE FILLING: Stir together filling ingredients in a heavy saucepan until cornstarch is dissolved. Bring to a boil, stirring constantly, then simmer, stirring 3 minutes. Cool completely, stirring occasionally.

MAKE RUM SYRUP: Bring water and sugar to a boil in a small saucepan, stirring until sugar is dissolved. Remove from heat and stir in rum. Transfer to a small bowl and chill until ready to use.

ASSEMBLE CAKE: Trim edges of cakes if necessary and cut each horizontally in half with a long serrated knife to form a total of 4 thin layers. Put 1 cake layer, cut side up, on a cake plate and brush top with some rum syrup, then spread half of pineapple filling over it. Top with another cake layer and brush with syrup, then spread with about ⅔ cup buttercream. Top with a third cake layer and brush with syrup, then spread remaining pineapple over it. Top with fourth layer, cut side down, and brush with remaining syrup. Frost sides and top of cake with remaining buttercream, then coat with coconut.

COOKS' NOTES: Cake layers can be made 2 days ahead and left unsplit. Keep wrapped well in plastic wrap at room temperature.

Pineapple filling can be prepared 3 days ahead and chilled, covered.

Rum syrup can be made 1 week ahead and chilled, covered.

Cake can be assembled 1 day ahead and chilled, covered. Bring to room temperature before serving.

Coconut Buttercream

Makes about 4¼ cups (enough to frost an 8-inch layer cake)

ACTIVE TIME: 15 MIN   START TO FINISH: 35 MIN

It's easier to make buttercream with a standing mixer, but it can be done with a handheld one.

4 large egg whites at room temperature

½ teaspoon salt

1¼ cups sugar

½ cup water

½ teaspoon fresh lemon juice

3 sticks (1½ cups) unsalted butter, cut into tablespoon
  pieces and softened

1½ teaspoons coconut extract

SPECIAL EQUIPMENT: *a candy thermometer*

Combine egg whites and salt in bowl of a standing mixer or other large bowl.

Stir together sugar and water in a small heavy saucepan and bring to a boil over moderately high heat, stirring until sugar is dissolved and washing down side of pan with a pastry brush dipped in cold water. When syrup reaches a boil, start beating whites with electric mixer at medium speed. When eggs are frothy, add lemon juice and beat until they just hold soft peaks. (Do not beat again until sugar syrup is ready—see below.)

Meanwhile, put thermometer into sugar syrup and continue boiling, without stirring, until it reaches soft-ball stage (238–242°F). Immediately remove from heat and slowly pour hot syrup in a thin stream down side of bowl into egg whites, beating constantly at high speed. Beat meringue, scraping down bowl with a rubber spatula, until meringue is cool to the touch, about 6 minutes. (It's important that meringue is fully cooled before proceeding.)

With mixer at medium speed, gradually add butter 1 piece at a time, beating well after addition until incorporated. (If meringue is too warm and buttercream looks soupy after some butter is added, chill bottom of bowl in a larger bowl filled with ice and cold water for a few seconds before continuing to beat in remaining butter.) Continue beating until buttercream is smooth. (Mixture may look curdled before all butter is added, but will come back together before beating is finished.) Add coconut extract and beat 1 minute more.

COOKS' NOTES: Buttercream can be made 1 week ahead and chilled, covered, or 1 month ahead and frozen. Bring to room temperature (do not use a microwave) and beat with an electric mixer before using.

If egg safety is a problem in your area, you may want to use either pasteurized egg whites in the carton or reconstituted powdered egg whites.

Gourmet Magazine, April 2001

Golden Grand Marnier Cake

Ingredients, at room temperature:
   ½ cup chocolate mini-chips or bittersweet chocolate
      chopped into ¼-inch pieces
   ¼ teaspoon Grand Marnier
   1½ teaspoons cake flour
   3 large eggs
   1 cup full-fat sour cream
   2 teaspoons orange flower water or 1½ teaspoons
      vanilla extract
   2½ cups sifted cake flour
   ½ cup + 1 tablespoon (ground) unblanched sliced
      almonds, toasted and finely ground
   1 cup sugar
   1½ teaspoons baking powder

1 teaspoon baking soda
¾ teaspoon salt
2 tablespoons grated orange zest
1 cup unsalted butter

Grand Marnier Syrup
½ cup sugar
¼ cup orange juice, freshly squeezed
⅓ cup Grand Marnier

One 9-cup fluted tube pan, greased and floured.

1. Preheat the oven to 350°. In a small bowl toss the chocolate chips and Grand Marnier until the chips are moistened and shiny. Add the 1½ teaspoons flour and toss until evenly coated.

2. In a medium bowl lightly combine the eggs, ¼ cup sour cream, and orange flower water or vanilla.

3. In a large mixing bowl combine the dry ingredients and orange zest and mix on low speed for 30 seconds to blend. Add the butter and remaining ¾ cup sour cream. Mix on low speed until the dry ingredients are moistened. Increase to medium speed (high if using a hand mixer) and beat for 1½ minutes to aerate and develop the cake's structure. Scrape down the sides. Gradually add the egg mixture in three batches, beating for 20 seconds after each addition to incorporate the ingredients and strengthen the structure. Scrape down the sides. Stir in the chocolate chips.

4. Scrape the batter into the prepared pan and smooth the surface with a spatula. Bake 55 to 65 minutes or until a wire cake tester

inserted in the center comes out clean and the cake springs back when pressed lightly in the center. *The cake should start to shrink from the sides of the pan only after removal from the oven.*

5. Shortly before the cake is done, prepare the syrup: Heat the sugar, orange juice, and Grand Marnier until the sugar is dissolved. Do not boil. As soon as the cake comes out of the oven, place the pan on a rack, poke the top all over with a wire tester, and brush on ½ of the syrup. Cool in the pan on a rack for 10 minutes, then invert onto a serving plate or cardboard round. Brush with the remaining syrup and cool completely before wrapping.

6. Serve room temperature with a light dusting of powdered sugar, if desired

The Cake Bible by Rose Levy Beranbaum. William Morrow Publishers, 1988.

Lady Baltimore Cake

For the cake layers
1 cup butter, at room temperature, plus additional for
    greasing pans
2 cups sifted sugar
3½ cups cake flour
4 teaspoons baking powder
¼ teaspoon salt
1 cup milk
2 teaspoons vanilla extract

½ teaspoon almond extract
8 large white eggs, at room temperature

For the frosting
2 cups sugar
4 large egg whites, at room temperature
Pinch of salt
1 cup walnuts or pecans, finely chopped
½ cup raisins, finely chopped
6 dried figs, coarsely chopped
1 teaspoon vanilla extract
1 teaspoon brandy or sherry (optional)

1. Preheat oven to 350°. Grease three 8-by-2-inch round cake pans with butter. Line the bottom with parchment. Grease parchment.

2. To make cake: Beat butter and sugar into a bowl at high speed until fluffy. Sift flour, baking powder, and salt into a bowl. Mix milk and extracts into a measuring cup. Add flour mixture into butter mixture a little at a time, alternating with milk. Beat after each addition.

3. In a bowl, beat egg whites at a high speed until stiff. Fold into butter mixture. Divide batter among pans. Bake for 25 to 30 minutes, or until golden and cakes pull away from pan sides. Cool cakes in pans on wire racks for 10 minutes before turning out.

4. To make frosting: Combine sugar and ½ cup water in a saucepan, bring to a boil and cook 5 minutes. Meanwhile, beat the egg whites with salt in a bowl until frothy. Continue

to beat and add hot syrup in a thin stream. Keep beating at high speed until the frosting forms stiff peaks. Mix in the nuts, raisins, figs, vanilla, and liqueur together and stir.

5. Spread the frosting between each layer and over the rest of the cake.

New York Times Magazine, April 21, 2002, from the article "Rich and Famous" by Julia Reed.

Lemon Layer Cake with Lemon Cream Frosting

Makes 1 (8-inch) layer cake

ACTIVE TIME: 1HR   START TO FINISH: 2 HR

For cake layers

2 cups sifted cake flour (not self-rising; sift before measuring)

¾ teaspoon baking soda

¼ teaspoon salt

½ cup whole milk

2½ tablespoons fresh lemon juice

1 stick (½ cup) unsalted butter, softened

1 cup granulated sugar

2 large eggs

For frosting

1 cup heavy cream

½ cup confectioners sugar

Lemon curd (recipe follows), chilled
Garnish: candied violets

MAKE CAKE LAYERS: Preheat oven to 375°. Butter 2 (8-by-2-inch) round cake pans and line bottoms of each with rounds of wax or parchment paper. Butter paper and dust pans with flour, knocking out excess.

Sift together flour, baking soda, and salt. Stir together milk and lemon juice (mixture will curdle).

Beat butter in a large bowl with an electric mixer until creamy. Gradually add sugar, beating until pale and fluffy. Add eggs 1 at a time, beating well after each addition. Alternately add flour mixture and milk mixture in batches, beginning and ending with flour, mixing at low speed until just combined.

Divide batter between pans, smoothing tops. Bake in middle of oven until a tester comes out clean, about 20 minutes. Cool in pans on racks 10 minutes, then invert onto racks, remove paper, and cool completely.

MAKE FROSTING: Beat cream and confectioners sugar with cleaned beaters until it just holds stiff peaks. Fold one third of whipped cream into lemon curd to lighten, then fold in remaining whipped cream.

ASSEMBLE CAKE: Put 1 cake layer, rounded side up, on a cake plate and spread with one fourth of frosting. Top with second layer, rounded side up, and spread top and sides with remaining frosting. Decorate with candied violets.

COOKS' NOTES: Cake can be assembled 1 day ahead and chilled in a cake keeper or loosely covered with plastic wrap (use toothpicks to hold wrap away from frosting). Let stand at room temperature 30 minutes before serving.

This batter can be baked in 16 (½-cup) muffin cups about 15 minutes; or in a 13-by-9-inch baking pan about 25 minutes. Halve cake crosswise to form 2 (9-by-6½-inch) rectangles and layer in same manner as above.

Lemon Curd

Makes about 1⅓ cups

ACTIVE TIME: 20 MINUTES   START TO FINISH 1¼ HOURS

½ cup fresh lemon juice
2 teaspoons finely grated fresh lemon zest
½ cup sugar
3 large eggs
¾ stick (6 tablespoons) unsalted butter, cut into bits

Whisk together juice, zest, sugar, and eggs in a 2-quart saucepan. Stir in butter and cook over moderately low heat, whisking frequently, until curd is thick enough to hold marks of whisk and first bubble appears on surface, about 6 minutes.

Transfer lemon curd to a bowl and chill, its surface covered with plastic wrap, until cold, at least 1 hour.

COOKS' NOTE: Curd can be chilled up to 1 week.

Gourmet Magazine, January 2001

Oatmeal Stout Cake with a Chewy Oat Topping

Serves 10

Cake

- 1 cup old-fashioned oats (not instant), also called coarse oatmeal or Irish oatmeal
- 1¼ cups oatmeal stout or other dark stout beer, such as Guinness
- ½ cup unsalted butter, at room temperature
- 1 cup tightly packed dark brown sugar
- 1 cup granulated sugar
- 2 large eggs, at room temperature
- ½ teaspoon pure vanilla extract
- 1 teaspoon finely grated orange zest
- 1½ cups all-purpose flour
- 1 teaspoon baking soda
- ½ teaspoon salt
- ½ teaspoon cinnamon
- ½ teaspoon freshly grated nutmeg

Chewy Oat Topping

- ¼ cup unsalted butter, at room temperature
- ½ cup tightly packed light brown sugar
- ¼ cup sweetened condensed milk
- ½ cup old-fashioned (coarse) oats
- ½ cup lightly toasted pecans or walnuts, coarsely chopped

1. Two hours before you plan to put the cake in the oven, combine the oatmeal and the stout and in a small, non-reactive bowl; cover with plastic wrap and chill.

2. Preheat the oven to 350°. Grease a 9-inch springform or other 9-inch round cake pan with 3-inch-high sides. In the bowl of an electric mixer or a large mixing bowl, cream the butter and both sugars until well combined and somewhat fluffy. Add the eggs, one at a time, beating well after each addition. Beat in the vanilla and orange zest.

3. Drain the chilled oat mixture, reserving the stout. Into a separate bowl, sift the flour, baking soda, salt, cinnamon, and nutmeg. Add the flour mixture to the creamed butter mixture in three additions, alternating with the reserved stout in two additions, beginning and ending with the dry ingredients. Take care at this point not to overmix; just make sure the flour is moistened and all ingredients are evenly distributed. Fold in the oats and scrape the batter, which will be quite thick, into the prepared pan. Place in the center of the preheated oven and bake for 55 to 65 minutes, or until the center of the cake springs back when lightly touched, and the wooden skewer inserted there comes out clean. Remove the sides of the springform pan and cool the cake completely on a rack before topping.

4. To prepare the Chewy Oat Topping, preheat the broiler. Combine all the ingredients for the topping in a small bowl and scatter over the cooled cake in its pan, pressing the mixture onto the surface evenly. Place the pan under the broiler and cook, watching closely, until the topping is bubbling and

golden. This sweet stuff can burn quickly, so don't leave the pan under the heat and walk away! Cool the topped cake for at least 10 minutes. Slide slender spatula under cake to remove it from pan bottom and slide cake to serving plate, then serve warm or at room temperature. Good with vanilla or orange ice cream.

In the Sweet Kitchen by Regan Daley. Artisan/Workman Publishers, 2001

Pistachio Cake

Makes 1 (13-by-9-inch) cake

ACTIVE TIME: 30 MIN   START TO FINISH: 1 HR

If you are using salted pistachios, omit the ¼ teaspoon salt in the ingredient list.

⅜ cup shelled natural pistachios (4 oz)
1 cup all-purpose flour
2 teaspoons baking powder
1 teaspoon ground cardamom
¼ teaspoon salt
½ cup whole milk
¼ teaspoon vanilla
1½ sticks (¾ cup) unsalted butter, softened
1 cup sugar
3 large eggs

Preheat oven to 350°. Butter a 13-by-9-inch metal cake pan, then line bottom with wax paper. Butter paper and dust with some flour, knocking out excess.

Pulse pistachios in a food processor until finely ground (be careful not to overprocess into a paste). Add 1 cup flour, baking powder, cardamom, and salt and pulse once or twice to mix.

Combine milk and vanilla in a measuring cup.

Beat together butter and sugar in a large bowl with an electric mixer until pale and fluffy. Add eggs 1 at a time, beating well after each addition. Alternately add pistachio flour and milk in batches, beginning and ending with flour, and mix at low speed until just combined.

Spread batter evenly in cake pan and bake in middle of oven until a tester comes out clean, about 20 minutes. Cool in pan on a rack 10 minutes, then run a thin knife around sides of cake and invert onto rack. Remove paper and invert cake onto a platter. Cut into squares and serve warm or at room temperature.

COOKS' NOTE: Cake can be made 1 day ahead. Cool completely and keep, covered, at room temperature.

Gourmet Magazine, May 2001

Ruth's Carrot Cake

1 cup corn or canola oil

1¼ cup honey

4 large eggs (room temperature)

1 cup cake flour

1 cup whole wheat flour

2 teaspoons baking powder

2 teaspoons soda

1 teaspoon salt

1 tablespoon cinnamon (be generous)
3 cups grated carrots (use large, sweet, peeled carrots)
1 cup chopped pecans or walnuts

Heat oven to 325°. Mix oil and honey well. Add eggs one at a time, beating well after each addition. Sift flour and other dry ingredients. Add to oil and honey mixture and mix until just blended. Fold in grated carrots and nuts. Bake in two greased and floured 8-by-8-inch Pyrex baking pans for 30 to 35 minutes or until pick inserted in center comes out clean and cake is beginning to pull away from edges of pan.

You might cut the cake into wedges and serve it warm as a vegetable, as Ruth does, or let it cool, remove from the pans, and frost with your favorite cream cheese icing for dessert. How about one of each?

Sweet Potato Bundt Cake with Rum-Plumped Raisins and a Spiked Sugar Glaze

Cake
¾ cup golden raisins
½ cup dark rum
2 large or 3 medium-sized sweet potatoes
4 large eggs
2 cups granulated sugar
1 cup mild-flavored vegetable oil
2 teaspoons pure vanilla extract
3 cups all-purpose flour

1 teaspoon baking powder
1 teaspoon baking soda
½ teaspoon salt, plus extra for salting the water
1½ teaspoons cinnamon
½ teaspoon freshly grated nutmeg
¾ cup buttermilk

Additional unsalted butter, at room temperature,
    for greasing the pans
Additional all-purpose flour, for dusting the tins

Glaze
½ cup tightly packed dark brown sugar
4 tablespoons unsalted butter
3 tablespoons whipping cream (35%)
Remaining rum macerating liquid from raisins

1. Preheat oven to 350°. Grease and flour a 10-inch bundt cake
    pan. In a small nonreactive bowl, soak the raisins in the rum
    for at least 30 minutes or several hours. Meanwhile peel the
    sweet potatoes, cut them in half and then cut each half into
    4-inch slices. Place the slices into a pot of cool salted water,
    cover, and then bring the water to a boil. Reduce to a gentle
    simmer and then cook until the sweet potatoes are very ten-
    der when pierced with a sharp knife. Drain off the water and
    allow the potatoes to air-dry for a few minutes, then use a
    potato masher or large fork to roughly mash them. Measure
    out 2 cups of the mash and set aside to cool.

2. In a large bowl with a whisk or the bowl of a stand mixer
    fitted with the paddle attachment, beat the eggs a little just
    to break them up. Add the sugar and beat until the mixture

is thick and pale, about 2 minutes with a mixer, 3 if whisking by hand. Add the vegetable oil and vanilla, then beat to blend. Drain the raisins and set aside, but add ¼ cup of the rum macerating liquid to the batter. Add the mashed sweet potatoes and mix until thoroughly combined, scraping down the sides and bottom of the bowl.

3. Into a separate bowl, sift the flour, baking powder, baking soda, salt, cinnamon, and nutmeg. Add the flour mixture to the batter in three additions, alternating with the buttermilk in two additions, beginning and ending with the dry ingredients. Fold in the raisins.

4. Pour the entire batter into bundt pan. Bake in the center of the oven 1 hour to 1 hour and 20 minutes, or until a wooden skewer inserted into the center comes out clean, and the cake is just beginning to pull away from the sides of the pan. Cool the cake in the pan set on a wire rack for 10 minutes, then invert onto the rack. Set the rack over a baking sheet or large plate to catch the excess glaze. This cake must be glazed while still warm, so it absorbs the maximum syrup—so don't take it out of the oven and go to the movies!

5. For the glaze, combine the brown sugar, butter, and cream in a small, heavy-bottomed saucepan. Bring to a boil over medium heat, stirring until the sugar dissolves. Continue to boil until the mixture thickens somewhat, about 3 minutes, stirring often. Remove the glaze from the heat and stir in the rum. With a long wooden or metal skewer poke holes all over the cake, concentrating on the top. Spoon about half the warm glaze over the cake and let the cake and remaining

glaze cool for 10 to 15 minutes, until it has thickened slightly. Pour the rest of the glaze over the cake, letting it dribble down the sides, then allow the cake to cool completely before cutting and serving or wrapping and storing.

In the Sweet Kitchen by Regan Daley. Artisan/Workman Publishers, 2001

Upside-Down Pear Gingerbread Cake

Serves 6

For topping

> 2½ firm pears (preferably Bosc)
> ½ stick (¼ cup) unsalted butter
> ¾ cup packed light brown sugar

For cake

> 2½ cups all-purpose flour
> 1½ teaspoons baking soda
> 1 teaspoon ground cinnamon
> 1 teaspoon ground ginger
> ½ teaspoon ground cloves
> ¼ teaspoon salt
> 1 cup molasses (preferably mild)
> 1 cup boiling water
> 1 stick (½ cup) unsalted butter, softened
> ½ cup packed light brown sugar
> 1 large egg, lightly beaten

Special equipment
    A well-seasoned 10-inch cast-iron skillet
    Or
    A 12-inch deep nonstick skillet (handle wrapped with a
        double layer of foil if not oven proof)

MAKE TOPPING: Peel and core the pears and cut each into 8 wedges. Melt butter in skillet over moderate heat until foam subsides.

Reduce heat to low, then sprinkle brown sugar over bottom of skillet and cook, undisturbed, 3 minutes (not all sugar will be melted). Arrange pears decoratively over sugar and cook, undisturbed, 2 minutes. Remove from heat.

MAKE CAKE: Preheat oven to 350°.

Whisk together flour, baking soda, cinnamon, ginger, cloves, and salt in a bowl. Whisk together molasses and boiling water in a small bowl. Beat together butter, brown sugar, and egg in a large bowl with an electric mixer at medium speed until creamy, about 2 minutes, then alternately mix in flour mixture and molasses in 3 batches until smooth.

Pour batter over topping in skillet, spreading evenly and being careful not to disturb pears, and bake in middle of oven until a tester comes out clean, 40 to 50 minutes. Cool cake in skillet on a rack 5 minutes. Run a thin knife around edge of skillet, then invert a large plate with a lip over skillet and, using pot holders to hold skillet and plate tightly together, invert cake onto plate. Replace any pears that stick to skillet. Serve warm or at room temperature.

Gourmet Magazine, February 2002

Permissions

GRATEFUL ACKNOWLEDGMENT is made to the following for permission to reprint previously published material.

Artisan: "Sweet Potato Bundt Cake with Rum-Plumped Raisins and a Spiked Sugar Glaze," "Oatmeal Stout Cake with a Chewy Oat Topping," "Almond Apricot Pound Cake with Amaretto," and "Black Chocolate Espresso Cake with Bittersweet Glaze" from *In the Sweet Kitchen* by Regan Daley. Copyright © 2001 by Regan Daley. All rights reserved. Reprinted by permission of Artisan, a division of Workman Publishing Co., Inc., New York.

Condé Nast Publications: "Upside-Down Pear Gingerbread Cake" (*Gourmet,* February 2002). Copyright © 2002 by Condé Nast Publications. All rights reserved. Reprinted by permission of Condé Nast Publications.

HarperCollins Publishers Inc.: "Golden Grand Marnier Cake" from *The Cake Bible* by Rose Levy Beranbaum. Copyright © 1988 by Rose Levy Beranbaum. Reprinted by permission of Harper-Collins Publishers Inc.

The New York Times: Recipe "Lady Baltimore Cake" from "Rich and Famous" by Julia Reed (*The New York Times Magazine,* April 21, 2002). Distributed by *The New York Times Special Features.* Copyright © 2002 by Julia Reed. Reprinted by permission of *The New York Times.*

eat cake

JEANNE RAY

A CONVERSATION WITH JEANNE RAY

Q. You've said that William Shakespeare inspired your first novel, Julie and Romeo, *and that Jane Austen inspired your second novel,* Step-Ball-Change. *Who inspired* Eat Cake?

A. Much as I'd love to tell you that T. S. Eliot inspired *Eat Cake*, it was really me. Both because I tend to bake or clean when I'm in emotional distress, and because my protagonist, Ruth, has a talent that her daughter helps her claim. For many years, I had a vague suspicion that I could write, but it wasn't until my daughter encouraged me that I was able to make it part of my life.

Q. You make Ruth's love of baking cakes so vivid and real in the novel, I wonder if you bake cakes, too. If so, what do you love about it? How did you choose the luscious cake recipes at the end of the book?

A. I love everything about baking cakes. I love going to the store and selecting the best ingredients, bringing eggs and butter to room temperature, measuring sifted flour and sugar carefully into clean dishes, whipping and stirring and folding. The whole process is enormously satisfying and usually produces a scrumptious cake, which I then enjoy giving away. It's a no-lose situation. The cakes in the book are not my "old standards." They were selected (and I've made every one) because each has a special something that sets it apart—color, flavor, or texture that make each cake a little different.

Q. Guy and Hollis are wonderful characters, and I enjoy getting hints about how their prickly relationship has evolved over time. Their relationship suggests that sometimes a man and woman might truly love each other, but simply be unable to live together. Was that your intention, and if so, can you comment more fully?

A. I do believe that love is not enough to sustain a long relationship. It takes a special respect for each other, a particular degree of appreciation and continuity to live together well over the years.

Q. Florence Allen, the nurse who is originally hired to help Guy and ends up helping Ruth as well, is a delightful character. Since you're a nurse, too, I wonder if you drew on your own experience in creating Florence.

A. In truth, Florence Allen is not a nurse but an occupational therapist. I did, however, draw heavily on my experience as a nurse when I created her. She epitomizes everything I find important in a caregiver: knowledge, professionalism, compassion, *and* the ability to laugh!

Q. Sam's desire to build wooden sailboats, Ruth's desire to bake cakes . . . Perhaps one of the reasons why readers find Sam and Ruth so likable is that many of us secretly yearn to pursue impractical dreams. Do you believe that it's truly possible to follow one's dreams without becoming financially irresponsible?

A. As crass as it might sound, we do need to live up to our fiscal responsibilities. That's just one of the reasons I think it's wonderful to try new things when we're older, have our children raised, and our homes paid down. It means delaying gratification sometimes, but it's a great feeling to begin to explore our creative selves after we've paid our financial dues.

Q. Each of your novels touches on aspects of contemporary life that we can all relate to, yet you add a gloss of warmth and wisdom. Do you consciously choose to tackle subjects that many families face, such as unemployment and caring for aging or disabled parents?

A. Absolutely. Having spent my life dealing with the more or less common grievances—my own and others'—I wanted to write about these things. It's important to me to let people know that they're not alone in their struggles.

Q. As this guide is being written, you've recently finished a month-long tour to promote the hardcover edition of Eat Cake. *Were there any particularly memorable experiences during your travels that you'd like to share?*

A. It's a beautiful thing to find out how many folks bake cakes when they're feeling stressed. One lady in particular told a great story about "dead man's cakes"—she had a relative who baked and froze cakes to present to families who had just lost a loved one. Better than flowers!

Q. *Do you think that as a society we need to take more time to figuratively "bake cakes"? Do you find yourself seeking ways to savor more of life's small pleasures?*

A. I think one of the causes of the eating disorders which abound in our fast-paced society is that we lose touch with the myriad pleasures associated with food: the growing, the picking, the buying of ingredients, the preparation, the smells in the kitchen. It's not enough to cram a bit of sustenance in your mouth and swallow until you're full. One needs to process the whole experience to be truly satisfied.

Q. *What are you cooking up these days—literally or figuratively, professionally or personally?*

A. I am still baking cakes, working one day a week as a nurse, and I have a new novel playing with my brain. I am enjoying my life in many different ways.

QUESTIONS FOR DISCUSSION

1. Ruth soothes her family conflicts with cake. Do you use food to soothe and comfort your family? In your particular case, is doing so more healthful or harmful?

2. The loss of Sam's job presents new challenges to his marriage with Ruth. Have you or your husband (or someone else close to you) ever suddenly lost their job? How did that affect your relationship(s)?

3. When the novel opens, Ruth's mother, Hollis, has moved in with Ruth's family because a robbery of her home, in which the door was kicked in, so destroyed her sense of security that she's no longer comfortable living alone. Many ordinary people are the victims of crime. Drawing from your own knowledge and experience, discuss what some of the long-term effects of nonviolent crime might be, and how as a society we might or might not underestimate the impact of those experiences.

4. Florence Allen has a healing influence on several members of the Hopson family. Has someone from outside your own family ever helped you during a moment of crisis?

5. Camille is sometimes utterly self-absorbed and at other times remarkably caring, confident, and capable. In fact, it's funny when she starts acting more responsible than her own parents! In what ways does Jeanne Ray's portrait of Camille jive with, or depart from, your own impressions of today's teenagers?

6. Once Ruth's cake baking business takes off, she's overwhelmed by the sudden need to fill all those orders. Have you ever been in a situation when success took you by surprise, and at first you didn't know how you would cope?

7. Do you think that we as a society need to take more time to fig-uratively "bake cakes"? How might you make more room in your own life for the small but significant pleasures that make life worth living?

8. Do you have a dream that you secretly long to pursue? Would you like to share it with the group, and discuss what might be hold-ing you back from going after it?

9. Have you tried the cake recipes in the back of the book? How did they turn out, and what response did you receive?

About the Author

JEANNE RAY works as a registered nurse at the First Clinic in Nashville, Tennessee. She is married and has two daughters. Together, she and her husband have ten grandchildren. She is also the author of *Julie and Romeo* and *Step~Ball~Change*.